THE FALLEN ONES
The War of Powers: Book Four

The war is over and lost...things are really desperate...and Moriana will do anything to regain her throne. She'll even go to a bunch of slimy aliens for help, with only a weird genie for company. So, ignoring the frightening rumors, Moriana steps resolutely over the bodies of her fallen comrades and marches on.

Fortunately for her lost lover Fost, his body is not among them. He's got other plans for it, if he can only catch up to her. But so far he's been attacked by a stone god, betrayed by a lecherous genie, killed by his lady love, and subjected to all-purpose mayhem. And now the latest problem is how to steal an ancient race's most prized possession...

"A good ripsnorting tale that whizzes along."
—*Isaac Asimov's Science Fiction Magazine*

THE WAR OF POWERS SERIES

THE FALLEN ONES

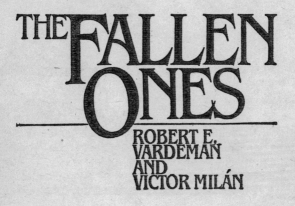

ROBERT E. VARDEMAN
AND
VICTOR MILÁN

PLAYBOY
PAPERBACKS

Published simultaneously in the United States and Canada by Playboy Paperbacks, New York, New York. Printed in the United States of America. Library of Congress Catalog Card Number: 81–82361. First edition.

Books are available at quantity discounts for promotional and industrial use. For further information, write to Premium Sales, Playboy Paperbacks, 1633 Broadway, New York, New York 10019.

ISBN: 0–872–16986–3

First printing January 1982.

To the person I'd most
like to be Shipwrecked with.

—rev—

To Barbara Miller,
who wanted to know
what happened next—
And to the whole crazy, wonderful Archon crew
who made me feel at home.

—vwm—

A Chronology
of the Sundered Realm

—20,000   The reptilian *Zr'gsz* settle the Southern Continent and begin construction of the City in the Sky.

—3,100   Istu sent by the Dark Ones to serve the *Zr'gsz* as a reward for their devotion.

—2,300   Human migration begins.

—2,100   Athalau founded by migrants from the Islands of the Sun.

—1,700   Explorers from the Northern Continent found High Medurim.

—1,000   Tension increases between the *Zr'gsz* and the human settlers.

—31   *Zr'gsz* begin active campaign to exterminate all humans.

—3   Martyrdom of the Five Holy Ones.

0   *The War of Powers*: Unable to wipe out the human invaders, the *Zr'gsz* begin to use the powers of Istu. Most of the Southern Continent is desolated. In Athalau, Felarod raises his Hundred and summons up the World-Spirit. Forces unleashed by the struggle sink continents, tip the world on its axis (bringing Athalau into the polar region),

7

cause a star to fall from the heavens to create the Great Crater. The *Zr'gsz* and Istu are defeated; Istu is cast into a magical sleep and imprisoned in the Sky City's foundations. Conflict costs the life of Felarod and ninety of his Hundred. Survivors exile themselves from Athalau in horror at the destruction they've brought about.
Human Era begins.

100   Trade between humans and *Zr'gsz* grows; increasing population of humans in the Sky City. Medurim begins its conquests.

979   Ensdak Aritku proclaimed first Emperor of High Medurim.

1171   Humans seize power in the Sky City. The *Zr'gsz* are expelled. Riomar shai-Gallri crowns herself queen.

2317   Series of wars between the Empire of Medurim and the City in the Sky.

2912–17   War between the Sky City and Athalau; Athalau victorious. Wars between the City and Athalau continue on and off over the next several centuries.

5143   Julanna Etuul wrests the Beryl Throne from Malva Kryn. She abolishes worship of the Dark Ones within the Sky City, concludes peace with the Empire.

5331   Invaders from the Northern Continent seize Medurim and the Sapphire Throne; barbarian accession signals fresh outbreak of civil wars.

5332   Newly-proclaimed Emperor Churdag declares war on the City in the Sky.

5340   Chafing under the oppression of the Barbarian Empire, the southern half of the Empire revolts. Athalau and the Sky City form an alliance.

5358   Tolviroth Acerte, the City of Bankers, is founded by merchants who fled the disorder in High Medurim.

5676   Collapse of the Barbarian Dynasty. The Sky City officiates over continent-wide peace.

5700   The Golden Age of the City in the Sky begins.

6900   General decline overtakes Southern Continent. The Sky City magic and influence wane. Agriculture breaks down in south and west. Glacier nears Athalau. Tolviroth Acerte rises through trade with Jorea.

7513   Battle of River Marchant, between Quincunx Federation and High Medurim, ends Imperial domination everywhere but in the northwest corner of the continent. The Southern Continent becomes the Sundered Realm.

8614   Erimenes the Ethical born. Population of Athalau in decline.

8722   Erimenes dies at 108.

8736   Birth of Ziore.

8823   Death of Ziore.

9940   Final abandonment of Athalau to encroaching glacier.

10,091 Prince Rann Etuul born to Ekrimsin the Ill-Favored, sister to Queen Derora V.

10,093   Synalon and Moriana born to Derora. As younger twin, Moriana becomes heir apparent.

10,095   Fost Longstrider born in The Teeming, slum district of High Medurim.

10,103   Teom the Decadent ascends the Sapphire Throne. Fost's parents killed in rioting over reduction in dole to cover Imperial festivities.

10,120   Jar containing the spirit of Erimenes the Ethical discovered in brothel in The Sjedd.

Mount Omizantrim, "Throat of the Dark Ones," from whose lava the *Zr'gsz* mined the skystone for the Sky City foundations, has its worst eruption in millennia.

10,121   Fost Longstrider, now a courier of Tolviroth Acerte, is commissioned to deliver a parcel to the mage Kest-i-Mond.

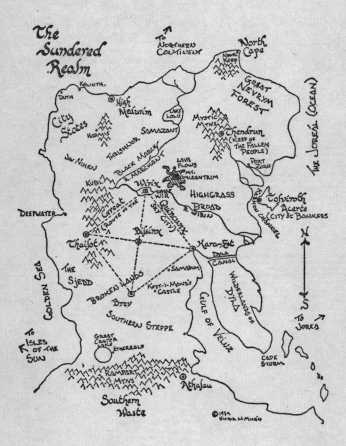

The Sundered Realm

To Northern Continent

North Cape

Kolinth

Duth

Niah Medunim

City Skates

Lake Lolu

Harmis

Thrishkor

Samazant

Jav Nihrn

Black March

R. Marchant

Kubil

Wirix

Lake Wir

Great Route of the

Mystic Mtns

Thendrun (Keep of the Fallen People)

Great Nevrym Forest

North Keep

Port Zorn

Lava Flows & Mt. Omizantrim

Highgrass Broad

R. Wirin

Quinnux Sky City

The Joreal (Ocean)

Deepwater

Thaisot

Dijinx

Kara-Fet

Dyla Canal

Tshviroth Acerte City of Bankers

Grion Channel

The Sjedd

Broken Lands

Dzzy

Samadum

Kest-i-Mond's Castle

Wildlands of Dyla

N

S

Golden Sea

Southern Steppe

Gulf of Veluz

To Jores

To Isles of the Sun

Great Crater Lake

Ethereals

Rampart Mtns

Athasau

Cape Storm

Southern Waste

© 1990 Victor Li Ming's

PROLOGUE

No light defiled the sacred darkness of the chamber cruelly gouged from the mountain's interior. With a sense that was not sight, the gathered worshippers knew the presence of their priest and leader, resplendent in his long robes of pallid, fine-textured leather and head-dress of obsidian and iridescent green metal. They perceived not the colors of Light, which were a lie; they knew the subtle shades of blackness.

The priest raised a strong hand and spoke to heads bowed in dark communion.

"In the secret places of the Mountain," he intoned, "pent in the stone that flows like water, that burns without the foulness of Light, the mother fluid of our race, there beats . . ." Ritually, he paused.

At once came back the ringing answer: *"A Heart!"*

"Our Heart." Another pause, then, "And it is lost to us."

"Lost!" The word scored the soul with a keening of pain honed fine by the grinding centuries.

"But when shall we forget?"

"When the Great Dark ceases to fill the space between stars."

He nodded gravely. The blackness he wore like a shroud about him brightened in the non-vision of the faithful as he built to the climax of the ancient ceremony.

"But know you it shall be returned to us, and its power will again pulse through the veins of our People."

"So shall it be!"

"And when that time comes, what will be our destiny?"

"*To conquer!*" The intensity of the shout caused the cavern walls to tremble.

"And when," he asked, growing in size and power as he spoke the climactic words of liturgy, "shall our time come?"

Eleven-score and ten mouths opened to give the final response. But no sound came. The subterranean chill of the chamber grew colder still, and an icy wind swept over the worshippers, a wind from nowhere, like the wind that blows between the stars.

His eyes widened in mingled fear and religious ecstasy, muscles cording in great knots on his neck and back, the leader-priest felt the nearness of a Presence his kind had not known for ten thousand years.

The Dark Ones' time came again.

Far to the southwest, the mountain Omizantrim trembled. Across long years it had built itself in fitful vomits of core-stuff from the planet until it stood thus, a black fang piercing the sky. Now it jetted a cloud of boiling hot ash and smoke, a roiling blackness shot through with flame and vivid lightning. A herdsman watching his flock of one-horned deer grazing the short grass that clung to the lower slopes of the mountain, was caught by surprise. He screamed as the awful heat enveloped him, boiling water from his tissues in an instant, mingling volcanic cloud and human body in a deadly stew.

The cloud rolled on, leaving the herdsman with his charges, now turned to gray ash statues scattered randomly on a lifeless hillside. The folk who dwelt lower on the slopes were luckier. They saw the cloud spew into the night like venom from a serpent's fang and retreated to special shelters dug in the cooled lava flows that jutted from the mountain like diseased roots.

Others, farther away, viewed the eruption with foreboding. Timid and wise alike made signs in the air and muttered fervent prayers to personal deities. But the wise were little comforted by their godly importunings. They knew that Those whose voice spoke through Omizantrim were mightier by far than the gods of Earth.

Farther south, all lights were extinguished at once in a City whose foundations rested on nothing more solid than the air itself. The Sky City's new queen, celebrating her fresh victory over her hated sister and rival to the throne, felt outrage welling within her breast. She sat in her great entertainment hall watching a subtle and sophisticated drama involving a half-dozen stalwart and naked young men, an assortment of implements of curious design and even more curious function, and a lovely young girl of a house which had dared oppose the queen's succession. The girl's screams marking that part of the program which the queen awaited most eagerly had only begun to echo through the hall when darkness fell abruptly.

Her pleasure thwarted, the queen ordered a hundred of the stewards of the Palace of the Winds, whose job it was to keep the lamps trimmed and filled with oil, exiled from the City in the Sky. The Palace Guard herded the unfortunates down the ancient avenue paved with skulls of past rulers toward the center of the City. Wailing, weeping, pleading for forgiveness, the stewards huddled at the lip of the Skywell. Her nakedness wrapped only in a lush fur robe, the queen had made a quick inspection of her City. In spite of the great festival she had decreed celebrating the victory at Chanobit Creek, she saw no lights. It meant that greater powers were loosed.

But it would not suit the majesty of the new queen to be indecisive and revoke the punishment she had commanded. Besides, having been cheated of the climax to which her private diversion had been building, she felt the aching need for some other release. The mass exiling would serve; the short walk from the Palace had made her sleek body hum with anticipation. A single hand gesture sent a hundred men screaming to their deaths on the snowy prairie a thousand feet below.

Later, when the drugged wine she had imbibed as part of her evening's merriment wore off, she wondered again why the lights had gone out all over the City. No comforting answer came.

And in that dark womb far to the north, the air began to vibrate and formed a single word from nothingness. That one word was the answer, the promise, the exaltation, the vindication of millennial faith.

That word was: *Soon.*

CHAPTER ONE

"Your Highness, Your Highness," called the dishevelled youth. The knight was young, his cheeks hardly touched with downy beard. Tears rolled unnoticed down his dirty face. It was not merely the unendurable anguish of defeat that made him weep. Only an hour ago he had seen the loveliest face he had ever known—snarling at him over the hilt of a Highgrass dog rider's saber. The tradition of chivalry dinned into him over a lifetime of training had almost stayed his hand, but loyalty to his princess and the ages-old urge to save his own life had acted with a will of their own. He had heard his own voice cry out in terror as his bright, straight blade hacked the woman's face into a ruin of blood, brains and gleaming bone.

He had passed the test he, like so many other warriors young and unblooded, dreaded above all: he had faced mortal danger and had not flinched. But he wondered if he had not failed another test in the same moment.

"We've brought you failure and disgrace," the youth almost sobbed. "How can we restore to you what our worthlessness has lost?"

Moriana Etuul brushed a strand of red-gold hair from her eyes and sadly shook her head. She gazed past the young knight at the man lying exhausted and in dubious safety beside the broad race of Chanobit Creek. The day had dawned as if especially tailored by this man. The sky had been filled with low clouds lying in a cool white blanket on the land to keep the bird riders grounded and out of the fray. Without their most deadly weapon, the Sky City soldiers would prove easy prey. Believing this, Darl Rhadaman, Count-Duke of Harmis, had taken the forefront with his sword held high, the eerily diffuse milky early light glinting from his sword's keen edge and the mirror-bright steel of his breastplate. Then, his face had been alive and almost boyish with the certainty that he fought for right and would triumph in its cause. Now his sword was nicked and blunted, his armor so hacked that the deep metallic cuts already scabbed red with rust in the damp air. Dull eyes stared out of a face as listless as a slab of meat on the butcher's block.

His brown eyes met her green ones, but no contact was made. Pity welled in her heart for him. It had meant far more than his life to him to bring victory for his Bright Princess, as he called her. Now, defeated, he faced her beneath budding branches ripe with the promise of spring and renewed life. The contrast tore at Moriana's emotions. If the battle had not been lost, Moriana would now be Queen of the Sky City, instead of her sister.

If only he had listened to me, we might have won. Unbidden, the words rang in her mind. Angry at herself, she tried to soften her thoughts. The lusterless brown eyes turned from hers, and she knew he had heard the reproach as clearly as if she'd shouted it. This knowledge added another fresh cut on her soul.

Shaking herself, Moriana returned to the reality of the moment. The young knight who had led the dazed Darl Rhadaman from the field still looked at her beseechingly. She recalled what he had asked.

"You cannot," she said without thinking.

He recoiled as if she had slapped him. Once more she reproached herself. He was a child and had just discovered that war was no glorious game. She had to give him something to cling to, or destroy yet another life in her fruitless quest.

"The best way you can serve me now is to live," she said.

He brightened.

"You will permit us to fight for you again some day?" A half-dozen eager young voices echoed the question.

"If you wish, perhaps you shall. Some day." She held back her tears with effort. "But that's not what I mean. I want you to survive. Live out this day and many more so that I'll not have your death on my conscience, too."

Bewildered, the youth blinked. Moriana turned to Darl. He regarded her through strange, old eyes.

"I'm . . . sorry," he whispered.

Emotion blocked her throat. She reached to take his hand and pressed it against her cheek.

"You tried."

"What will you do now?" Darl spoke listlessly.

"I can do two things. I can quit—which I shall never do as long as I draw breath. Or I can go elsewhere for assistance."

"Where will you go?" he asked distantly. "I have used up my stock with the folk of the North. Where will you find the men for a second army?"

Her lips drew back in a grimace.

"I will not use men. Or at least, not humans."

"I don't understand."

"The builders of the City—*Zr'gsz,* as they call themselves. They live at Thendrun in the Mystic Mountains."

A gasp burst from her listeners.

Still possessed by the awful calm of shock, Darl asked, "What can you offer the Fallen Ones? You can't offer them the City."

"By the Five Holy Ones, no! It's a matter of personal interest to the rulers of the City in the Sky to know how things go with them. There are artifacts, sacred relics, which the Fallen Ones would be overjoyed to recover. Without human aid, they have no chance of regaining them. And I think those trinkets a small price to pay for my City."

"But what of your soul?" asked another underaged knight with a bloody-bandaged arm. "They are evil. They are the soul of evil! How can you bargain with them?"

"The *Zr'gsz* are not the *soul* of evil, friend. You know little of the Dark Ones if you think any earthly evil can surpass theirs." The intensity of the feeling with which Moriana spoke caused her to shudder. "I hate the Dark Ones and fear them far more than you know. More than you can know. But I would sell myself to them. . . ." Her listeners gasped again and drew back. "Yes, I would do that if it would free my City from my demented sister Synalon. She seeks to return the City in the Sky to the Dark Ones, then give them the entire world. Do you think my soul too great a price to save your wives and friends and children from that?"

The young knight looked away in confusion and dismay at what he'd just heard. Moriana swayed, suddenly weary to the point of collapse. Almost by instinct, a hand went to clutch the Amulet within her bodice.

She felt a fierce impulse to tear the Amulet off and throw it into the clear, cold waters of the creek. Its mystically changing mixture of dark and light in the central stone had brought nothing but doom and death. Then she recalled the impossibly high price she had paid for the talisman bestowing eternal life. She took her hand away.

"We must go," she said, casting an uneasy look at the sky. Leaden and sullen in the dusk, the clouds hung close overhead. But not close enough to keep the Sky City bird riders from quartering the countryside around the battlefield looking for survivors.

A knight gave her a spare riding dog he'd caught

fleeing across the ridge. He had already fastened in place small bags containing provisions and the earthenware jug which housed the spirit of her long-dead companion Ziore. Moriana mounted the huge animal, hiking up the skirt of her gown. To please Darl, she had worn this finery rather than the tunic and breeches and boots that were her accustomed garb. Now the delicate lacebird silk was ruined, stained with mud and blood and sweat, and she had hacked it off at the knees so that it wouldn't bind her legs. The Northern knights blushed and looked away as she settled unchastely astride the black and white dog.

They didn't understand she was a Princess of the City in the Sky, a warrior of great skill, not like the pampered hothouse flowers that were the Northern ladies. Moriana had no time for their affronted mores. Defeat knew no dignity; nor did death.

The party had just set out following the creek as it curved gently northward toward its eventual rendezvous with the River Marchant when the bird rider squad swept over them like a glowing cloud from the guts of Omizantrim. The boy knight who had guided Darl to safety fell with an arrow in his back. Others cried in surprise and pain as feathered messengers of death winged downward from above. Only Darl and Moriana survived, saved by thickening twilight and the almost naked branches overhead that screened them from the eagle riders.

Moriana looked back. The Sky City troopers hadn't realized any escaped their new slaughters. They passed once more above the bodies of their victims looking for signs of life. One figure stirred, trying to raise himself from the mud of the riverbank. A sheaf of arrows drove him down facefirst.

Moriana clenched a fist and ground it against her forehead.

Oh, my daughter, my poor daughter, a voice sobbed

in her mind. But the princess took no solace even from the comforting presence that rode in the jug at her hip.

Turning their backs to the slaughter, Moriana and Darl Rhadaman rode north. North to the Mystic Mountains and the last stronghold of the ancient enemies of mankind.

"We're too late." Fost Longstrider slumped in the high pommelled saddle atop his riding bear. The beast grunted sympathy with his master's despair. "The battle is already lost."

His companion made a bitter sound. She was a tall woman, with a brush of cropped red hair, high cheekbones, slightly slanted eyes of brown. Her mail hauberk clanked as she raised one arm.

"No, 'tis won," she said, pointing. "For them." Her outstretched finger indicated carrion crows gathering like mourners around the bodies. Larger birds stalked among them, naked heads bowed and aggressively pecking for a larger share of the fine meal. Fost smiled in grim appreciation of the rolling wheel of death and life. One side, the other side, human, dog, eagle—it was all the same to the vultures. Whatever misfortune befell others, they fed. And prospered.

Fost and Jennas rested their tired bears in a copse beyond what had been the right flank of the Sky City army. The field lay deserted now, save for the dead— and the feeding vultures.

It had been a long, desperate journey from the south where his lovely and beloved Moriana had left him dead in a city swallowed by a glacier. It seemed half a hundred years since his sorcerous resurrection by the Amulet of Living Flame, since he and Jennas, hetwoman of the nomadic Ust'alaykits, had arrived in Tolviroth Acerte, the City of Bankers, to find that the Princess Moriana had departed days, hours even, before they appeared. Now they had missed her again.

Fost considered Moriana's possible fate. Fled? Killed? Captured? The thought of the latter possibility turned him cold. Capture meant return to the Sky City to face the vengeance of her sister Synalon—and of her cousin Rann, warrior, genius, sadist.

Death would be better by far.

They rode on through the eerie stillness of dusk. Fost couldn't rid himself of the sensation that the limp bodies strewn so recklessly about would rise up at any instant with a friendly greeting or outstretched hand. He was no stranger to death; he'd dealt it himself on occasion. But he had little experience with such whole-sale slaughter. And no stomach for it at all.

He had been horrified at the carnage at the battles of the cliffs, when he'd helped the People of Ust defeat the Badger Clan and their foul shaman. That had been the mildest of diversions compared to this awful carnage. Together in a heap to Fost's right lay more men and women than lived in either Bear or Badger tribe. He shuddered. He wanted to throw up.

Though they kept careful watch they saw no eagles. The bird riders were off chivvying the defeated, butchering stragglers and the wounded. The wind babbled to itself of the sights it had witnessed that day, stirring fallen banners and mocking the dead. The wind even spoiled the clean and optimistic odors of early spring with the gassy rankness of corruption. Fost took hold of the strap slung over his shoulder, held a leather satchel high.

"See, old smoke," he said to the bag. "This is the reward for your passionate desire for bloodshed. Don't your nonexistent nerves pulse with excitement at the sight?"

A sniff came from the satchel.

"What could I possibly find to excite me here?" a voice asked peevishly. "This is rubbish."

Furious at the spirit's callousness, Fost swung the satchel up to dash the jug it contained to pieces on the ground.

"No," said Jennas. "Let him be."

Ashamed at his angry outburst, Fost pulled the strap back over his shoulder and let the satchel fall to its riding position. He knew he was only venting his ire at not finding Moriana on the genie in his jug.

Following the path the routed army and its pursuers had taken, they passed the hill with its crumpled pavilion and heard the murmur of running water.

"I'm thirsty," said Fost, "and there were too many corpses in that stream back there for even the bears to touch the water. Let's see if this one is less clogged with dead."

Jennas nodded. They rode toward the sound, angling toward a stand of trees well beyond the hill. Though none of the bird riders had shown themselves so far, neither felt like taking chances.

They were almost to the water when they heard the moan.

Without thinking, Fost booted Grutz's sides. The big bear rolled over the bank and into the water, never breaking stride. The icy water numbed Fost's legs. He barely noticed in the urgency that gripped him.

Another sad knot of bodies lay at the treeline. Dogs and men in the distinctive armor of the City States had been struck down by the equally distinctive arrows of the Sky City. The missiles protruded at angles that told they had come from above.

Fost pulled Grutz to a stop beside a young man who stirred feebly. His fingers raked furrows in the mud. An arrow had penetrated his backplate and jutted horribly from the center of his back, as if that, in all the broad earth, was where it belonged.

The knight had been trying to reach the creek. His

first words to Fost confirmed this.

"Water. Need . . . need water."

His voice rattled like a handful of pebbles on a tile roof. Fost dismounted and squatted by his side, studying the extensive injuries. A trail of bloody spittle ran from the corner of the young man's mouth. Fost doubted the youth was twenty.

"You're in a bad way," said Fost, trying to remember the rough but practical healing lore he'd learned in his career as a courier on the highroads of the Sundered Realm—literally a lifetime ago. "I don't know if you should have water."

"You don't honestly think it matters, do you, you dolt?" asked Erimenes acidly from his jug.

Fost shrugged. The shade was right, though it surprised Fost that Erimenes had responded in this fashion. Compassion was not a trait he normally associated with the long-dead philosopher whose ghost rode in the jug at his hip.

The youth drank greedily from Fost's water bottle, which had been taken and filled by Jennas and tossed back to the courier without comment. Fost held the blond head cradled in his lap as the dying boy drank. Jennas urged her mount out of the stream and slid off beside them. Her boots went deep into the cold mud. She was as tall as Fost and just as strongly built.

The boy coughed. The fit came so violently that he jerked himself free of Fost's arms. To Fost's horror, he fell backward onto the arrow still in him. His weight drove it deep and snapped it off. He stiffened, coughed up bloodshot phlegm, then sank back with a sigh, as though sliding into a warm and soothing bath.

Fost bit his lip. The boy's chest rose and fell raggedly within his armor.

"The princess," Fost said, hating himself for troubling the dying man. "Do you know who I mean? The Princess Moriana."

"Princess?" The boy nodded, then frowned, his face a bloody mask. "Failed her. Failed her. . . ."

Fost felt a cold black hand clamp his throat.

"She didn't—she's alive, isn't she?" he demanded. To his relief the youth nodded. A grimace twisted the young features as if the slight motion had pained the boy. "Where did she go?" The knight did not respond. By dint of great effort, Fost kept himself from shaking him. "Where did she go?" he asked again.

"The . . . three of them."

Fost frowned up at Jennas.

"Three?"

"Ah—aye. Princess, Lord Darl and . . . Great Ultimate, is it getting dark so soon? And the spirit . . . the woman in the jug. . . ."

"Woman in a jug?" asked Jennas, as confused as Fost.

"It must be the other spirit that Guardian told us about," said Fost, trying to remember more of what the speaking, sorcerously living glacier had said. "The glacier's name is Guardian," he told Jennas, seeing her baffled look. "When we left Athalau, the glacier told us Moriana had a spirit jug with her. He said something about the genie inside, but other matters pressed me then. Guardian had mistaken the other spirit for Erimenes. It put him into a fine rage." Fost glanced at the blue form wavering by his elbow. He did not remember having uncapped the jar to let him out. Erimenes's face acquired a faraway look.

"A woman," the spirit said musingly. "As I live and breathe, a woman! This has interesting aspects I had not considered. Imagine, another such as I!"

"By Ust's snout," muttered Jennas, "one of you is more than enough. And you do *not* live and breathe."

"A woman!" cried the philosopher. "I can at last vindicate my teachings! What the two of us might do together. . . ." The misty body of the shade glittered with dancing blue motes of light, spark-bright in the darkness.

"Be quiet, you," snapped Fost. "This man is dying, and you rant about another genie."

"Not just any genie, friend Fost," crowed Erimenes. "A female! I wonder if it might be possible that we. . . ." His face glowed with a lechery so luminous it astonished even Fost, though the courier knew the shade's ways by now. Erimenes had preached stark abstinence throughout his life, and then had thirteen hundred years to think better of it. The long, lonely centuries trapped in his ceramic jug had been devoted to developing a totally hedonistic philosophy; disembodied, Erimenes could only experience his newfound ideals as a voyeur. Until the promise of another—female—genie.

Jennas scowled.

"The boy, Fost, the boy is dying."

Fost swallowed and turned back to the dying knight. Erimenes's crude enthusiasm shamed him. And he was no closer to finding out what had happened to Moriana. He leaned closer to the youth.

"Where did she go?" No response. Fost dribbled water across the parched lips and asked again, slowly, "Where—did—she—go?"

The young knight tried. In his fading mind he was glad that with his dying breath he could help his princess, the Bright Princess whom he and his friends had let down so badly.

"She went to . . ." His blurred, fading mind struggled to concentrate. "Went to . . ."

Another coughing spell wracked him. He sprayed bloody foam all over the front of Fost's tunic. Fost gripped the boy's shoulders, trying to steady him.

The boy tried to say, "To see the ones who built the City in the Sky," but the coughing hit him again.

"To . . . City . . . Sky," was all Fost Longstrider

heard in the instant before the boy's head lolled back on lifeless muscles.

Gently he lowered the boy. He rose and looked at Jennas.

"The fool," he groaned. "She went back to the damned City."

"And you will follow her."

"And I'll follow," Fost said. "I'll follow."

CHAPTER TWO

The fugitives rode north following the course of Chanobit Creek as it flowed toward its meeting with the mighty River Marchant. Moriana intended to keep to that course until they could cut northeast to the Mystic Mountains and avoid passing through the lava flows surrounding Mount Omizantrim like a skirt. Those dead lands of tortuous folds and black stone tentacles were well avoided at the best of times. Fell creatures stalked human prey there. Besides, Moriana had no appetite for a meeting with the Watchers, descendants of the loyal few entrusted by Felarod after the War of Powers to guard the flows of skystone. The Fallen Ones had used that gray igneous rock to build their flying rafts of war and commerce, and huge chunks of the skystone formed the base of the City in the Sky itself. The Watchers had passed long ago into legend, keeping vigil over the lonely centuries against a return of the Fallen Ones. How could she look any of them in the eye knowing she went to enlist the aid of their ancient enemies?

Nor was this the best of times to approach Omizantrim. Sometime during the night after the Chanobit Creek debacle the volcano had belched into deadly life again. Lightning and choking poison vapors now ringed the jagged crest of the mountain, and a spume of black smoke grew from it like a bloated, ghastly phallus raping the sky. Such was the power of that single eruption, that from time to time Moriana and Darl passed through areas rendered gray and unreal by falls of ash from the crater two hundred miles to the east. Glancing uneasily

at the vast smudge defiling the eastern sky, Moriana
wondered what unholy message the mountain had
uttered.

She had the gut feeling that it boded her no good.

In another year Moriana might have appreciated the
soft beauty of early spring. Leaves burgeoned on the
trees, and fields and meadows exploded with a profu-
sion of wildflowers, pink canthas, ovuei as gold as the
sunset on placid waters, even the rare royal minsithen
mimicking the colors of the Empire of High Medurim.
In contrast to Moriana's grim mood, those minsithen
shone cheerfully, each a bright yellow star inset in
five rounded petals of blood-rich maroon, enriching the
air with subtle scents. The trees were deciduous, mostly
sturdy spreading anhak, their bark as brown and shaggy
as a hornbull in winter coat. Interspersed with the
anhak rose stands of Upland tai, straight, slim yellow
boles as graceful as elf dancers against the great gnarled
shapes of their neighbors. Birds molted to show rainbow colors to the new season and sang to the travellers.

But neither the princess nor Darl had eyes or ears for
the splendor all about them. The bulk of the Sky City
army had hurried south the day after Chanobit, but that
did not mean she and Darl were spared the horrors of
pursuit. With breaking of the weather, the war eagles
once more had the freedom of the sky. They could
range north to harry the refugees and then wheel southward to catch up with the lumbering columns of dog
riders and infantry in time for a hot supper and boots
of mulled wine. Moriana's every sense concentrated upward, eyes scanning the sky for sight of wings outstretched in the distance, ears cocked for the cry of a
death-giving war bird carried to them on the spring
breeze already laden with the smells of spring flowers
and moist fertile earth. She wished Darl would rouse
from his stupor long enough to take some of the burden
of the searching off her.

If anything, his depression grew worse with every

mile. His thoughts turned inward and he seldom responded, even when directly spoken to. After two days, Moriana ceased trying to communicate with him. She decided it was best to let him work alone through his depression, if he could. She knew no magic to pull the man back to the world outside his skull. Darl seemed momentarily a lost cause to her, lost like the battle, lost like her precious City, lost, lost, lost.

On the third day, they approached the juncture of Chanobit Creek and the River Marchant. As they rode, Moriana had collected dazed stragglers, tatters of her once-proud army. Her battered army was now sadly composed of knights in dew-tarnished armor turned as gaunt as their quarrelsome, hungry dogs by fear and deprivation; of Great Nevrym foresters slipping on foot through woods flanking the riders, graceful and lethal as panthers even in defeat; of peasant footmen stunned and stumble-footed; and of adventurers hard-eyed and angry at seeing their dreams of conquest and plunder evaporate with the morning mists at Chanobit. Some still hailed Darl as their commander, in spite of his temporary mental infirmities. Gratifyingly, others called out her name with fervent loyalty on encountering the party. She felt small and soiled at the satisfaction she took in knowing that some, at least, gave allegiance directly to her instead of to her through the charismatic wandering hero who had taken her cause at Tolviroth Acerte.

Tolviroth Acerte. So long ago. Lifetimes ago. And a lifetime of struggle lay in front of her.

Since that first day after their defeat, Moriana had said nothing more of her intention of journeying to the keep of the Fallen Ones. Part of her disliked being less than candid with men so loyal. The practical side pointed out that there would be plenty of time to leave for those who disapproved. But that had to be later, when they were beyond the joining of the rivers, and most likely beyond the vengeance of the City in the Sky. Besides, her cynical self observed, even among the survivors were many who followed whomever was in motion at a given moment, not caring where they headed. They were like Darl, who needed to be led. Others realized that their numbers and the princess's intimate knowledge of the bird riders who pursued them gave the best chance of survival. Moriana knew the callowness of attributing faith to all who followed her simply because they followed.

The woodlands rose gently to a ridge that dropped off steeply toward the northwest. Moriana rode point with a bow in her hands. She felt responsible for the fate of these groundlings who followed her.

Before she reached the crest of a rise, she slipped from the back of her war dog. She patted the beast's blunt muzzle and whispered encouraging words in one cropped ear. The animal was trained to stand stock still and to make no sound. She had no fear of it running off or betraying her presence with barking when she scouted the ridgeline on foot.

It's a sign of becoming human, child, a calm, gentle voice said in her mind. *This concern for those you once would have deemed beneath your notice.*

Moriana paused, still hunkered below the crest of the rise.

"Aye, perhaps I'm not fully human. Perhaps my people had lived in the splendid isolation of our City too long." Her mouth twisted bitterly. "Certainly I can send humans to their deaths as easily as if I were of some other race."

Don't use that stick to beat yourself, the voice said. *That is the most human trait of all.*

Moriana smiled briefly. Ziore of Athalau had spent her entire long life cloistered in a convent devoted to the ascetic teachings of Erimenes the Ethical. Like Erimenes, the nun had survived the death of her body, living out long, dusty centuries as a cloud of mist contained within the enchanted red clay of an Athalar spirit jar. Moriana had found the genie while stumbling in a haze of exhaustion and self-hatred through the streets of the glacier-entombed Athalau. Though Ziore's existence had been remote from human experience, the spirit was wise with a wisdom as deep and placid as a sheltered pool. Her soothing presence and loving words had been all that enabled Moriana to keep her tenuous grip on sanity through the brutal trials and disappointments of the last few months.

"Thank you," Moriana whispered, feeling an immediate answering caress in her mind.

Arrow nocked but undrawn, the Princess of the City in the Sky moved up the slope. She placed her feet carefully to avoid slipping and falling headlong on the slippery mulch of fallen leaves underfoot. The anhak trees grew right to the crest where the soft black earth fell steeply to a broad flood plain. Here and there she saw great raw gaps in the terrain where the spring flood had undercut the bank and toppled a hunchbacked anhak. None was recent. Winter had been too brief for the melting snowpack in the far-off Thail Mountains to engorge the Marchant till it overflowed its banks.

She dropped to her belly. Nothing in the act struck the princess as incongruous. In years past when an heir apparent to the Beryl Throne and not an outcast, she had trained as a bird rider of the elite Sky Guard, a course designed to break all but the fiercest, most determined and toughest in mind and body.

Moriana had passed without the slightest favor being accorded her due to her station. Under the command of the youthful leader of the Guard, her cousin Rann, she had led a flight of Sky Guardsmen into battle against the Northern Barbarians. Now Rann was head of all Sky City soldiery, and Moriana's sworn enemy. But Moriana had not forgotten the hard lessons she'd learned from him. Not the least among them was that survival never took second place to dignity in the field.

With bits of sodden leaf and rich black loam clinging to her belly, she snaked to the crest of the slope. Above her and to the left grew an oval-leafed urylla bush. The short shrub sported no flowers and would not blossom until the white sun of high summer glowered down from overhead, but it provided excellent cover. The princess knew not to silhouette her head against the sky.

Noiselessly she wriggled to the bush, raised her head to peer through the branches. To her left the Chanobit made its final dash to meet and merge with the Marchant. Man-high rushes marked the banks of the river. She scanned them carefully. If the Sky City forces wished to mount a final ambush on the ground, this would be an ideal place to do it.

For ten long minutes she lay staring intently from between the leaves of the bush, eyes scanning the river, the mile-broad flood plain, the sky. The surface of the river rippled strangely clear. This time of year it usually clogged with flotsam, branches, barrels, scraps of cloth. The decaying corpses of trees, animals and feckless men were often carried downstream on the spring torrent, too. As she completed her thorough reconnaissance, Moriana pondered the shortness of the winter. Though it lengthened the growing season for the groundling farmers, a magnificent boon in the cool Sundered Realm where the planet's three-hundred-day year rendered the fertile time between frosts precariously brief, she found only ominous portent in it. Powers were afoot that interfered with the very order of the universe.

"And I'm about to unleash still more powers," she said to herself, "and fell ones indeed, unless the legends lie."

Nothing moved on the plain, and Moriana saw no movement among the reeds other than the restless scurrying of a southwesterly breeze. High piled clouds rolled across the sky, but Moriana's practiced eye placed them many miles away. If the fluffy cumulus contained the wheeling shapes of war eagles, the birds would be too distant for her to see. Finally, as satisfied as she could be with an inherently risky situation, she nodded to herself and slid back down from the crestline.

She rolled onto her back to descend the hill and instantly froze. Reflex drew the bowstring halfway to her ear before Moriana recognized the tall, broadshouldered form who had stolen up to stand a handful of yards behind her.

"Walk warily, Stormcloud," she said throatily. "I might have let fly without thinking had I not heard you approach."

The man smiled. His face was that of a fallen angel surrounded by a nimbus of curly golden hair. There was a decidedly not cherubic light in the cat-green depths of his eyes, but he nodded and courteously refrained from pointing out that the princess hadn't heard him.

"I trust your capabilities, Bright Lady," he said.

In spite of herself, Moriana smiled back and smoothed a wisp of sweat-lank hair from her eyes.

"I'm glad somebody in this party does."

"Oh, but all admire you, Your Highness. The way you rallied us together after the slaughter at the creek is commendable. No man could have done better."

Moriana frowned. Was this some implied criticism of Darl? She saw no sign of guile on that open face. But then she suspected that Iatic Stormcloud could plot foul murder and continue to beam like a seraph in a religious mural.

Still, she had no firm reason to mistrust him and many to be grateful. It was the young mercenary, Stormcloud, who had led the reserves in turning back a flank attack that by rights should have been the final desperate thrust of the Sky City army. Had a war dog not panicked at the smell and upset the brazier Moriana used for her weather magic, the princess would have been able to maintain the ground-hugging clouds that

kept eagles from the sky, and handsome Iatic Stormcloud would have taken his place beside Darl Rhadaman as architect of a great victory.

In spite of a lingering unease about the young mercenary, Moriana had been happy when she and Darl
had encountered Stormcloud and ten survivors in the
woods a few miles from the battlefield. Alone of the
Northblooded officers of her army, he had taken her
military abilities seriously. He had proven invaluable in
persuading the other survivors of the rout that she knew
what she was doing and that her commands should be
heeded. And with Darl lost in a fog of melancholy,
unable to cope with this first shattering defeat of his
career, Moriana had found herself relying more and
more on Iatic Stormcloud's air of authority and calm
counsel.

Moriana became aware of the way her truncated
skirt had ridden up her hips, baring pale skin. She wore
nothing beneath the soiled, faded garment. Moriana's
fine silk undergarment had chafed her unbearably as
she rode, so she had dispensed with it. Deliberately, she
drew the ragged hem of her skirt down to cover herself
better.

"As far as I can tell, the crossing is clear," she said,
relaxing the bow, clamping the broadhead arrow to the
staff with her thumb while pushing herself to her feet
with her other hand. "There's no knowing whether bird
riders wait above the woods for someone to venture out
on the open flats." She paused, considering. "I'll scout.
Stay here and cover me."

Iatic frowned.

"My lady, is it wise for you to risk your . . ."

"Down! Get down!"

The shrill warning sang from the satchel at Moriana's hip. Without hesitation, Moriana cast herself forward, rolling down the slope into a clump of tai near
Stormcloud. The mercenary hesitated, looking dumb-

founded by the sudden voice from nowhere, but quickly recovered and threw himself into the scrub.

An instant later a flight of eagles swept overhead in a thunder of wings. The bird riders barely cleared the treetops, and leaves rattled on branches from the wind of their passage. Gazing upward, Moriana counted a score of them in chevron formation, javelins and short-bows ready to slay the unwary.

Let me out, a voice urged in the back of her skull.

Knowing how slight a movement the great Sky City eagles could detect, Moriana reached down, groped in the satchel without taking her eyes from the deadly formation swinging out over the flood plain and pains-takingly untwisted the basalt cap of Ziore's spirit jar. She sensed the genie flowing like mist from her jug. Moriana concentrated and sent a thought warning to Ziore not to assume her usual form. A pink apparition swaying among the trees would be certain to attract the attention of any eagle looking that way.

The compact cloud of the nun's vaporous being went swirling into the bushes that hid Moriana, lending an almost imperceptible rosy glow to branches, leaves and the bole of a tai by the princess's elbow.

Never fear, my child, came Ziore's familiar thought pattern. *I've learned a few things since meeting you.*

"What are you doing?" whispered Moriana.

Trying to control the leader's emotions, came the mental reply. *I can read his intentions clearly enough. He means to hide his men in the reeds by the river and wait until you try to cross the open space.*

"Can you control him at such a distance?"

My powers grow greater with use. I think I can. Now hush and let me concentrate.

Flashing the shadow of a wry smile at the thought of being reproved by the cloistered, innocent spirit, Mori-ana lapsed into silence. Straining her every sense, the princess detected small, furtive sounds of the forest, little creatures scurrying from cover to cover or digging holes against the coming of night and predators. She felt a definite kinship with the tiny, hunted woods beasts.

So acute was her hearing that she heard the slow rise and fall of Stormcloud's breath ten yards away. She heard the wind whispering above the murmur of the river, heard the mighty throb of distant wings, heard now and then a scrap of human voice as the riders called to each other. The squadron turned slowly above the southeastern bank of the Marchant looking for a likely place to land and lie in ambush without the necessity of remaining airborne for long, tiring hours.

They've seen no sign of us since immediately after the battle, Ziore said in Moriana's mind. *I'll try to convince the leader that we've passed long since, or crossed by another route.*

Moriana nodded. She watched the flyers through several more of their aerial circuits. One dropped out of formation, his bird's claws stretching down to seize the earth. Another rapped a command at him so sharply that the sound came clearly to Moriana's ears, though she couldn't understand its sense. The meaning became clear soon enough: the landing bird hammered the air with its spread wings and soared again, tucking its talons up against its pale belly feathers.

A bird rider peeled from the formation and arrowed his bird straight at Moriana's hiding place. Moriana caught her breath. Had her sister protected these men with a spell that allowed them to sense magical tampering with their senses? Was it possible they detected Ziore's subtle compulsions and now homed in on the source? Synalon and the sorcerors of the Sky City were cunning and knowledgeable. Moriana alone knew of the long hours of arcane studies her sister had devoted to such matters. But the lead eagle rose quickly, the others rolling into a long line after it, climbing toward the heights of the southern sky. They were a thousand feet up when they passed overhead and vanished from Moriana's view in the treetops.

A long sigh gusted from Moriana's lips. A branch tickled one cheek and she brushed it away. Still cautious, she rose from the bushes.

A moment later the foliage stirred off to her left and Iatic Stormcloud rose from his own cover, as silently as she. His eyes widened as he looked past her. Stormcloud blinked at the sight. Moriana turned to see Ziore's form hovering at her side.

"I take it we owe your familiar thanks for the warning," the mercenary captain said, jerking his head in the direction the departing bird riders had taken.

"Yes, but she's not my familiar. Ziore is my friend."

Stormcloud nodded polite acknowledgement at her emphasis.

"I was able to control the emotions of their leader," Ziore explained aloud.

Moriana looked sharply at her spirit friend. Was the flush of success rendering the shade too talkative? Then she relaxed. If she couldn't trust Stormcloud with the knowledge of the genie's power, there was no one left she could trust. Not unless Darl came out of his damned self-hating fog.

"That could prove handy," said Stormcloud, eyeing the pink figure appraisingly.

"Yes," Moriana agreed curtly. Tugging down the hem of her skirt, she walked past him into the woods, aware of the man's eyes on her all the while.

CHAPTER THREE

Preoccupied, Prince Rann Etuul walked along a back street of Bilsinx, his stride eating up a surprising length of ground for one so short. Bulbous towers loomed on either side of the cobblestoned street, and in the distance in front of him rose tall minarets. Pale, drawn faces peered out at him through glass rippled with age and purpled by the sun. He gave them no more attention than he gave his surroundings. All his thoughts centered on the great gray oval of the City in the Sky floating a thousand feet above his head, drifting to the east like an immense stone cloud.

He similarly paid little attention to his companions, the three armed men in black and purple swaggering in a loose wedge before him and the thin and pimply adolescent mage who trotted behind. Hard-pressed to keep up with his prince despite longer legs, the young wizard Maguerr half stumbled and half ran while managing to stroke a wisp of ginger-colored beard and cradle a geode the size of a human head against his hollow chest.

Rann hummed a wordless tune as he walked and thought. The events of the past few days amounted to nothing more than history for him now. Past glory faded with the promise of future triumphs. His destiny, the destiny of Queen Synalon, the destiny of the City in the Sky lay to the east.

East. The City in the Sky, by some process forgotten even before men wrested control of it from the reptilian Hissers who had built it, could have picked one of three directions to move after it floated into Bilsinx from the west. From the central city of the Great Quincunx, the pattern it had followed immutably over the center of the Realm since Felarod had confined it after the War of the Powers, the Sky City could have gone north to Wirix, south to Brev, or east to Kara-Est. Brev was the smallest of the Quincunx cities and had already made proper obesiance to Synalon. Wirix raged defiant and strong in the midst of Lake Wir, almost as remote from the land as the City itself. There would be little profit in conquering Wirix immediately.

The city that Synalon must subdue next was Kara-Est, richest seaport of the Realm, most powerful of all the five Quincunx cities. And it was toward Kara-Est that the City now headed.

On its last transit of Bilsinx, the Sky City had dropped a deadly rain of stones on the ground city's defenders, as bird riders wheeled down unleashing a steel-shod storm of arrows. An attack by the Highgrass Broad mercenaries had completed the defeat of Bilsinx, along with a commando attack on the Mayor's Palace by Sky Guardsmen under Rann's command. The city had fallen quickly under his brilliantly waged campaign and fighting prowess.

And more important than the fighting, the prince's honeyed words had soothed the anxieties and resentments of the subject Bilsinxt. They had even sent a body of their light cavalry to fight Moriana's army beside the very bird riders and heavy dog-mounted lancers and bowmen who had stormed their city. His diplomatic ways had turned a defeated enemy into a wary ally.

Now giant shapes grew in the large central plaza of Bilsinx like arcane fungi, turning into vast bloated sausages and rising upward toward the City silently floating overhead. Eagles harnessed to long, stout tethers guided the cargo balloons with a precision otherwise impossible. Time weighed heavily. Preparations for further battle occupied all of Rann's waking thoughts and even haunted his dreams.

He nodded in silent pride. Below the elongated shapes swung gondolas fairly straining with their cargoes of arrows, foodstuffs and a hundred other necessities in preparation for the coming battle of Kara-Est. Alone of all the Quincunx cities, to say nothing of the cities of the Sundered Realm, Kara-Est had substantial defenses against attack from the air. As it was the greatest prize of the Quincunx, so it would be the dearest won.

Everything proceeded well ahead of schedule. He had been inspecting warehouses of goods assembled since the occupation began, among them bundles of rare and expensive herbs sent over the Thails from Thailot, westernmost Quincunx city. Rann smiled wickedly as he thought of the aromatic bundles. Perhaps the smug engineers gazing through the complex ring sights of the rooftop-mounted ballistae of Kara-Est would have a few surprises as they strove to bring down their swift-winging Sky City foe. And the men of the seaport's aerial defense force, riding in light platforms beneath the living gasbags called ludintip—Rann had plans for them as well.

A high wash of shirred white clouds drifted between the City and the sun. Rann's sensitive nose sensed the promise of rain sometime that afternoon. He must expedite the loading. The Sky City eagles hated to fly in the rain, and it was injurious to their health to do so. The specially bred, intelligent birds were mighty engines of destruction, but they had definite vulnerabilities. For the birds' lungs, strained from hard flying, to breathe in cold damp air could lay them low as readily as iron darts from Estil catapults.

Rann needed his eagles if the assault of Kara-Est were to succeed. And he would have them.

"Maguerr," he barked, not bothering to look back at

the weedy journeyman mage who trotted at his heels. He scarce could stand to look at Maguerr, with his lank hair that seemed stranger to comb and soap alike, his inadequate beard, his beaklike nose with nostrils that seemed to exert an unbreakable fascination for his fingertips, his watery eyes and spiderleg fingers and pimples without number. But the boy was a genius in that special branch of magic that enabled the Sky City's forces to communicate verbally over great distances, and hence, indispensable. There were times when he annoyed Rann so much that the prince began to itch uncontrollably with the need to tie the horrid youth to some handy fixture and flay the skin from his wretched and unsightly face. Yet because of Maguerr's undeniable ability, and in a perverse way as partial penance for his own failure to make an end of Moriana and her clever groundling, Rann had attached the wizardling to himself as his personal amanuensis.

Maguerr's slippers scuffled along the cobblestones.

"Yes, Your Highness," he whined. A tic twitched beneath Rann's left eye.

"Pick up your feet when you walk," he rapped, "and for Istu's sake try to learn not to talk through that damned proboscis of yours."

"Yes, milord." Maguerr's tone was obsequious and unruffled by his master's brusqueness.

Rann bit back a curse. He saw the slight head motions of the three escorts who walked before him. The prince seldom had need to raise his voice, yet here he was on the verge of screaming at his own secretary. Rann knew quite well that his Guards made sport of him, and he promised silently they would pay for it. At the same time, he toted up yet another debit owing to Maguerr, a debt he planned to collect with the most usurious interest once the mage was no longer necessary to his plans.

It had been long since his taste for torture had been sated.

"Take a memorandum," Rann said. "To Her Excellency Gomi Ashentani, Governor of Bilsinx by grace of Synalon I Etuul, Mistress of the Clouds, First among the Skyborn, of the Dark Ones Most Favored, and all the other usual honorifics." He chopped the air with one hand.

Behind him Maguerr murmured to himself, impressing the words on his spongelike mind. Among his other unbearable attributes was numbered an eidetic memory. Rann gritted his teeth and continued.

"Milady Governor: You are hereby instructed to dispatch the ground forces left at your disposal, holding back a suitable reserve, to Kara-Est by no later than nightfall—"

Although Bilsinx was not just a conquered city but a thoroughly subjugated one, the hands of Rann's three Guards rested on sword pommels, and their eyes were never still. Bowstring-taut alertness was the rule of the Sky Guard elite, and even though they expected no trouble they scanned the street and storefronts with eagle-sharp eyes. They made no idle chatter; Rann would not permit it. They allowed themselves a measure of relief that the prince, impatient with crowds clogging the main thoroughfares, had chosen this side-street where no assassin could sidle to dagger range of Rann in the anonymity of a mob.

But they allowed themselves no laxity.

Yet it was the prince's sharp eyes that caught the telltale gleam of sunlight on steel in a doorway ahead and to the left.

"Down!" he shouted, hurling himself to one side, tucking in his shoulder and rolling to the stoop of a shuttered bakery, closed by the Governor Ashentani's rationing decrees. When Rann came to rest, his scimitar glistened in a wicked arc from his left fist.

The Guardsmen's honed reflexes snapped at Rann's command. But not quickly enough. Arrows whined, went home with deceptively soft sounds. Sword in hand, a Sky Guardsman sank to his knees, eyes fixed on the red fletched shaft sprouting between them. Beside him a comrade choked on the steel point embedded in his throat.

"Get the bastards!" a harsh voice cried.

A man and a woman broke from the cover of doorways on opposite sides of the street and cast aside shortbows. The man straightened his left arm, causing a hornbull hide buckler strapped to his forearm to slide into his hand. His other hand brought forth a broadsword. The woman drew forth a rapier and maingauche with identical fretwork hilts. Two more men materialized behind them, weapons in hand. A fifth figure stepped from a farther doorway as the remaining Sky Guardsmen ran to engage the killers.

Rann gained his feet. He started forward in a crouching glide, only to stop and clutch at his chest as agony shot through him.

"Dark Ones!" he gasped, "I've torn something loose!"

He had undergone terrific punishment in recent months. Broken ribs had been his reward when he sought to interpose himself between a raging Vicar of Istu and his helpless queen. His chest barely wrapped with bandage before he was off in the saddle again, Synalon had ordered him to Athalau and a nearer brush with death. An immense block of ice had fallen from the vaulted roof of the living glacier in which Athalau lay, striking down Rann and the Sky Guardsmen who had trailed Moriana, Fost Longstrider, and their treacherous spirit companion, Erimenes. Only the wildest luck had prevented the prince from being mashed into red gruel by the ice fall. And only the fierce, driven vitality and determination of the man and his lineage had enabled him to survive, with a dozen bones shattered and a score of muscles torn loose.

He had had the best healing sorcery of the Sky City; but not even the peerless mages of the Soaring World could make him altogether whole again in the short time alloted them.

Conquest for queen and City had repeatedly called him forth half mended, still hurt and hurting. Now his wounds betrayed him.

He fought for balance as blackness veiled his senses.

"Your Highness!" he heard Maguerr call in alarm.

Rann struggled against the darkness threatening to swallow him. He saw his remaining bodyguard surge forward to perform his duty. With a musical skirl, the Guardsman's curved blade met the straightsword assassin. The woman with the rapier circled, watching for an opening. The next two assassins went wide to bypass the combatants, making for the prince with deadly intent shining on their faces.

"Come forward and meet your death, dog lover," snarled the Guardsman, Ahue. "At least you'll know a good death from City steel."

The assassin was a good man, strong wristed and supple, but his foe was of the superbly trained Sky Guard. Ahue's scimitar beat the larger blade aside. The killer screamed shrilly as the caress of steel severed veins and tendons of his swordarm. His blade fell, ringing on the cobblestones as his cry drowned in blood bubbling from slashed throat. Before he fell, the Guardsman was lunging for the woman, launching a vicious hail of blows that she was hard-pressed to fend off despite her paired weapons.

"Your turn, bitch," Ahue cried, recovering to slash out again.

"Bitch, am I?" she snarled. "Better than you who defends a eunuch! Or are the two of you lovers? Do you share his bed?"

Ahue viciously attacked, angered by the slurs both on him and his prince. Rann was a eunuch, castrated by the Thailint barbarians. The Guardsman's pride prevented him from accepting this insult calmly, even though he knew it was intended to enrage him and thus force him into a deadly mistake.

He slashed fiercely, incoherently screaming out his anger.

The black-haired swordswoman gave way. Her two companions hesitated. The one on the right, a lean straw-blond man who kept a pair of rapiers twitching before him like the antennae of some giant insect, feinted a lunge. The Guardsman's scimitar shot sparks off the twinned blades and sent the man reeling backward.

Ahue spun and lunged, almost gutting the burly redbeard who tried to dart by on the left and give his friend time to bring up his dirk for a parry. The redbeard lashed out with his spiked ball mace. Holes tapped in its haft made it whine like a banshee, a high, unnerving sound. The Guardsman was not distracted. He ducked nimbly below its lethal sweep and returned a cut that opened a long red dripping slash in the olive-drab fabric stretched taut across the maceman's thigh.

The three killers retreated. The Guardsman faced them with a wild laugh. A killing frenzy was upon him, and even seasoned slayers such as these quailed before his madness.

"Stand back!" barked the same harsh voice that had ordered the assassins forward. A tall woman strode forward. Her pale blonde hair was cut square across the brows, though it swung free behind, brushing broad shoulders. In her hands she held a curious implement, the like of which the Guardsman had never seen before. He continued to smile defiantly, but his eyes narrowed at the peculiar weapon.

Though exotic, the device was not unfamiliar to Rann. By titanic effort of will he forced himself away from the pilaster he used to prop himself upright.

"Ahue, *get back!*" he shouted desperately.

In his frenzy, Ahue did not hear. Or perhaps he

heard and for the first time defied an order from his prince and commander. It was the first and last time. Ahue brought his scimitar up from guard, preparing to hurl himself upon his new antagonist. The blonde woman swung something around her scarred left hand. A black blur whined toward the Guardsman.

Ahue cursed as a chain wrapped itself around his throat. A fist-sized leaden ball smashed into the side of his head, staggering him. He caught the chain in his gauntleted left hand. The blonde woman jerked the chain with all the might of her beefy shoulders. Ahue plunged forward, swinging wildly with his scimitar. The blonde fouled it with her chain. Her right hand turned and swept upward. Breath and life gusted from Ahue's mouth as the upturned sickle blade tore through his light mail shirt into his guts, ripping upward. The tip of the sickle curved within his ribcage to cleave his heart. For a long moment Ahue stared past the woman's left shoulder, breast pressed to hers as though in comradely embrace, his gore gushing onto the front of her body as his wide brown eyes gaped in final surprise. Then he fell.

The killers sighed. They had stopped to watch the dance of death between their leader and the berserk Sky Guardsman. Now they started forward again, watching Rann with grim singlemindedness. The blonde drew her sickle blade free, disentangled the chain from the corpse with a musical tinkle and stepped forward.

With unnatural clarity Rann heard the sounds: Maguerr muttering in horror behind him; the many-throated murmur of crowds in Bilsinx's main street, oblivious to the deadly drama being enacted a few hundred feet away; the scuff of soft sole leather on stone; even the hissing of gasses venting from the cooling corpse of Ahue.

"I am Prince Rann Etuul and you shall not have me so easily," he said, pushing the tip of his chin toward the dead Ahue. Rann hadn't expected any of these

killers to follow the direction of his gesture. They were
too good for that. But he'd lost nothing by trying.

He collected himself, pushed pain aside, forced the
darkness from his vision. Battle lust sang its adrenaline
song in his veins. He knew that for the next crucial few
moments he would be able to function at almost full
capacity. His mind had the cold clearness it always did
when he went into battle. The sickness and desperation
he had felt just heartbeats ago had been transmuted
into exultation and anticipation. Fall he might, but he
would drink deep of blood and pain before yielding to
the Hell Call.

"Die, eunuch," said the man facing Rann. The straw-
haired young man danced forward, grinning, rapiers
questing. Rann glided to him. The soles of his calf-high
moccasins never left the street. The rapier points
darted in a quick one-two attack. Rann's scimitar
dashed them aside with contemptuous ease.

The youth raised an eyebrow and began to circle.
Rann knew what he attempted; the assassin wanted to
get the prince to circle with him so that one of his
fellows could slip a blade in from behind. Rann circled
in a direction counter to the other's motion so that their
left sides came close and the man's body stayed between Rann and the deadly sickle and chain.

That was the weapon Rann feared most: *aizant-eshk*
it was called, the devil's claw. The name was appropriate.

The blond man stopped circling a few steps before
his right arm would have begun crowding the gray-
green stone of a facade. Rann faced him coolly, left
arm half extended with his blade, right hand open and
held by his hip in readiness for a grab at the other's
weapon.

Rann sorely felt the lack of a parrying weapon.
Normally he carried a spike dagger of his own design
tucked into his right boot. But he was in Bilsinx today
as a Sky Guardsman as well as Prince of the Sky City.

Sky Guardsmen prided themselves that they never carried daggers, except for those rare occasions when they fought on foot. In flight they never came closer than sword's length from a foe.

"Are you going to fight or wait for me to die from old age?" demanded Rann as the man continued to circle.

Something in the words affected the blond man. Rann saw his eyes glaze slightly with rage. An opportunity. Now all he had to do was capitalize on it.

He waited until he saw the other tense for a lunge, then snapped the scimitar in a whining overhead wrist cut. With a clash, the rapiers met in a defensive cross and caught the descending blade. The triumphant grin on the blond man's face changed to a look of astonishment as Rann deftly turned his wrist and thrust the curved sword down inside the other's guard. The point went into the assassin's neck where it met the notch of his clavicle. Blood fountained, his knees buckled, and the confident light in his eyes faded in an instant.

Experience and coolness had aided the prince. He doubted the others would fall prey so easily.

Rann ripped his sword free and spun, whipping the scimitar in an eye-high cut parallel to the ground. The black-haired woman was almost upon him. Her rapier fended the stroke, but her comrade's blood spattered into her eyes. As she blinked frantically to clear her vision, Rann brought the scimitar in beneath her main-gauche in a quick backhanded return. The woman howled and doubled over, dropping both weapons to clutch at the ropy intestines spilling from her belly.

The whisper of steel on steel warned the prince. He flung himself headlong, jarring every bone in his body. The lead ball of the devil's claw clattered by inches above him, drawing its chain after like a comet's tail. The weight ricocheted off stone polished to a high gloss by innumerable feet. Rann rolled fast as the blonde woman reeled in the ball. As soon as he was clear he pulled himself to his feet. His head spun; the adrenaline rush was fading fast and when it went, so would his already slim chance of survival.

"Now it is time for you to die, little man," the blonde told him. He cast a quick glance at the redbearded man and dismissed him as a real danger. The woman was a different case.

Rann needed to know more about the blonde if he was to successfully defeat her. Gathering that information would prove difficult. She was good, too good. As she neared, twirling the ball on a half yard of chain, holding the sickle loosely, her hand protected by a brass strap fastened to the haft as a sort of knuckle-duster, he clearly made out the indigo mark on her right cheek. It was a convolute squared mandala.

From his limited experience in the City's commerce, he knew it for the tattoo of the Dyers' Guild in High Medurim. That explained her deadly expertise. The hereditary guilds controlled that city's industry with an iron hand. Those born outside of a guild were forced to live on the dole or by outlawry; those born into a craft for which they lacked aptitude or interest, unless they bought out of their birth guild and into another, were doomed to the same fate.

But the guilds needed enforcers to keep power over their members, and to prosecute their ever-changing rivalries and feuds. They kept large contingents of professional killers. Some imported masters from Jorea, the North Continent, or the Far Archipelago. Others trained native Medurimites, providing opportunity for lucrative employment even for those forced to live outside a guild. But whether imported or domestic, the Weapons Masters of High Medurim were among the most perfect murderers to be found anywhere in the world. The blonde-haired woman with the feral look to mouth and eyes was one of that kindred.

That knowledge didn't cheer Rann. If anything, it drained some of his determination. At his fighting best he knew he was more than a match for gutter killers like her. But now . . .

"Yes, little man," she cooed, moving closer. "Your death is at hand. Come. Don't fight it. Let me dispatch you without pain. I promise you won't feel even a twinge."

Over his left shoulder Rann heard low incantation. Maguerr was trying to summon help on his geode. Rann grimaced; the mage had more nerve than he would have credited him with. Small good his unexpected steadiness would do. The only people who might receive his call were in the City overhead. Even the swift eagles were unlikely to arrive before the issue was settled. Rann sidestepped toward the center of the deserted street, need for room overriding the worry that one assailant might get in back of him. He felt the first twinges of pain in his chest and knew help would not arrive in time.

"It is you who will die," he said. Rann fought down giddiness. His words rang hollow in his ears, and he knew she laughed at him, this blonde killer from High Medurim.

"Your pet wizardling's magic will avail him naught," she said, moving closer. "Your eagles will take too long to arrive. Your corpse will be stretched out on the street for an afternoon repast. Your eagles *do* eat human flesh?"

The adrenaline rush was past. Rann fought on nothing more than dogged determination. It wouldn't be enough.

He had no warning of the attack. One instant he faced the relaxed blonde, the next her sickle came spinning through the air toward his face. He dodged, hacking at the weapon as it whined past. The tip raked his right shoulder and left a burning wound. He felt warm blood pour down his arm onto his tunic.

The blonde's face twisted in rage at her missed stroke as she yanked hard at the leaden weight in her hand. She deftly spun the sickle back to her hand. Rann's blurred eyes were too intent on her. The big red-bearded maceman came for him. The prince's sword darted past the spiked ball and sheathed itself an inch in the man's left eye, almost by accident. His sword felt as if it weighed a hundred pounds now.

Bawling, the redbeard fell back. The blonde's arm moved in a blur. The chain of her weapon whipped about Rann's ankles. She uttered a cry of fierce delight as she pulled it tight, jerking the prince's feet from under him.

But even as he fell, the prince's right hand shot out to seize the chain. The blonde leaned forward to close with her intended victim; he pulled with a supernatural might born of desperation. The tattooed assassin lost her balance, fell. Rann served her as she had served his Guardsmen, face twisting in a wild grin as he felt his curved blade penetrate her flesh.

But his life was done. The huge-shouldered man with the red curly beard loomed over him, face now a horrid mask, a single blue eye glaring wildly. The mace went high. Rann snarled in futile defiance as the spiked ball was silhouetted against the clouds.

The red-bearded man's head exploded in a welter of blood.

He fell heavily beside his leader's body. Rann lay gasping like a beached fish. He was aware of the distant sound of screaming, and another sound less identifiable.

Regaining his breath, Rann struggled out from under the blonde woman's body. Maguerr knelt in the street, clutching his midsection and retching dryly. Unsteadily Rann went to him and laid a gory hand on his bony shoulder.

"You have my gratitude, boy," he said in a voice that hardly seemed to be his own. "Don't feel shame at being sick. It happens often when first one slays a fellow man."

Such tender words from the fearsome Prince Rann

would have shocked any of his Sky Guard. Maguerr merely shook his head.

"N-not that, lord," he choked. "The geode communicator. Was—aggh, my stomach!—was in tune with it. What happens to it . . . I feel."

Numbed and slow to comprehend, Rann fell back a step. His bootheel crunched on a fragment of the geode which Maguerr had hurled to burst the skull of the red-bearded assassin. Maguerr screamed.

"Breaking! Gods, it's shattering me!"

Understanding the mage's plight at last, Rann leaped to one side, lost balance, reeled, and stepped on yet another fragment. The mage fell over with the wail of one damned.

When the bird riders arrived, they found Rann Etuul, Prince of the City in the Sky, Marshal of the Sky Guard and commander of all the City's forces, dyed dark red with drying blood and scrabbling on all fours on the Bilsinx backstreets, diligently searching for pieces of Maguerr's shattered geode.

CHAPTER FOUR

Boisterous merriment boiled and soared, filling the great audience hall of the Palace of Winds clear to the vaulted ceilings far overhead. The festive week proclaimed by Synalon in celebration of her victory over her sister had dragged into its sixth day, only to have its vigor renewed once more by fiat of the queen, in honor of the miraculous escape of Prince Rann from the High Medurim assassins.

Torches guttered in sconces, splashing orange light on walls and making the ancient figures carved into them seem to writhe in the grip of nameless, unsettling emotions. Captive fire sprites thrashed inside crystal bell jars as tall as men, their furious hissing and killing heat contained by the thick greenish enchanted glass. All that escaped from the bell jars and into the great hall was their hellish blue glare. Great tables of veined green stone stood everywhere, piled high with the finest food and drink. The revellers circulated, drinking, eating, sniffing vapors from bubbling bowls of potions, trying to adopt the appearance of being successfully and spontaneously amused. Some danced a stately pavane to the strains of an orchestra brought up from Bilsinx. Others stood around discussing what a marvel it was that the mercy of the Dark Ones had preserved Prince Rann from the treacherous attack while their eyes searched for likely partners for later assignations.

But the sound of merrymaking had a false note to it like a gilded pot-metal coin dropped on a table. There were those in the Sky City who were not altogether overjoyed at their queen's victory over her twin, who by right of inheritance should have sat on the Beryl Throne in Synalon's stead. And even those who supported Synalon for reasons of conviction or expedience found it difficult to work up much cheer over the prince's survival. His was not a personality to attract tender sentiment.

On the highbacked throne carved of a monstrous single green beryl crystal Synalon sat at her ease, idly scooping berries from a silver bowl and feeding them to the ravens who perched on either arm of the throne. She wore her glossy black hair curled into an intricate knot atop her head. A thick unbound strand fell to either side of her beautiful, sculpture-perfect face, lending it a decidedly misleading air of innocence.

Of all the revellers in the vast, crowded audience hall, she was the freshest looking. She had changed into a new gown only moments before ascending her throne, a gown woven of shimmering green and blue and pearl and silver threads. Depending on light, the viewer's perspective and the motion of the lithe limbs and body to which the garment clung like skin, the colors subtly changed. Debauchery, particularly of the sort mandated by Synalon, was hard work. Watching courtiers and subjects move about in a low haze of fatigue, Synalon smiled, a wicked light touching her cobalt eyes. A life of determined dissipation, interspersed with the harsh disciplines of black sorcery, kept the queen as fit as the toughest of Rann's Sky Guard.

The dancers strutted through the complex patterns of the Virgins' Recessional, commemorating the coming of spring. Synalon covered a yawn with a slender hand. Her subjects proved most tedious. If left to their own devices for an instant they lapsed into supremely trivial activities. It was ever up to her to make sure their celebrations held at least some semblance of life.

For a time she contemplated calling for the hornbull she'd had ballooned up from the surface and giving a demonstration of what she considered properly vivid recreation. Certainly her subjects were abusing the dance area with their . . . tedious meanderings.

Then a better idea came to her. The smile returned to her lips. It was much like the expression of a great cat that comes upon a tender and helpless kid.

She set the silver berry bowl on a stand beside the throne. Sensing their mistress had some new diversion in mind, the ravens beat their wings and chuckled evilly. Propping her chin on her right hand, she held her left in the air before her eyes, forefinger extended. A glow appeared at the tip. Slowly the finger began to turn in a circle, leaving a silvery trail in midair. Instead of dissipating, the trails remained and began to form a ball shape, as a caterpillar would spin a cocoon.

Eyes turned toward the throne now. Motion ceased on the floor as couple by couple the dancers stopped to see what magics their monarch performed. Fear and anticipation mingled on the faces of the celebrants, giving Synalon a warm flush of pleasure. Like most of her favorite amusements, the one she concocted now would bring delight to some and stark anguish to others. The revellers, well aware of this, felt a thrill of expectation.

When she had woven a ball of light in midair, Synalon brought up her other hand. Both palms cupped the glowing globe, shaping it, massaging it, infusing it with pseudo-life. Like her gown, it shimmered with myriad opalescent colors.

"What do you dream?" she asked her subjects. Her voice was as smooth and strong as silk. At the sound of it the musicians ceased their efforts, though the words were clearly audible above the melody. "This is the Ball of Dreams, my children. In it you shall see your deepest, darkest thoughts, summoned forth for all to see."

She gave the globe a push. It drifted away from her, seeming to test the air like a scenthound casting about for a trail. The revellers fell back from the ball, trying to be unobtrusive. No one was overeager to be the first

to have thoughts, desires, deep secrets called forth for
the cruel amusement of the rest.

The scintillant ball darted toward a knot of courtiers
gaily caparisoned in silks and the furs of animals specially bred by the genetic sorcerors of Wirix for the
color and quality of coat. It hovered above the head of
a paunchy, black-haired youth. The young man studiously looked away from the ball as its surface began to
shimmer, then swirl with colors like oil on a pond. An
image within the ball snapped into sharp focus: the
young man naked on a luxurious bed grappled ecstat-
ically with a blowsy older woman.

"Why, that's Sunald's mother!" exclaimed a burly,
bearded comrade. The women in the group tittered.
Laughter was taken up by the hall as a whole, laughter
too hearty, momentarily releasing tension of those who
know they may yet feel the axe. Furiously red to his
high-flounced collar, the youth stalked out, head drawn
down between his shoulders like a bird seeking a
worm's hole.

"And where does the Ball of Dreams cast next?"
asked Synalon in velvety tones. "Will it be you? Or
you? Or even you?" Her finger stabbed forth each time
indicating revellers. As their expressions turned from
mirth to horror, Synalon laughed delightedly.

With a perversity like that of the sorceress who had
summoned it into existence, the ball ignored all of
Synalon's prospective victims and swung next to float
above the blonde head of the burly man's escort, who
had laughed first and loudest at the revelation of
Sunald's secret lust. She gaped in mute horror as the
ball seethed with color again to reveal her, as naked as
Sunald had been, spreadeagled on her back across a
furry hassock receiving the eager attentions of a great
black war dog. Bannered on the dream sphere's surface
for all to see was the woman's face, a face showing
every indication of almost religious ecstasy. She

screamed and fell to her knees, hands tearing at her bodice as laughter rained on her like blows.

The burly man tried to comfort his lady but she pulled away. He turned angry eyes toward the throne. Synalon lounged back, amused.

"Is this not more interesting than your pathetic little dances?" asked the black-haired Synalon, idly playing with a strand of her hair. "Now that you know Lady Emele's most secret desires, perhaps you will accommodate her."

Laughter rolled through the great audience hall.

"Or," Synalon said, "was the large black canine image in the sphere yours? Are you then a shapeshifter?"

Again the resounding laughter, a bit too loud, a bit too long. Synalon waved a long-fingered hand in acknowledgement of the success of her sorcerous entertainment, then turned back to the sphere.

The ball moved on, pausing at random to blight the mirth of one or another who had been roaring with cruel laughter only moments before. A tall, lean banker was revealed adjusting his institution's accounts to bleed funds into his own pockets; a matronly woman noted for announcing frequently, loudly, and at inordinate length that a woman's sole duty was motherhood was shown strangling the latest of her dozen brats in its bassinet, a look of orgasmic glee transfiguring her plump features; a civil functionary loathed by the populace for over-punctilious enforcement of statutes regarding the conduct of small businesses appeared nude, wallowing in a great heap of his own excrement, smearing it over his body and cooing like a giant baby; a noted cavalry officer was seen spurring his famed red war dog to the rear against a backdrop several veterans recognized as the ridge by Chanobit Creek.

The laughter rose to a hysterical crescendo. The matron lay on the marble floor in a faint. The banker

hurried off to slit his wrists. As the cavalryman backed
away from the half-dozen comrades in arms moving in
his direction with lethal purpose and the bureaucrat
stood laving his pudgy hands against one another while
tears cascaded down his cheeks and chins, Synalon only
sat on her throne watching with an amused smile on her
face, feeding bits of spiced meat to her ravens.

The ball stopped, rose, as if seeking fresh prey. It
descended in a gentle slope toward a clump of older
celebrants who stood near one of the buffets. It settled
at a point a foot above the head of the tallest of the
group, a woman whose short reddish hair was dusted
with white streaks.

Gilinon dun Krit, a powerful member of the Council
of Advisors to the Throne, snorted disdainfully as she
glared up at the shimmering sphere. Her companions,
other advisors and their hangers-on, backed away from
her as if afraid to be marked as having stood by her
side. For a long moment the woman gazed up at the
particolored roil of the sphere, the muscles standing out
on her neck as stark as pillars, a vein beating visibly in
her broad forehead. Then with a shriek of fury and
despair beyond words, she drew a long dagger from her
sleeve and flung herself at Synalon.

Palace Guards and Monitors anonymous behind
brown iron sallets lunged from their waiting places by
the walls, cursing and driving the illustrious assembly
from their path like so many cattle. Synalon threw back
her head and laughed, a sound unutterably pure and
sweet.

Her face a red demon's mask unrecognizable in its
hatred, the Councillor reached the foot of the royal dais
and raised her arm to strike. The two ravens swept
down upon her, striking with beaks and black-tipped
claws. The woman reeled back, beating impotently at
the bird sinking its claws in her scalp and stabbing at
her eyes with its beak. Its fellow lit on her dagger arm
and dug its nails deep.

The venom on the birds' talons took effect. With an anguished scream, dun Krit straightened so spasmodically that both large black birds were flung aside. She began to twitch, then hop, until she was spinning about the pattern inlaid in the floor's center with her arms flung wide, a ghastly parody of the calm dance that had occupied that place scant moments before. Her face turned bluish-black and her tongue protruded between bloated lips. With a last garbled outcry she fell to her back. Her body arched, flopped, black foam gushed from her nostrils, and then she lay still.

The silence of ghastly death filled the great hall. All cheer was stilled—except for the pealing laughter of the beautiful young queen.

Four Monitors made their way through the crowd and gingerly bore the body off. The revellers turned away.

"Come, the gaiety has just begun," cried Synalon, clapping her hands for the orchestra to start afresh.

The Bilsinxt musicians looked at the faceless men bearing out their limp burden, and fell into a light and happy air. At a nod from Synalon a small army of servants invaded the hall, bearing fresh platters of meats and pastry and great tureens of wine and essences. Slowly the tide of conversation began to flow once more.

High above the assemblage floated the pearly sphere. Synalon looked to it again, motioned with a finger. It dropped.

Conversation ebbed. Another clique of Councillors stood not far from where the ball had found dun Krit, and it was toward them the sphere now moved. Once more it seemed to single out the tallest person present, this time a portly man whose red face was fringed by a white beard that grew to meet the rim of equally white hair circling the base of his great skull. A shorter, stouter companion in a blue robe and black slippers with flaring gingery sidewhiskers and rough cheeks

spoke urgently to him in a high-pitched voice that
quieted as the sphere descended.

A commotion at the entrance brought heads around.
Prince Rann strode in without so much as a glance at
the heralds who bawled annunciation of his arrival.
Moving without apparent haste he quickly came to the
cleared space before Synalon's throne. The crowd
melted to give him way.

At a finger wave from Synalon, the sphere veered
from above the Councillors' bald heads and followed
the prince. Hearing an intake of breath from the crowd,
the prince turned to see the shimmering ball floating
toward him. Instead of kneeling before his sovereign,
he crossed his arms and stood waiting, watching the
approaching object with neutral eyes. It came to a stop
over his head. The swirling crossed its face again. The
tantalizing hint of a picture had begun to appear when
Synalon clapped her hands smartly and the ball vanished tracelessly. Her pale skin was flushed all the way
down the revealing front of her bodice.

One eyebrow raised, Rann knelt to make the customary obeisance.

"Rise, cousin," Synalon said throatily. "Accept the
plaudits of the crowd gathered to offer thanksgiving for
the survival of our most valuable servant."

He crossed his arms again as the hall rang with applause.

"I thank Your Majesty," he said dryly when the
clapping ebbed. "But I cannot stay to partake of your
amusements." The leaden inflection of the last word
told what he thought of her ideas of diversion. They
had some tastes in common but fetes and grandiose
display were not among them.

Synalon pursed her lips.

"And why not, honored cousin?"

"I have only come to inform you that the preparations of your mages are complete. The conjurations are

done. Magically, we are as prepared for battle as ever we'll be."

A murmur of whispered comment ran through the hall. It was rumored that Synalon herself would take part in the coming battle with Kara-Est. The Dark Ones had bestowed new and frightful powers on her. She wanted the world to behold them, and to know fear. Those in the great audience hall already knew that fear.

"But why must you rush away, then?" asked Synalon peevishly.

"The mystical preparations are but a part of making ready for the battle," said Rann. "I must see to our men and arms."

Synalon waved a hand languidly. As usual no rings adorned her fingers. Any ring she might wear interfered with the dangerous spells she cast so casually.

"You burden yourself overmuch, cousin. Is our victory over the wretched groundlings not assured?"

"By no means, Majesty." The crowd gasped. They expected Synalon's face to distort in anger, for her slim hands to clap furiously to summon guards to haul Rann off to torture and death for his defeatism. Instead, she rested her chin on one hand and regarded him calmly. Above her shoulders the ravens carefully preened blood from their wings.

"And why not?"

"Kara-Est is the most powerful of all the Quincunx cities. They have their aerial defenses and they know quite well we mean to take them on our next transit. Further, our ground forces are still en route back from the north. We'll have to rely almost totally on our bird riders." He took a deep breath. "I think we shall win, O Queen. But assuming that our victory is assured can only weaken us."

Synalon gave him a mocking smile.

"Our cousin instructs us with his customary wisdom," she said. "Very well, Prince. You have our permission to return to your chores."

He bobbed his head and knelt again.

"Oh, and how fares the loyal young apprentice mage Maguerr, through whom the Dark Ones acted to effect your rescue?"

"He does well, Majesty. He should be able to return to full service by the time the prow of the Sky City crosses the Cholon Hills outside of Kara-Est."

"You are a man indeed, Prince Rann, to inspire such loyalty in your followers," Synalon said with a razor-edged smile. Rann colored furiously. Synalon alone could torment him with that knowledge with impunity. He rose and stalked off, the heel taps of his boots clacking angrily on the marble flagging.

"Oh, and one more thing, cousin." Synalon's voice halted him just before the great double doors of graven green jade. "Might you be able to spare a flight or so of your most stalwart Sky Guards for the evening? They need not bring their mounts. They, ah, shall have a mount supplied them." She licked her lips which gleamed as red as fresh blood in the light of torches and captive salamanders. "I feel the need of some slight stimulation."

Rann did not turn, but the whole hall marked how his neck went red. His own favored diversions notwithstanding, he was a notorious prude and disapproved vigorously of his cousin's extravagant public displays of her sexual prowess and libido. He nodded jerkily and went out. The great doors swung closed with a resounding thump.

Flushed with happy anticipation, Synalon settled back on the crystal of her throne and called for more wine. Servitors hastened to her bidding.

The tall, red-faced Councillor turned to his companion. The smaller man's hands were still shaking with reaction and dread.

"Well, here's a curiosity, Tromym," said High

Councillor Uriath, smoothing the fringes of his white beard. "I never would have thought I'd be *glad* to see that devil Rann."

Tromym did not answer. Instead he lifted his goblet to his lips for a hasty gulp. Though he used both hands, a torrent of the purple wine cascaded down the front of his blue robe.

Off in the dappled distance of the woods a bird sang. Moriana walked a cathedral-like path beneath mighty trees, seeking some rest for her weary, tortured soul.

In every direction she looked grew trees. Most were yellow tai but every now and then the graceful tai stood aside for a tree giant, a shunnak with red bark shining on boles twenty feet thick, lifting blue-green clad boughs five hundred feet off the forest floor.

It was a scene of primeval beauty. Birds with long, brightly hued tails flew between the trees, small animals scurried about on missions known only to themselves. In the midst of all this tranquility walked Moriana, troubled and upset.

Ziore rode in her jug at Moriana's hip, doing her best to caress the worries from Moriana with comforting thoughts and her special gift of empathy. It should have been impossible for Moriana to remain wrapped in gloom, tormented by thoughts of past and future.

But a few miles to the northeast, an invisible presence beyond the leafy treetops, the Mystic Mountains loomed like eidolons, ancient, enigmatic, evil. Within them slumbered Thendrun like some dormant beast, the sole remaining stronghold of the Fallen Ones. Their nearness banished peace from the fugitive princess.

"But you know full well you've no other choice," the nun Ziore said. She spoke aloud, feeling that in her present mood Moriana needed sensory reaffirmation that she was not alone, though her mind was ever aware of the presence by her side. "And what can the danger be? The *Zr'gsz* will have dwindled over the centuries and most of their magic is no doubt long forgotten. They could prove no great menace to the Realm, even if they harbored such designs—which I'm sure they no longer do.

"The *Zr'gsz* are long-lived but their memories are longer still." Moriana's voice hardened. "I'm betting they haven't lost much of their power. I will need redoubtable allies to seize the Sky City by force of arms."

Ziore held still a moment, mulling this.

"You are right. But still, you mustn't worry. It's been ten thousand years since the War of Powers and eight thousand since your ancestors drove the lizard folk from the City. Surely after all that time they cannot nurse futile hopes of regaining their power? Their time is passed. If they are so long-lived, surely they are wise enough to acknowledge that?"

Moriana shrugged. "It's what I'm gambling on."

"And you are thinking of your other recent gambles that haven't worked," said Ziore.

"I . . . yes, you're right. Darl is no better, even after he and I went into that small village to purchase new clothing."

"He accompanied you. That is a sign of some progress," pointed out the genie. "It is the first indication of interest in the world around him since his defeat."

"Our defeat." The words fell like bitter droplets from the princess's tongue. "And he showed only passing interest in these." She looked down at the new clothing. Moriana had selected a wardrobe of the kind she had come to fancy in her own years of faring through the Realm: rugged tunics that laced up the front with leather thongs, canvas breeches with dog leather linings sewn inside the thighs to cushion the chafing of long hours in the saddle. The colors were russet, muted orange, burnt umber, the earth tones she favored, that set off her golden hair and vivid green eyes so well.

"Darl still thinks of you as his fairy princess,"

pointed out Ziore. "Seeing you clad thusly might have shattered his illusions."

"Damn him!" flared Moriana. "I'm not a toy to be put on display. I'm a woman and a princess. Not a fairy princess but one with the need to regain my City. How dare he pretend I'm anything but what I am?"

"Not all have your drive, Moriana," quietly pointed out Ziore. The genie paused. Moriana felt fleeting touches over the surface of her brain, feathery tickles, light samplings. "And Darl reads your thoughts as surely as I. He realizes the burden you carry over Fost Longstrider."

"I killed the man I loved. And all for this." Her fingers went to the black and white Amulet hung around her neck: the Amulet of Living Flame, which legend said would bring the dead back to life. For the promise of eternal life she'd killed Fost, driven her knife firmly into his heart, as they fought for possession of it.

"Your reasons were noble. The Amulet will allow you to best Synalon. Without it, your powers can never be used. She knows so much more of the black arts than you. Even if she slays you, with that in your possession you will live on and succeed."

"Darl reads more than guilty knowledge," Moriana said bitterly. "He knows I can never love another man as I loved Fost. Not even Darl Rhadaman."

"You are wise, my child. What you say is true. Darl's depression is great because of the loss. He hoped to win your favor with victory. He knows no other way of gaining your heart. His most romantic gestures and words carom off the shell you've built around your heart."

"I loved Fost," she said simply, a tear welling at the corner of her eye. She brushed it away, then rubbed the wetness from her finger onto the black and white Amulet. Even as her fingers touched it, the colors swirled in slow motion, black battling white for supremacy.

"You can love Darl—if you try," said Ziore.

"I have my duty to the Sky City before me. After Synalon is defeated and I've regained the throne, *then* will be the time to consider affairs of the heart. Darl's withdrawal, painful as it is to me, isn't the worst of my problems."

Though she had not spoken of it again since the evening of the battle, word had filtered through her small party that she intended journeying to Thendrun to ally with its denizens. That word was not well received. Her fellow refugees had begun slipping away, in ones and twos, walking away from sentry duty in the midst of darkness or falling back on the march until turning off unobserved into the woods. Among those who stayed there was talk; Moriana heard—or thought she heard— terms such as "witch" and "traitor to her kind" hissed behind cupped hands around the campfires when they halted for the night.

"I don't understand."

Moriana started at Ziore's words, though they rang softly in the quiet of the woods. When Moriana writhed in the grip of a mood like her present one, the nun's shade would read her thoughts carefully unless Moriana asked her not to. The princess had made no such request. But she had forgotten that her dark musings were shared by another.

"What don't you understand?" she asked stiffly.

"Why the terrific resentment among the others about your going to the Fallen Ones? I doubt more than a handful of humans have so much as seen one in the eighty centuries since Riomar Shai-Gallri seized the Sky City. Why the intensity of feeling?"

Moriana stopped, allowed the forest stillness to settle about her for a dozen heartbeats before answering.

"Have you heard of the Watchers?" she asked.

"Well . . . yes," answered Ziore hesitantly. "My knowledge is second-hand through what I've overheard from others."

"Then your education contains gaps," said Moriana, grateful for the chance to speak of things other than her feelings for Darl and Fost. "When Felarod and his Hundred drew forth the wrath of the World Spirit and broke the might of the *Zr'gsz,* they imprisoned the demon Istu sent by the Dark Ones to aid the Hissers in the foundations of the Sky City. This was only one of the deeds he did before the World Spirit departed. Some of the lava that has flowed in centuries past from the Throat of the Old Ones—Omizantrim—is a stuff called skystone. Worked properly with spells known to *Zr'gsz* adepts, the skystone floats on air like chaff. The City itself is built on a huge raft of it. The much smaller war rafts the Hissers rode into battle were a source of their strength as important as Istu himself. So Felarod summoned up a creature from the belly of the earth called Ullapag, whose cry, though inaudible to humans, is death to the *Zr'gsz.* And to aid the Ullapag and insure that the Hissers should no longer have access to their skystone, Felarod set a band of heroes, men and women strong and keen-sighted and skilled with bow and spear, to watch over the skystone flows until the Fallen Ones should be no more. These are the Watchers of legend.

"After ten millennia," Moriana added, "the descendants of the original Watchers remain on their lonely vigil at the foot of Omizantrim. Can you imagine the dedication that implies?"

"Yes, it disturbs me greatly. For three hundred generations to circumscribe their lives willingly to keep an ancient faith—it makes my own deprivation trivial, doesn't it?"

Moriana felt Ziore's bitterness at her own life. She could sense the troubling of her friend's thoughts and wondered if some of Ziore's gift had worn off on her. Being a nun in life following Erimenes's self-denying teachings and missing the rich realms of human experience had stunted her in many ways.

"Each person's problems, no matter how trivial, are enough and more for that person," said Moriana, smiling wanly at being able to quote one of the genie's aphorisms back at her.

"But it's more than just the Watchers," the princess went on. "I take it you're not acquainted with children's fairy tales."

"No," Ziore replied. "I was sent to convent at an early age. We had no time for such mundane trivia." Her words rang as harshly as any Moriana had heard her speak.

"The favorite of them, even now, concerns the bravery and dedication of the Watchers in standing off attempts by the Hissers to regain their precious skystone mine. Whether there's any truth in them, I don't know. And when children cry or balk at eating their greens, what do mothers tell them? 'The Vridzish will get you if you don't behave!' "

"So the Hissers are the legendary embodiment of evil to the people of the Realm."

"And the Watchers the embodiment of heroic dedication," said Moriana.

"Now I see why your men fear your destination— and why you do, as well."

Moriana bit her lip. "And have I reason to fear my course of action?"

"Have you any other?" came the sharp reply. "I—"

The nun's voice cut off, to resume in Moriana's mind: *Someone comes.*

The princess went into a fighting crouch, hands on hilt of sword and dagger. She heard whistling, a jaunty carefree tune, and the crunching of leaves under boots.

"Well met, Lord Stormcloud," she said as the tall blond youth strode into view.

He smiled, as radiant as the sun shining above.

"You requested that I not sneak up on you again," he said. "I saw fit to follow your advice."

Straightening, Moriana took hands from weapons and smiled.

"I . . . I wanted to tell you, Iatic, that I am most grateful for the assistance you've given me. It wouldn't have been possible to come this far."

He stood arm's length from her, smiling.

"Then perhaps the time has come for you to tender payment," he said, lunging as he spoke.

Caught off balance, Moriana fell back against the trunk of a tree. Strong fingers clawed at her belt. She felt the brass catch give, felt her swordbelt torn away bodily and flung into the brush. Her fingers struck at his eyes. Laughing, he easily caught her wrists and threw her down.

Moriana felt a pulse of energy surge from Ziore. The spirit was trying to quell the mercenary's passion. Iatic's face purpled in fury. He savagely kicked the satchel, parting the strap and sending Ziore's jug spinning after Moriana's swordbelt. Moriana heard the jug strike a tree with crushing force. She screamed.

The air exploded from her lungs as the mercenary flung himself atop her. Moriana wasted no time demanding what he was doing; she felt the hardness of him prodding into her thigh as his fingers tore at the fastening on her breeches. She brought a knee up. He twisted his hips expertly to block and grinned at her. The Amulet, torn free of her bodice, shone like obsidian.

"I've wanted this for so long," he panted. "Watching you flash your breasts and thighs in that flimsy gown . . . ah! You've wanted what I can offer you. There we go! Now, down with your trousers and in—you'll be begging for more, Bright Princess, by the time I'm done!"

He held both wrists pinioned in one powerful hand while the other tore open her breeches. His body had the power of a seasoned warrior. But so did hers, and she was coming out of the numbness of shock she'd first felt at his attack.

"No, no, you've got no right to hold back." He groaned in her ear like an avid lover, but in words no lover would utter. "You've made your pact with blackness, you've sold your soul. Now collect some of the wages!"

He thrust. Snarling like a war dog, she tore her hands free. His smile widened sardonically as she grabbed his throat. Then, as her thumbs began inexorably to press his head back, the smile disintegrated and a look of disbelief came into his eyes.

Stormcloud clutched at her wrists with both hands. Sweat poured down his face. Her eyes blazing with insane rage, Moriana gathered her strength and heaved.

When armed men ran up from the camp, led by Darl looking fully his old self with broadsword bared in his hand, they found her huddled half-naked against the slick trunk of a shunnak, cradling Ziore's jug in her lap. The Amulet, now the purest white, hung quiescent between bare breasts. The genie hovered by her side. A few feet away Iatic Stormcloud lay sprawled, as limp as a child's ragdoll, eyes touched with the lifeless cast of porcelain.

His neck was broken.

CHAPTER FIVE

"And what forecasts have you for me?" Duke Morn, ruler of Kara-Est, slumped on his throne, speaking into his beard and not looking at the stubby figure who stood before him. "Are we ready to meet the onslaught of ah, the, ah, Sky City?"

Rising from her knees, Parel Tonsho, Chief Deputy of Kara-Est, wrinkled her nose in distaste. The wind was in from the north, blowing directly across the great fen called the Mire. Not even the Ducal Palace in the Hills of Cholon overlooking the city was exempt from the sour reek of decaying swamp. Heightened by unseasonable heat, the smell overpowered even the pomades carried by the deputy's half-dozen armed and painted retainers. One of the youths caught her expression and tittered, thinking it directed at the duke's vagueness. She shot him a glance that froze him to silence.

"As ready as we shall ever be to trade with them on the battlefield," she said, "unless our *brave* partners in Wirix see fit to send us some of their mages to help ward off the spells of that damned bitch-slut, Synalon."

Bony fingers stroked gray-shot beard.

"Oh, but our, our trading friends the Wirixers, ah, they're cautious," he murmured as if to himself. "They wish us to deal with the Sky City, bleed them penniless, that they do, and at the same time they marshal strength in case we fail in the exchange. Clever . . . clever business, indeed."

Tonsho moistened thin lips. She gave the boy who had snickered a meaningful glare. Though for the most

73

part Duke Morn was the distracted, feckless dodderer he appeared, sometimes he gave evidence that the shrewd statesman he once had been had not wholly died with his wife and only son two years ago. The boy pouted and stroked a golden bangle depending from one ear. Tonsho made a mental note to get rid of him at the first opportunity. He was obdurately stupid, and she could not abide that, even in her kept pretty-boys.

In the drafty throne room atop the Palace's highest tower they made a curious contrast, the duke and the commoner who actually ruled the dukedom. Morn's once mighty frame had shrunk to a spindly, emaciated shadow of its former self. His leonine head, once long and fierce, was parchment-skinned and hollow at the temples. Despite the sticky noonday heat unrelieved by the rank breeze crawling through open windows, he wore a heavy robe of yellow velvet trimmed with the fur of the rare *gazinga* of the Dyla Wilderlands. He huddled within its confines as though afflicted with chill. Whether heat or senility caused it, Morn virtually ignored Tonsho and idly rustled fingers among the maps and charts that covered the tables set by the curving stone wall to his side.

She stood before him, as stubby and ugly as a tree trunk but equally unyielding. Her slit-eyed face resembled that of a pit-bred fighting dog, her eyes watery gray and hair an indeterminate color suggestive of mice. Her lumpy body was decked out in an outrageous robe of scarlet and electric blue, and her shoes were yellow, curling upward at the toes. Tonsho was the most senior and powerful member of the Chamber of Deputies which administered the wealthy port of Kara-Est. She had clawed her way to that lofty position from the lowest gutter of the city's slums.

"The artillerists manning our roof engines can hit an osprey on the wing," she told him. "And our ludintip can hoist aloft gondolas filled with archers. For the first time in generations we will carry the war to the enemy in his own element. Most of Synalon's ground forces are still straggling back from the north, and her bird riders are diminished by two hard-fought battles in the last several weeks. Only the dog cavalry the City held in reserve in Bilsinx, the greater part of which already has marched on us according to our spies, is reasonably fresh. And they can be discounted."

The huge, narrow head slowly moved up and down in a nod. Tonsho had no idea whether he comprehended her words or not. His lucid moments were both infrequent and unpredictable.

"On the debit side: their bird riders, particularly the Sky Guard, are consummately skillful and have the morale to absorb huge losses without breaking. We will have to inflict frightful slaughter on them to turn them back. And as they have made all too clear in recent days, they are more than adept at wreaking slaughter themselves. They have Synalon, who has announced to all the world that the Dark Ones have given her Their favor, and traded her increased powers. This may be true. Lastly, they have Rann. I credit him a greater advantage to them than the favor of the Dark Ones, or of the Three and Twenty Wise Ones of Agift into the bargain." She smiled grimly at the thought of such an unlikely alliance.

"Well. . . ." Duke Morn stuttered at a loss for words. "Do what you can. Yes. Let this be your watchword: do what you can."

"We will," the deputy rasped. A cold knot gathered in her belly at the prospect of battle, but she held her mind rigidly from her fear. "We may not win, Your Grace. But we will cost the City in the Sky dearly in this armed negotiation. Perhaps enough to render moot their dreams of conquest."

She made abasement and prepared to leave.

"Yes," the duke said slowly. "I know what my part

must be. You may leave now, Chief Deputy Tonsho. I will consult the weather. Meteorological data will be of vital importance in the coming conflict. Vital."

She hid her grimace with another inclination of her head. He had been a strong leader, wiser than many and perhaps less destructive of his subjects than most strong rulers. Then a freak storm had blasted up the sheltered Gulf of Veluz overturning the tiny skiff in which his adored wife and son were taking a pleasurable day's sailing. For a week the duke and his navy searched the waters of the Gulf. The bodies of his wife and sole heir were discovered washed against the first lock of the Dyla Canal. The duke had seemed to shrivel on beholding them.

Since that tragedy he had been obsessed with the study of weather. He had his throne room transferred up to this pinnacle, inconveniently far up flights of stairs for Tonsho's short legs, and the charts and brass meteorological instruments, telescopes and barometers and astrolabes cluttering the cramped chamber were the only things in life that held any interest for him. Tonsho had ambiguous feelings about his fixation. It was sad to see a basically able man so reduced, but at the same time his infirmity cleared her way to power in the richest city of the Realm. And when all was said, she knew she was a more capable ruler than any highborn.

"I'm sure your observations will be of great value," she said, and left. Her boys trooped obediently behind her, trailing a hint of perfume and the tinkling of weapons harness and gilt finery.

Fost laughed at the wind in his face and followed Jennas at a gallop down the long, sloping plain. Evening came down blue and cool all around, and the vast fields of flowers closed petals of white and yellow and crimson against the coming dark. It felt good to be alive, better perhaps than at any time since the courier had died and been reborn in Athalau.

"Come on!" Jennas shouted back at him. "Grutz will be as sluggish as a fattened boar if he doesn't exercise. Make him work!"

Fost thumped his heels against the bear's furry barrel of a body. Grutz shot him a reproachful look over one churning red shoulder and dutifully lengthened his stride.

Riding the enormous steppes bear was like riding an avalanche in full slide. Fost no longer felt the horrible queasy gut-clutching of motion sickness, nor did the constant back-and-forth whipping of his body threaten to part him, head from neck. He had never been much of a rider, but months in the saddle of the unorthodox southern mount had given him far more skill than he would acknowledge to himself. And it had toned him up as well. There hadn't been much exercise in simply riding the runners of his wheeled dog sled, as he had for most of his career as courier on the highroads of the Realm. Wenching and fighting had kept him more trim than most men then. Now he was conscious of a strength in neck, loins and belly he'd never before known.

Jennas had been riding Chubchuk, her own brown war bear, since both were cubs, as she put it. Pound for pound—and she outweighed the courier by a healthy margin—she was stronger than Fost, or any man he'd known. It wasn't plumpness; the feminine layer of sub-cutaneous fat, helpful insulation against the vicious chill of antarctic winter, merely softened the outlines of her powerful muscles, making her appear sleek and as strong as some great aquatic creature. Her greatest strength resided in her thighs and solid stomach, thanks to a lifetime of riding. The first time her muscles had clenched in orgasm around him, Fost's eyes had nearly popped out of his head. Since then many were the times when in the heat of passion she'd clamped him so fervently with her legs that he literally cried for mercy.

Tall green grass whipped at his legs. He was a handsome man, another thing he would not admit to himself. His face was more rugged than his years accounted for, showing signs of having been well-buffeted about and occasionally hacked open. His shoulders were broad within a hauberk of mail, his carriage erect, black hair blown back wild and free. When angered Fost looked like death on the prowl, but there were laughter lines prominent about his mouth and ice-gray eyes. He made a splendid barbaric pair with Jennas.

She grinned and waved as Grutz puffed up alongside Chubchuk. Her own chain mail shirt was unlaced down the front displaying a single swatch of canvas tied about her ribcage to keep her large breasts from bouncing uncomfortably.

Fost looked at her and thought how beautiful she was. He had considered her merely handsome before, and wondered now at his former blindness.

But she's not Moriana, came the pursuing thought. Fost knew deep down that no one could ever compare to his Sky City princess. No one, not even Jennas.

The light went out of his eyes and he let Grutz fall behind. He owed his life to the hetwoman of the Bear Clan. Wise and clever, an incomparable companion in bed and battle, she even laughed at his jokes. But Fost loved the golden-haired, green-eyed heiress to the Beryl Throne, she who had killed him to possess the gem both thought at the time to be the Amulet of Living Flame.

However, the gaudy bauble Moriana had taken from Athalau was not the Amulet but the Destiny Stone. This fey device had the power to alter the luck of its wearer, swinging between extremes of good and bad according to its own mysterious whim. The undistinguished pendant Fost had seized in his dying reflex had been the Amulet they both sought.

The Amulet exhausted the last of its power bringing Fost back to life.

Fost had to reach Moriana and tell her of her mistake. If she wore the Destiny Stone into battle with Synalon, thinking it made her invincible, she could perish. That thought formed a cold lump in the pit of the courier's belly. No matter what she'd done to him, he loved her.

He and Jennas rode north of the lava flows around Omizantrim, coming down off the Central Massif of the continent through the dark foothills of the Mystic Mountains. Following the Black River which flowed from the Mystics to meet with the Joreal at Port Zorn, they planned to take passage there through the Karhon Channel around the headlands of the Wirin River delta, and through the Dyla Canal to Kara-Est. It would be much quicker than faring overland as long as the army of the Sky City was interposed between them and the seaport.

They stopped on a high bluff overlooking the Black River. It was Jennas's turn to cook the evening meal. Fost, weighed down by his thoughts, went off by himself in search of his earlier lightness of heart.

Though he'd become an experienced rider, Fost still felt the day's jostling most poignantly in the kidneys. He wandered downstream through twilight touched with the scent of wildflowers and dead fish. He whistled as he searched for a likely spot out of sight of the encampment.

"I do so wish you would leave off that noisemaking," Erimenes said sourly from his pouch. "You can't carry a tune in a sling."

Fost laughed. It was true enough. "Whatever you say, old spirit," he said, opening his breeches.

"If you did anything I said, you'd be much better for it," Erimenes said loftily. "For instance, right now you'd march back to camp and put what you've got in your hand to *much* more pleasurable use trying out certain variations I've designed especially for you and Jennas."

Reflexively, Fost thumped the jug with his free hand. He resumed whistling.

"Ouch! You're a townsman, Fost. No country-born lad would ever urinate in a running river."

That was true, too. Though he'd spent most of his adult life under the stars, he had been born a child of High Medurim's slums, and such he would remain. He shrugged.

And almost died.

Erimenes squawked a warning. Fost froze. When first he'd met the genie, Erimenes's inclination was to let Fost discover approaching danger as it jumped out at him. Erimenes declared this was in the interests of a rousing battle. He often derided the courier for his lack of adventurous spirit, his "cowardice" in the face of overwhelming odds. The change in Erimenes's habits had come slowly after his brief return to Athalau. Fost didn't yet trust the ghost's reformation.

Water parted in a surge. Fost had a glimpse of toothed jaws opening wider than his own height. He backed, frantically trying to cut off the stream of urine. A four-foot-long beak slammed shut inches from his stubbornly spraying wand.

"Great Ultimate!" he cried, still scrambling for footing. "What is that?"

"Something you're best away from," advised Erimenes. "*Far* away from. It appears most hungry. I certainly don't cherish the idea of my jug ending up in that maw."

Fost sat down clumsily in his attempt to escape. A black head reared above him. Eyes like slits of red fire hungrily appraised him. Fost beheld his attacker as a bird like a black cormorant, but gigantic beyond imagining. Its neck reared a dozen feet from a body of unguessable size. Its head and pointed beak protruded eight feet. Fost had a few more brief seconds to see that the dripping monster was dark above and light below, and then it struck.

The beak drove down with lightning speed. Fost rolled desperately. The lancelike beak buried itself three feet deep in the soft earth where he had lain an instant before. Then the courier was up and running, fumbling to stuff himself back in his trousers and bawling at the top of his voice.

"Down!"

This time Fost knew better than to doubt Erimenes. He dived forward, gasping at an impact that drew a searing line of pain along his back.

Tucking his shoulder, he rolled. As he twisted, he drew sword from scabbard. The beak cracked with a sound like the gates of Hell closing. Dying sunlight glinted from teeth like spikes. The bird voiced a triumphant, whistling scream. The awful jaws descended.

A furred, dark form struck them like a bolt shot from a catapult. The monster went down with Grutz snapping and clawing at its head. In an instant the bird had its webbed talons beneath an oily body and snaked its neck out of the bear's embrace. The head cocked itself back preparing for another strike, eyes burning with unnatural hatred.

Grutz scrambled nimbly away from a vengeful thrust of the beak. Though they weighed a ton each, the bears were as agile as dancers on their feet. But as immense as Grutz was, he was dwarfed by the nightmare black birdshape that stood over him poised to kill this new interloper.

Roaring, Chubchuk lumbered down the slope to aid his companion. The hellbird turned its head; instantly Grutz darted in and swiped it on the side of the head. The head reared, shrilling agony. Streaming black ichor dripped from parallel slashes below a burning eye.

Fost regained his feet, breathing heavily, sword held double-handed with one hand gripping the outside of its silver basket. He heard Jennas's angry cry as she charged into battle waving her greatsword.

The head darted at Fost. He leaped away, barely

keeping his footing on the wet grass. His hauberk swung freely at his sides, its fabric of interlocked iron rings rent as easily as paper by the deadly beak. He felt wetness drench his back and knew it was his blood.

"Fost!" cried Jennas. "Are you still in one piece?"

"Mostly," he gasped, feeling the first waves of pain from his wound. "Watch yourself. This thing's strike range is phenomenal." Even as he spoke, the creature unleashed itself like a steel spring straight for the courier.

The monster's strike at Fost gave the bears a chance to close in on it, ripping and biting and snarling up a storm. The monster retreated toward the bank in an ungainly waddle. But it was not defeated. Its head moved with blinding speed. Chubchuk bawled as the beakpoint pierced his shoulder.

Grutz grabbed a scaly leg and bit. The bird collapsed, an unearthly keening echoing out over the rush of the Black River. It was up again on one leg in an eyeblink, holding its wounded leg to its belly, but Grutz's sally had given Chubchuk a chance to scurry to safety. The bears worked well as a team, but Fost realized that even those ponderous, furry engines of destruction were outmatched by this avian menace.

Fost saw Jennas circling wide behind the monster, coming up on its blind side. He knew then what he had to do. Ignoring Erimenes's shrill cheering, interspersed with demands to be freed in order to get a better view, he took the stoutest grip he could on the sword and sucked in a huge breath.

The flaming gaze fixed on him. Strength left him in a flash. His soul was being sucked out through his eyes, drawn out to fall into a void, into fiery scarlet suns.

"You limp-peckered, frog-witted son of a catamite!" shrieked Erimenes in tones ill-suited to the Realm's most distinguished dead philosopher. *"Move!"*

Fost moved.

"Yaah!" he screamed, soul snapping back into his

body in a blaze of fury. "Come and get me, buzzard!"

He had fully intended to draw the hellbird into a strike at him, dodging aside at the last moment while Jennas attacked from the opposite side. But instead of leaping out of the way, he stood his ground as the needle-sharp point of the monster's beak arrowed at his chest. Time slowed as his whole being focused on the black blade of the bird's beak. When it was an arm's reach away, he swung his sword. Power flooded him now, adrenaline-backed power. His lips stretched back in a maniacal grin. The beast made a horrid flutelike sound of surprise and agony as Fost's sword smashed its beak in two.

The head jerked back. Air hissed like a venting fumarole in the night as Jennas chopped half through the long, snaky neck with a slash of her greatsword.

Stinking black fluid spattered over Fost. The shattered beak opened and closed in mute agony as the head flopped at random on the half-severed neck. The monster waddled back two steps and slid over the river bank. Fost ran forward to see it come to rest partly in the water. It kicked twice, trying futilely to make one last attack. Then the light went from its eyes and it lay still.

Fost turned and threw up.

After a time he felt Jennas's touch on his shoulder.

"Are you hurt?"

He felt as if the left side of his back had been splashed with liquid fire.

"Not seriously." He gratefully accepted a sip of water from her canteen, rinsed the warm water around his mouth and spat.

"A new War of Powers is in the offing. My divinations are being proven correct," Jennas said solemnly. "Evil creatures go abroad on the planet again, as the Dark Ones make plans to reclaim their dominion."

The world spun around Fost.

"No, no, no," he repeated over and over in stubborn

denial. He couldn't live in a world where the gods took active part in the affairs of men and where powers beyond comprehension played and lost human beings—and monsters—like pawns.

"I've heard of such giant birds before," he managed to choke out as bile rose in his throat.

"Nonsense." The cap of Erimenes's jug had slipped off in the fracas. The genie's column of mist wavered by Fost's side. The shade eyed him disdainfully. "The natural helldiver is appropriately named. They were too common in my day, though I gather they've died off." He gestured at the Black River, murmuring unseen in the growing darkness. "But that bird is strictly a salt water creature. Might I point out that the Black River is fresh this far up from the ocean?"

Still Fost shook his head, too tired for words, mutely denying that which he could not bear. With surprising gentleness Jennas took his hand and helped him rise.

Grutz and Chubchuk hunched like fat gargoyles at the edge of the bank. Fost heard an odd, low moaning, an uneasy despairing sound that he took first for a roaring within his head and then for the wind in the reeds. But as his head cleared he realized it came from the bears. The long hairs on their necks and shoulders stood up like spiked harnesses and their wicked yellow teeth were bared toward the water.

Clutching Jennas's shoulder, Fost staggered to the bank's edge and looked down at ... nothing.

"See?" Jennas said. "It's gone."

Fost pulled away.

"That doesn't mean anything. It slid into the water and was carried away by the current. The river's swift here."

"No, look at the grass, Longstrider. The monster fell flat. The grass is crushed in all directions. Had it slipped into the water the grass would lie in that direction."

The courier squinted. The lesser moon peeked up

from the horizon, Omizantrim piercing its side like a dagger. Its rosy light showed black smears on the grass with steam rising in wisps from it. As Jennas said, the grass had been mashed down straight.

His knees gave way beneath him.

"Gods!" he cried.

"Yes." Jennas was as grim as an executioner. "The gods. And we are bound to fight their battles for them."

CHAPTER SIX

The path into the Mystic Mountains was little more than a haunting memory. When the low, humped foothills had started to grow into jagged mountains the party had hesitated for a moment among the stunted ugly bushes of the ravine where the trail had petered out. Moriana stared up into the heights while the others rested their dogs and sweated.

Finally she said, "This way," and rode on. The party that followed her was three less than that which had stopped.

So it had gone. Half the remaining contingent had deserted after the death of Iatic Stormcloud. Though what had happened was apparent enough to all, and though Darl argued in Moriana's favor with all his old skill and verve, more than twenty knights and footmen had turned their mounts to the northwest and ridden back for the River Marchant and the City States of the Empire that lay beyond. This journey lay under far too many ill omens for even the strong of heart.

Another factor entering into the dwindling of Moriana's force was the cultural background of the men. These were northern men unused to women who could slay warriors as strong as the young mercenary captain with their bare hands. By her own testimony Moriana was a sorceress. Stormcloud's death convinced a number of her followers she was a witch.

Others had lost battles with conscience or courage as they neared the ramparts of the Mystic Mountains, low and uninviting. Now besides herself and Darl, who remained in a state of watchful quiet that was less alarming that his earlier detachment, Moriana's retinue consisted of five dog riders and eight footmen. All left in her band now, for reasons of their own, were not afraid to penetrate the citadel of mankind's ancient enemy.

She questioned none of them as to their motives. The princess wasn't sure she wanted to know why they chose to accompany her. All her attention had to be directed forward—and up, up into the Mystic Mountains.

The path mounted quickly along crooked switchbacks up almost sheer granite faces, straightening out now and again to follow the spine of a razor-thin ridge.

"The drop—it must be five hundred feet," came a fearful voice from behind. Moriana didn't turn to see who spoke.

"No, not five hundred," came still another voice. "By the gods, it has to be closer to a thousand." The second speaker laughed boisterously, an action not shared by the others in the party.

For Moriana, a mere thousand-foot drop was like home. In the Sky City she often peered out from the forward prow down at the terrain as it slowly slid beneath her. No one in the City in the Sky harbored any fear of heights, not when their everyday existence depended on separation of City and ground of at least a thousand feet. Her training aboard the war eagles had accustomed her to much loftier vantage points with even less substantial footing than that enjoyed by the dog she rode.

"Your men fear," came Ziore's quiet voice from the pouch at Moriana's side. "Is there nothing you can do to calm them?"

"You are the empathic one," pointed out the blonde-haired princess.

"I have tried. It is a wearying job. The fears of several of the men are acute."

"Those from the forest of Nevrym?" hazarded Moriana.

"Yes. They are more accustomed to the closeness of their forests. The precipitous drops of these mountains work against their courage."

"With luck, we won't have much longer on the trail." Her fingers lightly touched the hidden black and white stone of the Amulet around her neck.

"Darl bears up well," added Ziore, almost as an afterthought. "He returns to his former self."

"With a little help from your powers?" asked Moriana.

"With very little help from my powers," corrected the genie. "He heals himself. It is for the best."

Moriana fell silent then, not wanting to speak further, even with Ziore. She no longer knew what was for the best. All she knew was what she had to do. Right, wrong, it made no difference. It was what she had to do.

She fell into the slight rolling motion of the dog between her legs as the creature struggled to climb ever higher into the mountains.

The sharp igneous rock of the mountains cruelly punished the pads of the dogs' feet, causing them to become slippery with blood. On trails often no wider than a strong man's shoulders such poor footing could be fatal. Knowing something of the geology of the Mystic Mountains, Moriana had prepared for this.

"Halt!" cried Moriana after another hour of the upward struggle. "Rest a while in the clearing yonder." She pointed ahead to what amounted to little more than a widening in the narrow trail. But the area proved a narrow canyon leading back into a sparse stand of trees. A small spring spurted from rocks and provided a much needed diversion from the sight of nothing but hard volcanic rocks.

"My Princess," said Darl, moving to her side. "Should we put on the leather boots now? Our dogs are beginning to suffer."

"Aye, pull them out and see to it, Darl," she said,

pleased that the man had taken the initiative to approach her on the subject.

"And," spoke up Ziore, "you might boil some of the *olorum* root found in the crevices yonder and apply the resulting sediment to the dogs' feet before putting on the boots. It will soothe and heal their torn pads."

"The *olorum* root?" asked Moriana. "One I am unfamiliar with. Thank you, Ziore. It shall be done." Darl bowed and silently turned to see to it. More and more he seemed his old self. Moriana hoped the change went deeper than his visible actions. It pained her greatly seeing the man suffer so—and all for her.

Several men brewed tea and others tried to ease their nerves with stinging draughts of Grassland brandy. Moriana accepted a cup of steaming tea—a pleasantly bracing Samazant strain, not the resinous amasinj of the steppes—and allowed a grinning Nevrym forester to lace it with colorless liqueur. She sat on a rock and stared back the way they'd come. The mountains fell away in toothlike peaks of gradually diminishing size, becoming foothills, spreading away to the south and west into an open plain. To her right yellow prairie gave way in the distance to the brown and pale green patchwork of cultivation; at the edge of vision the black line of the forests that had sheltered them for the vital first days of their flight swam in heat haze.

Ahead of the princess rose Omizantrim straight and stark from the plain. As always in the last weeks, a plume of smoke grew from its maw, steely gray today. By a fluke of the weather—or something more, a possibility Moriana studiously avoided thinking about—the wind blew from the Throat of the Old Ones straight into the Mystic Mountains. They had been tasting ash on their tongues all morning, and some of the dogs sported reddened, running eyes from it.

To her left, away and southward, the scrubby shortgrass plain was abruptly interrupted as the land dropped a thousand feet to the Highgrass Broad below. Far-off smoke spires lifted above the tall grass prairie. The Grasslanders engaged again in their favorite sport, it seemed, which was massacring one another in internecine feuds that kept them honed for mercenary work.

Darl saw that the dogs watered and canteens were refilled from the tiny artesian spring, always making sure that no one got out of sight of the resting place without accompaniment. In more and more ways was Darl returning to his former self.

Moriana was relieved at the precaution. These mountains had a feel about them she disliked, and she knew it went far deeper than mere superstition engendered by cradle fables. The *leitmotif* of the Mystic Mountains was black: black soil, black-stemmed shrubs, black birds wheeling on spring thermals overhead. The anhak here grew black, more gnarled than in the woods below, and higher up grew black pine, whose very needles were as much black as green.

From the woods upslope came a screeching, a rising-falling unearthly sound. The dogs started and growled. One whined and tucked tail between its legs. The four archers with the party, three Nevrym foresters and an Imperial borderer from Samazant, looked to their bows. Moriana did likewise.

"I don't like this place." Ziore's subdued voice came from the pouch. Neither she nor Moriana felt her misty presence would do other than aggravate the others' uneasiness over the princess's sorcery.

Moriana shrugged, finished her tea and stood.

"Nor do I," she said simply. "Let's ride."

Hissing, the monster lurched from a hidden draw beside the trail. The lead dog reared and leaped back, almost unseating his rider. Moriana drew the nock of her arrow to her ear in a single fluid motion. Her dog growled deep in his chest. The others set up an excited barking as the vast green shape slid across their path.

It was a monstrous lizard, twenty feet long and more. A crest of yard-long spines, yellow and curving, grew down its back, diminishing in size as they approached the tail tip—still out of sight up the gulley. Moriana recognized it as a sprawler, its immense body suspended between its legs rather than supported atop them. It turned a bony triangular head toward them and regarded them dispassionately with a yellow eye the size of a man's head.

Horrific as the creature was, it wasn't the giant lizard that drew muffled exclamations from the travellers. Three iron-hard spines had been removed where the wattled neck flowed into its shoulders. Where they had been sat a rider.

Tall and manlike, the being stared at them from within an elaborate casque of green metal that shimmered in the sun. His helmet and breastplate revealed few details of head and body, except a pair of flat black eyes as emotionless as the lizard's yellow one. On the being's left arm rested a great spiked target shield, whose rough surface suggested construction from the scaled hide of a beast such as the alien warrior rode. The right hand's three black taloned fingers and thumb gripped a lance. The stranger wore no boots; the feet the startled humans saw sported three toes, also tipped with black claws. The largest was hooked in a ring serving as a stirrup.

With reptilian patience, rider and mount gazed upon the travellers. Behind her Moriana heard a low wail, rising into a shrill frightened yapping as a war dog panicked at the smell and nearness of the monstrous lizard —or perhaps of the being who rode it. Easing her bowstring forward, she clipped the arrow to the bowstaff with her thumb and snapped the fingers of her right hand.

"Enough," she said, and the dog was still.

Her companions looked from the monsters blocking

their path to the princess, sitting tall in her saddle, her golden hair thrown fearlessly back. A mixture of fear and confidence radiated from their gazes.

Before Moriana said another word, the lizard rider spoke.

"Men." The word came out oddly protracted, with an almost tubercular wheeze. "Expected. Come." With that abbreviated greeting, the lizard man goaded his mount with one knee. The monster lifted its belly from the dirt, turned its head and began crawling laboriously upslope. Moriana paused for a few seconds, considered and then followed, her dog shouldering past the cringing mount of the knight who had taken the lead. She forced herself not to look back. Not a soul of her party might be following her, but at this of all moments she couldn't show fear.

Only the emotion-sampling Ziore knew the princess's true condition.

She concentrated on studying as much of their peculiar guide as possible from the rear. He wore a breastplate and back of the same unfamiliar metal as his casque, and a skirt set with strips of the same stuff. His arms and legs flashed bare. They were dark green, almost black, like the needles of the pines that grew to either side of the wash they followed up the mountainside. From where she sat, the musculature looked human enough and the skin flexed as supplely as any human's. Now and then sunlight broke on the curve of the thigh muscle in a metallic glint, and Moriana guessed the being—the *man,* though unlike any she'd ever seen before—was covered in fine scales. The only jarring overt sign of his alienness, aside from his complexion, was his feet and hands. Somehow, Moriana found those small divergencies more unsettling than more obvious ones would have been.

"What do you think?" she said softly, directing her question to Ziore.

She felt the genie's puzzlement before the mental answer came.

I cannot tell. I sense no emotion that I can read. Or none that makes sense. A dark inchoate churning, shot through with—yes, with longing. And a feeling of fulfillment.

"Fulfillment? How so?"

Ziore paused long before answering.

I can tell no more, she thought. *The thoughts and passions of the creature are so . . . so other. The dog we ride is far more easily accessible than this* Zr'gsz.

Moriana slid a hand inside her tunic and pulled the Amulet up so that only she could see it. Its surface was evenly divided between black and white. She grimaced in both annoyance and relief. She saw only ambiguous omen in the odd stone.

Letting the Amulet drop back cool and hard between her breasts, she marvelled at the craft of the long dead Athalar savants who had created the Amulet. Not only did it return life to the bearer but in some way it monitored the state of ther fortunes. It seemed a facility of limited application. After all, someone blessed with good luck or afflicted with bad as a general rule needed no portents to tell her so.

But not always. And so she had come to consult the gem in situations such as the present that might bode good or ill.

And like now her answer was often no answer at all. Equilibrium of black and white mocked her.

They neared the top of the round-crowned mountain. The lizard hoisted itself over the top, tail sweeping from side to side in a swirl of black dust. Moriana leaned forward and goaded her balky dog after.

What she saw made it hard to breathe. A horn of black rock rose before her, separated from the round-topped peak by a chasm so deep its bottom was lost to view in mist and shadow. Hung about the peak was a wreath of what she first mistook for cloud. With a quickening of her pulse Moriana finally realized it was in fact gray smoke from Omizantrim.

Far beneath them she saw a thin line spanning the void. A bridge? She scanned the peak with her eyes but saw no sign of keep or tower, nothing raised by hands, human or otherwise.

The princess became aware of the black-jasper scrutiny of the lizard man. She peered at the smoky wreath, finally catching some anomaly within. Slowly she made out shapes—but nothing like the battlemented walls she had expected. Instead, clinging to the mountain's shoulder was a clump of dark geometric shapes, blocks and angles jutting in disorder that appeared almost organic. A single emerald green gleam shone through the smoke.

The *Zr'gsz* did not turn at the sound of the rest of the party scrabbling up onto the mountaintop. Still gazing impassively at Moriana, he raised his lance and pointed it unerringly toward the outcrop on the distant peak.

"Thendrun," he said.

"You are welcome, humans." The words were spoken with flawless diction, vowels duly voiced, plosives and labials properly enunciated. "You may take for granted that many years indeed have passed since those words were uttered here." Khirshagk, Instrumentality of the People, raised his goblet and smiled.

Before the beaten gold rim of the cup covered his mouth Moriana glimpsed blue-white teeth. Like the rest of him, they were almost human, incisors to the front, flat and shovel-tipped, and blunt grinding molars in the back. But his eyeteeth protruded like sabers, with a hollow behind the upper pair into which the equally formidable lower ones could socket when he locked his jaws. Humans and Khirshagk's ancestors had shared a diet of both flesh and vegetation—but more of the former.

Otherwise, its owner was what Moriana could only

honestly call handsome. His face, narrow and finely boned, sported high cheekbones and a lordly knife blade nose that she found oddly familiar. His skin was bluish green, darker still than the sentry who had guided them across the narrow bridge to the keep. His startling cat-green eyes shone with intelligence in the light of torches flickering in black wrought iron sconces on the walls of the chamber.

To her surprise the reptile man had hair, black and lustrous, combed back from his high, broad forehead. All in all, he had the appearance of a perfectly human male of more than average comeliness.

Except for the clawed hands and feet.

Moriana sipped bitter green wine. Behind her she heard a whisper. Her head snapped around. She saw nothing but the curved wall of the Instrumentality's audience chamber. The wall was unadorned, of a dark green crystal. There were no hangings for furtive listeners to hide behind, and her eyes made out no seams revealing secret doorways. Moriana puzzled over the source of the sound.

Nor do I know, came Ziore's soft thought mingling with her own.

She was conscious of cool eyes on her.

"I am grateful for your hospitality, Lord Khirshagk." He smiled.

"You pronounce my name quite well, Your Highness," he said. "But you need not name me lord. I am Instrumentality of the People; I am a tool in their hands. Not master over them."

Moriana returned the smile, letting some of her skepticism show. Most human rulers claimed that it was the people who reigned, and that they themselves were merely servants of the popular will. The reality was inevitably the reverse. She doubted whether the *Zr'gsz* and humans differed much on that score.

Khirshagk had met them at the gate of Thendrun in a green-trimmed robe of what Moriana at first thought to be unadorned black. Now in the flickering light she made out faint hints of patterns and arcane figurations. To her eyes they appeared black on black; she assumed he saw the contrast more clearly.

"Lady Moriana," he had said, "and Lord Darl. In the name of the People, I bid you enter Thendrun." After the inhuman accent of the lizard rider, the cultured perfection of Khirshagk's words was as startling as his knowledge of their names, and of the rest of the party as well, whom he named and greeted one by one as they filed between the great black gates into the keep.

All those who had started the ascent into the Mystic Mountains accompanied her into Thendrun. Perhaps her men felt that in this lair of ancient magic and evil the presence of a sorceress was more asset than liability. She didn't question this small bit of good luck on her part. It was about time things ran smoothly for her.

Lizard men whom Moriana took for servants, lighter of skin than the Instrumentality and the gate guards who stood by with two-handed maces and tall rectangular shields, stepped forward to lead the tired dogs to kennels. The beasts snapped at them so viciously that the riders had to lead their own mounts.

The retinue was led to a great table in an apartment carved out of one of the many jutting blocks of crystal that formed Thendrun. The block tilted at thirty degrees from the perpendicular, though the dining chamber was hewn out parallel to the ground. The princess's men cast dubious glances at the nothingness beyond the windows and surveyed the steaming joints served them on black jade platters with varying degrees of uneasiness; rumors abounded about the manner of meat the Hissers savored most. But it proved to be good, hearty dog, served with piles of boiled greens and potatoes— basic Northland fare. When Khirshagk led forth Moriana and Darl, smiling sardonically at the men's scrupulousness, they had fallen to with a will.

"Come, Lady Moriana, Lord Darl," said the reptilian Instrumentality. "Here is food that might be more pleasing to your palates."

"What my men eat is good enough for me," said Darl.

Moriana hastily cut in. Strange feelings worked inside her, feelings that had no easily definable name. Going along with Khirshagk seemed more important than sharing the table of her stalwart band.

"What Lord Darl says is true. But if you have prepared special dishes for us, we would be honored." Moriana cast a look at Darl telling him not to argue. He bowed his head slightly in acquiescence.

"This way, then," said Khirshagk, a tiny smile dancing on his all-too-human lips. He led them down a long corridor and into another part of the keep, a part obviously different from the spot where they left behind their human comrades.

More refined fare awaited the highborn pair: small birds baked in leaves, served whole and smoking; brittle crusted black bread; mushrooms; and a bowl of savory sauce so spicy that Darl and Moriana clutched their throats and hastily swallowed wine at the first taste.

The Instrumentality's circular chamber was forty feet across and carved in the center of a pyramidlike extrusion of green stone. Moriana judged it to be one of the highest points within the keep. A waist-deep circular well was cut into the center of the room. It was here that Khirshagk had seen his guests served on low tables carved of black onyx, while they reclined gratefully on luxurious furs.

Lounging back, Moriana noticed that Khirshagk was drinking only wine. He hadn't joined them in their meal.

"Aren't you hungry, Instrumentality?" she asked

warily. "Surely, such a feast isn't commonplace in Thendrun?"

"It is specially prepared for you," admitted Khirshagk with some amusement. "But I have already supped. As you might know, the dining habits of we *Zr'gsz* differ from yours."

By no means ignorant of the rumors concerning the *Zr'gsz* culinary preferences, Moriana forebore to comment.

She noted that Darl ate with an appetite he hadn't shown for some time. She caught his eye and smiled and was happy to see the corners of his mouth turn briefly upward in reply. She turned back to Khirshagk.

"Since you expected us," she said, meeting Khirshagk's gaze and the challenge she read there, "no doubt you already know our errand."

Wine swirled as Khirshagk rotated the goblet in lazy circles.

"Our divinations told us much, and we deduced some, as well. We are not wholly unaware of what goes on in the world beyond the limits of our admittedly limited preserve." He spoke without apparent bitterness.

"Then you know what we've come to ask."

"We do." The Instrumentality smiled. "What remains to be seen is what you have to offer us."

She nodded deliberately. Her wine cup was empty. She bent forward to set it on the table, aware that Khirshagk's eyes followed the sway of her breasts inside her tunic. She had loosened the lacing in front to allow herself to breathe; now she wondered if that had been politic.

A *Zr'gsz* woman, slightly built and pale of skin, came to refill her cup. Moriana wondered how she walked across the stony floor without her nails clicking. By human standards, the lizard woman was attractive. A bit blunt of feature, black-eyed and thin-lipped, her jet hair confined at the temples with a stone circlet carved to imitate plaited strands, she moved with inhuman cadence, limbs swishing softly inside a lead-colored smock.

"I assume that mere riches mean little to you," said Moriana, retrieving her goblet.

"More than you might think. Not that we care for gold as such. Living stone means far more to us than rock killed by over-refinement, tainted by fire, sullied by movement from one hand to another. But we do have dealings with your kind, more than you probably expect. The yellow metal comes in quite handy at times." He sipped. "But your point is well taken. We wouldn't aid you for any wealth you could offer."

"I haven't much to offer." She grinned. "Have your divinations told you that?" She shook her head; the wine made it feel light. "No, what I have to offer you will value much more than a few gold klenors, I think."

She leaned forward. This time his eyes held hers.

"When my . . . my ancestors drove yours from the City in the Sky, your folk were constrained to leave behind certain items of ritual significance."

"At risk of being slaughtered should they have tarried to retrieve them, yes." His manner was languid, but his eyes glittered with interest beneath half-lowered lids.

"If we win, you'll get them back."

He drew a deep breath. Setting down his goblet with a clink, he leaned on furs and steepled his fingers before his face.

"Ah, the relics of my people," he murmured. "The Jade Mace, the Bell, the Scrolls of Eternity, the Idol of the Blessed Child." Reverence rang in his words. "Yes, we value them . . . much."

"All are intact, awaiting only you to reclaim them." She spoke before realizing that the "Idol of the Blessed Child" referred to what her people called the Vicar of Istu, the ugly stone effigy that squatted in the Well of Winds. The Rite of Dark Assumption, banned since Julanna Etuul had seized the Beryl Throne almost five millennia before, made the idol live for a short period with the spirit of the Demon of the Dark Ones, whom Felarod had imprisoned in sorcerous sleep in the depths of the Sky City. Moriana's sister had revived the Rite—with Moriana meant to be the Vicar's sacrifice and bride. Only the timely intervention of Fost Longstrider saved her life. Moriana's thoughts tumbled and swirled thinking of Fost and his valor in saving her from that vile fate.

Ziore's gentle touches on the perimeter of her mind soothed and steadied her.

Moriana licked her lips. Khirshagk watched impassively. How much had his divinations revealed? He had an aura of vast power; she almost tasted it.

"For such inducement we would aid even the get of those who stole the City from us," said Khirshagk. "But we can offer little aid if neither of us can reach the City, is it not so?"

"Yes." She had to fight to say the next words. "We will help you regain access to the skystone mines, as well." Darl let out his breath in sharp exhalation, but said nothing.

"You know what that entails."

"I do." The words hurt her chest.

"And the Heart?" He curled his fingers down, save for forefingers tipped forward to aim at Moriana like a weapon. "The Heart of the People, which damned Felarod cast into molten lava in the Throat of the Old Ones, where his monster could keep it ever beyond our grasp? You'll help us retrieve that as well?"

The Heart of the People!

She had thought the tale of the huge night-black diamond, which smoked like a heart plucked beating from a breast and laid on the sacrificial brazier, to be mere legend. Fear seized her. The Heart was reputedly one of the most powerful of all the Dark Ones' gifts to their chosen. Only Istu himself was a greater sign of favor of the Lords of the Elder Dark. She didn't wish to think what bringing the Heart back into the world might imply.

But she had to trust the lizard folk. Closing her eyes and forming a thought, she asked a single question of Ziore.

The nun responded.

I cannot read this being. His motives are hidden behind a veil of blackness.

The princess had to make the decision on her own; even knowing that decision would affect the entire continent—the world!—she had to make it.

"We will," she whispered.

A soundless shout of exultation rang through Thendrun. Moriana started, looked around. Khirshakg showed no emotion. Darl sat holding his wine goblet negligently in one hand. He had obviously heard nothing. It had been her imagination and nothing more.

"Then let the bargain be sealed." Khirshagk rose and offered his hand. It bore a ring on the index finger, a dark emerald set in graven obsidian. The gem was worked in likeness of something only barely discernible, a face or a mask. Moriana made herself take his hand with no display of the reluctance she felt.

He lifted her hand, kissed it. His lips were dry but surprisingly soft. He then turned and offered his taloned hand to Darl, who got to his feet and gripped forearms heartily with the Instrumentality. Moriana gulped her wine. The imprint of Khirshagk's kiss burned on the back of her right hand.

They passed the evening in inconsequential talk. Khirshagk spoke with animation and wit, and displayed a surprising knowledge of the affairs of the outside world. Moriana guessed that the Hissers had some intercourse with true men (this made her feel better somehow), though the latter took pains to keep this a secret.

Professing a love for human music, the Instrumentality prevailed on Darl to sing, which the Count-Duke then did in a lovely mellow baritone. It was the lay of a rootless wanderer who beholds a wondrous lady and consecrates his life to her. He cannot possess her, for she is pledged to another. In the end he gives his life for her and dies with a smile on his lips. It was a common enough theme, but phrased with a bittersweet poignancy that brought tears to her eyes. Her reaction was odd in its way; the princess had no ear for music and cared little for it as a rule.

"Your own composition, I believe," said Khirshagk when the song was done.

Blushing slightly, Darl nodded.

Moriana bit her lip. At once she understood. He had written the song for her. Darl confirmed it by avoiding her eyes.

"Well," Darl said, rising and stifling a yawn with the back of his fist. "I'm worn down with travelling, I don't mind admitting. I think I'll retire. Your Highness?"

"I'll wait a while," said Moriana before she could stop herself. She wondered why she'd said that. It wasn't just pique at him for performing such a song in front of the lizard man. Her motives went deeper—and Moriana didn't wish to examine them too closely.

He looked at her for a long moment. Then with a wan smile, he nodded.

"I wish you a good rest, my Lady. Your, uh, Instrumentality, I thank you for your gracious hosting."

"You've more than repaid me with your song, Lord Darl." He hissed flat syllables to a *Zr'gsz* female, who wordlessly lifted a torch from its bracket. "Rissuu will show you to your quarters." The tall man bowed and departed.

Moriana lay back. Her lips were dry, but she had no desire for the wine. Nervously the princess ran her hand along the black and silver fur beneath her.

"It's the hide of the greater weasel of Nevrym," said

Khirshagk. "A cunning, deadly beast. We trade for them with the foresters."

Moriana nodded. The men of the Great Nevrym were known to be reckless, enamored of danger. Of all the folk of the Realm it was easiest for her to imagine the Nevrym foresters trading with the shunned and dreaded Hissers, not through any love for them or for the Dark, but because of the essential lawlessness of their natures. It occurred to her that most of the footmen who remained with her were Nevrym men. She had thought it because of the toughness of the breed. Perhaps it was also because the keep of the Fallen Ones was not such a mystery to them.

Khirshagk walked to the wall as gracefully as a hunting beast. He reached a hand to the single torch burning beside the curtained doorway and snuffed it as a human might snuff a candle flame between thumb and forefinger. Moriana winced in sympathy, but he displayed no sign of pain.

"What you are about to see," he said quietly, "has been seen before by only one of your kind. And she was of your *kind* indeed."

Hsst! went another torch. The room descended another step toward utter darkness.

"She?" asked Moriana. The word came out huskier than she intended. She watched him move. In motion, Khirshagk had the stop-and-go rhythm of a lizard, she noted. It was exotic and not at all repellent to her. Deliberately, he doused the remaining torches in the same way. She gave a little gasp as the jaws of blackness closed.

"Wait," he bade her.

She waited. Gradually, she became aware that the chamber did not lie in total night. As her pupils expanded she began to discern the details of the room's spare furnishings once more, this time illuminated by a suffused green glow that seemed to come from all around.

"Thirty thousand years ago my folk came to this continent. Of all the vastness of this land you call the Sundered Realm, this was the place they chose as their first home. And they grew themselves a keep, nurturing crystals by arcane means until they formed the vast blocks and protrusions that are the Thendrun you see all about you. Crystals of emerald, Princess, such as the giant single crystal that is your Beryl Throne." She saw the white gleam of his smile. "You can see why we don't value what the Pale Ones call riches."

A suspicion formed in her mind.

"And the City in the Sky . . . ?"

"You are perceptive. It is no more than to be expected." Before she questioned the cryptic remark, he went on. "Yes, we grew the Sky City in much the same way from a bed of skystone. It's of a different substance, of course. It grew vertically in spire and towers instead of the angular shapes of our keep. And you're aware that it's not made of emerald. Nor does it glow with its own light, as do the walls of our dwellings."

"It's beautiful," she said. It was the literal truth, but it was a soul-disturbing beauty, a beauty redolent of the Dark Ones.

He came toward her. She stood, arms limp at her sides. Moriana forced her mind into the calm necessary to form the thought to the nun: *Ziore, what does he intend?*

You need me to tell you that?

Khirshagk put out his hand till his forefinger touched the untied lacings of her tunic. Her breath came shallow and rapid as the finger pulled down, drawing forth the leather thong. His claw touched the place where the garment came together below her breasts, and continued downward. The leather parted as if he used a knife.

"You are not the first Moriana to visit Thendrun," he said in a rich, low voice. "Nor the first Etuul."

She blinked.

"A Moriana Etuul aided shai-Gallri, it's true," she

said. Her voice was almost as breathy as a *Zr'gsz's*
now. "I am descended from her. I'm the first of my clan
to bear the name Moriana since. . . ."

Her words trailed away as he lifted his finger to her
breast. The finger stroked. Moriana stiffened, remem-
bering the way the black talon had sliced her tunic.
But the touch on her nipple was gentle. She shuddered
with surprised pleasure as the nipple grew erect.

"Since that Moriana came to Thendrun to gain the
secret of true magic," he said. He took his hand from
her breast, dropped it. Her swordbelt fell to the furs
with a muffled clatter. A moment later her breeches
joined it, pared from her like the peel from a fruit.
The razor claw didn't so much as touch the skin beneath.

She started to reach for Khirshagk. She had early
guessed how the evening would end and had been steel-
ing herself for it. Now there was no need for her fortitude. She had not lain with Darl since before Chanobit.
Desire was a keen edge in her loins.

Khirshagk stepped back.

"In those days the Pale Ones had little magic besides
that of Athalau, which is no real magic at all, merely
the exercise of mental powers."

"And what is true magic?" She felt the coldness of
the Amulet between her breasts but did not look down.
A cool breeze fondled her nakedness.

His hands went to his robe.

"*Power*. The ability to manipulate the beings of this
world and the Dark beyond. That gift was given to the
People alone. The earlier Moriana came to purchase
that gift, and so she did."

"And how did she pay for it?" Moriana almost whispered.

He laughed.

"She found the paying no ordeal," he said, and
parted his robe.

Moriana stared. Not one but two great penises jutted

from his groin, one above the other, each one swollen-headed and wrapped with veins like a vine-wrapped column.

"We are similar, your kindred and mine," said Khirshagk. "But my folk are the greater breed."

She sank to the furs and lay back. Her eyes were wide with expectation. His double erection was impressive, but she was not altogether certain what he intended to do with it.

He knelt between her thighs, took a member in either hand and pushed forward with his hips. Moriana lifted her hips to meet him.

"That way," she groaned. "But I've never done that before. . . ."

In a moment, pain and pleasure mingled and overlaid one another. He lowered himself until he loomed over her like an idol supporting himself on muscular arms. Even in the wan emerald light his eyes shone like windows into blackness. He began to move to and fro, slowly. The skin of his members had the slightest roughness. The friction thrilled her almost beyond toleration.

Light began dancing before her eyes. Breath came short. Hot and cold chased tails through her body, touched her with fire, with ice, and the pleasure moved within her, possessing her utterly.

When the icy explosion came within her, she screamed with the fury of her own release.

She drifted from consciousness, floating timeless in darkness and satiety. At length her eyes focused again. Khirshagk still hung over her, and she felt the twinned rhythm of his heart yet within her. She didn't know how long she lay in her daze. She sensed he could have kept that same position for hours, days—and more.

He slipped from her. Even the withdrawal gave intense delight. She gritted her teeth as climax seized her lithe body again. Winded, she lay back looking up as he put on his robe. For some reason the black against black figures were clearer to her now. They seemed to move with a life of their own. Or was that only a trick of the emerald witchlight?

"That first Moriana," she asked. "How long did it take her to gain the true magic?"

He looked down at her, his expression totally unreadable.

"*She* never gained it at all," he said, leaving the chamber with noiseless tread.

Moriana stared up at the ceiling. It was concave and faceted like a gem. It focused her mental energies and flooded her with both vitality and unease. She blinked several times and looked away from the disquieting ceiling.

"Ziore?" she asked softly. "What do you make of it?"

"I know not what." The voice came from somewhere amid the furs strewn in the pit.

Moriana put her hand to the Amulet, clenching it hard. She couldn't make herself look to see whether the stone shone white—or black.

CHAPTER SEVEN

On that day appointed for battle by forces none living could comprehend, it seemed as if Nature herself rejoiced at the prospect for slaughter. When dawn poured itself over the horizon like soured milk, the Sky City floated some ten miles west of Kara-Est, where it was spotted by pickets posted in gondolas held aloft by ludintip, huge airborne jellyfishlike creatures. As they reported, the City showed no sign of warlike intent. No war birds circled its tall towers or winged in arrowhead formation to meet the aerial guardians of the seaport. To the immense disgust of Parel Tonsho, and Hausan and Suema, Senior General and Sky Marshal of Kara-Est respectively, a number of Deputies immediately expressed relief and demanded that their city's military alert be called off.

The alert remained in force.

At ten in the morning, aerial reconnaissance reported ground troops massing on the plain west of the Hills of Cholon. Smiling grimly—largely for the benefit of the court sculptor come to immortalize what the general was sure would be an epic victory with a heroic bust in marble—General Hausan ordered two thousand cavalry and three thousand foot soldiers, including almost a thousand archers, to come forth from the Landgate to meet the foe. Sweating, itching and weak-kneed within her ornamental armor, Tonsho watched the couriers ride out from the Hall of Deputies with considerable misgiving. At her side her covey of youths strutted and made muscles, bragging about how *they* would deal with the enemy.

Tonsho knew victory would not be so easy. Battle never was, especially battle against the fearsome Sky City. She silenced her chirping boys with an impatient wave of her hand. On this of all days she didn't want their arrogant prattle distracting her from the serious business of worrying, something no one else in Kara-Est appeared capable of doing.

Standing on the skywall beside the huge mandibular jut of the City's forward dock, Rann and Synalon watched the tidal race of armies in collision. Synalon held a heavy white robe closely about her against the wind. Her hair blew like black stormwrack around her pale face. Rann wore the black and purple of the City with the gold brassard on his left arm identifying him as one of the elite Guard. He needed no badge of rank; the blazing crimson crest on the head of the black war eagle was device enough.

"We shall be victorious, cousin," said Synalon smugly. "I feel it. I *know* it!"

Rann glanced sidelong at his queen. "Is this assured by the Dark Ones?" he asked in a monotone.

"The Dark Ones?" answered Synalon, wildly, almost insanely. "*I* assure this day's victory, cousin dear. *I* am the one with the power. *I* will crush those crawling insects, those larvae, those pathetic creatures daring to oppose my will!"

Rann said nothing of his own preparations, of the army, the eagle riders and the part they would play, the magics performed by scores of mages in the City. For all he knew, Synalon might be correct. This day might belong to her and her alone. Shaking his head at the prospect, he turned attention back to the slow jigsaw merging of armies below.

Ghostly with distance, the sounds drifted to their ears: barking, shouting, trumpets ringing, the beat of drums. The white and azure banners of Kara-Est snapped above orderly rectilinear arrays, heavy spearmen massed in the center with archers on the wings and squadrons of cavalry on the outermost flank. Against them came the Sky City ground troops, twenty-two hundred dog riders from the City and her subjugated "ally" Bilsinx. The attacking force travelled in a shapeless, fluid formation that the regimented commanders of the Estil army thought disorganized.

In advance swarmed the Bilsinxt light cavalry hurling darts and arrows to disorder the close-packed ranks of the Estil. The heavier City riders couched lances and charged through, the skirmishers parting easily to either side like a bow wave from a war galley's prow. The lines met, purple and black against blue and silver. Several seconds later the observers in the City heard the dull hammerblow followed by a many-throated shout as the hours and weeks of waiting were consummated in steel and blood and death.

Rann smiled grimly. His nostrils flared and he imagined the coppery smell of blood. Beside him Synalon stood as pale and stiff as a marble statue, her thoughts alien.

Inexorably, the City floated east. The striving mass of men and beasts passed beneath. Though outnumbered and less massively armored than their foe, the Sky City forces held their army in savage deadlock. The Bilsinxt streamed past the enemy's flanks like quicksilver, driving arrows into the unprotected flanks and rumps of the Estil knights' war dogs. Between the skirmishers surged an inchoate, writhing mass pushing now this way, now that.

Ran nodded. Turning to an aide who stood by, he said, "Order the artillery to commence firing. It'll give our crews good practice for what's to come." The aide nodded and rushed away. "Besides," Rann said, leaning forward to grip the windworn stone of the wall, "the Estil must be encouraged to reinforce."

Less than a minute later, a rain of rocks and ballista darts spattered among the Estil. Dogs screamed and men choked, dying as the two-yard-long shafts pinned men to mounts and mounts to sod. A few riders and footmen fleeing for the rear became a trickle, a stream —and threatened to turn into a torrential rout.

Ludintip-borne observers signalled news of impending disaster. Hausan barked orders and scattered demotions like seedcorn. Reinforcements began to flood in from the hills.

"Cease bombardment," Rann ordered. Several of his aides remarked among themselves he had not smiled so since he had come up from a diverting evening torturing the virgin daughter of Mayor Irb, late of Bilsinx.

The prince walked to where the apprentice mage Maguerr sat in a bishop's chair peering into a new geode.

"Get me Dess." The visage of the City's ground commander peered forth one-eyed from the geode communicator. Rann spoke briefly; the other nodded. He had been a colonel of the Guard until an arrow robbed him of one eye and the binocular vision essential to bird-back warfare. Rann trusted Dess to carry out his orders, no matter how distasteful.

Reinforcements joined the Estil battles, roaring lustily with eagerness to be at the foe. No sooner were fresh troops engaged than the black and purple lines began to waver. In a matter of heartbeats, the City forces had turned their dogs' tails toward their enemy in headlong flight.

Back in the Hall of Deputies Hausan crowed with delight at the news and restored the ranks he had been pruning mere moments before.

"But, sir, the ludintip report that many of our reserve forces are marching forth to join the pursuit."

"Are they now? Spirited lads! I shall see a medal struck to commemorate this day." He turned to Tonsho and the Marshal with an expansive wave of his hand. "Did I not tell you the fight would be decided on the ground? Let them fly their pet gerfalcons against us now. The day is won!"

Tonsho and the roundcheeked Suema exchanged thoughtful looks. Without a word, the plump little Sky Marshal left to issue commands of his own. Ludintip rose from the city, titanic animated gasbags, some as large as a hundred feet across. The oblate spheroids of their hydrogen sacs glared orange-red in the sun. Shield-sized nuclei moved freely across the surface of the sacs avoiding only the tightly held sphincters the ludintip used to steer. The vast fernlike feeding fans were folded beneath the creatures. Tentacles as thick as a man's thigh clung to special brackets set in the gondolas; much slimmer tentacles studded with sting cells carrying an agonizing nerve poison waved in agitation. The gondolas swinging below the creatures bristled with spearpoints and engines of war.

Smiling oddly for a man who has just seen his army routed, Rann went to his war bird and accepted the reins from a cadet, who danced back with obvious relief. The eagle scowled at him.

"Easy, Terror," Rann soothed. The bird spread its wings once with ineffable emotion as the diminutive prince swung into the saddle. Rann gripped the shaft of the implement that rode in the lance stirrup by his left leg. He hoisted it in salute to his queen. Synalon returned his salute with a small, haughty upward motion of her chin. It was all Rann could expect in way of acknowledgement now that the Power was on her. He kicked vigorously and Terror exploded into the air with a boom of wings. Seeing the red-crested war bird soar, the bird riders of the City took flight as one.

A score of gold brassarded riders formed on Terror. Each carried a shield in one hand and a lancelike object similar to Rann's in the other. The implements were wood shafts ten feet long, each tipped with an eighteen-inch cylinder of red fired clay, capped and sealed with a curious glyph. A wire ran back from the cap to a ring set on a lever at the point where each rider's hand gripped. Through vents in the bottom of each cylinder came a dazzle of flame.

Bolts arched gracefully from the cloud of ludintip. Prematurely loosed, they dropped harmlessly into the Hills of Cholon beyond the lordly palaces and great houses. Rann's grin widened, but he did not fail to note that more of the Estil artillerists had prudently held fire than loosed in panic.

A shaft went by to the left, its whine lost in the thunder of Terror's wings. Rann let his "lance" drop level, pressing the butt to his ribs with his elbow.

From the clay vessel came an agitated chittering. Guiding the eagle with his knees, Rann swerved in full flight until the tip of the cylinder pointed at a gasbag so immense that a full two score men and two catapults rode the gondola beneath. The chittering increased to a frenzy of liquid syllables just the far side of coherent speech. Taking measured breaths, Rann waited until the sound reached a crescendo.

His forefinger tugged the ring.

The cap snapped open. A blue nimbus of flame sprouted from the end as the sealing glyph was broken. An instant later the fire cloud became an arrow-straight line of fire between lancetip and ludintip.

The ludintip exploded in a brilliant blue flash as the fire elemental buried itself lustily in the hydrogen inflating the gasbag. Screaming, the Estil aviators began their last long journey home.

Lines surged on either side of Rann, one red, one green, to converge on a second ludintip. Terror fought the thunderclap buffeting from the first explosion with powerful wings as another blossomed, and another.

With the wind at his back, Rann distinctly heard the tunk! tunk! tunk! of the City's own artillery, even above the screams and blasts and the tremendous noise of

Terror's passage. A black bundle soared by, trailing smoke, to fall among the pitched rooftops at the western fringe of the City.

Rann glanced back. His cheeks grew taut. Only ten bird riders still followed him, spread in a loose echelon. The aerial artillerists of Kara-Est were proving formidable foes indeed.

Explosions splashed all over the sky as bird riders launched fire salamanders against the ludintip. The Palace mages of the Sky City had spent weeks conjuring small fire sprites into specially enchanted containers that would trap the creatures and their killing heat inside until the lids were opened and the magic seals broken. No more efficient weapon for eliminating the animated airships of the Estil existed.

Rann let the staff with its special spirit jar drop in a lazy spiral to the cobbled streets below. Other bird riders would circle back to munitions carriers for more staffs. He had other concerns. With the unconscious skill of great practice, he performed the acrobatic feat of reaching for the recurved Sky City bow slung across his back while taking in the situation around him.

The tight formations of eagles had scattered themselves all over the sky on their firing pass through the ludintip. Smoke trails grew like vines into the sky on all sides. A score and more of the gasbags had been set aflame by the salamanders. Rann's own forces were too spread out among the remaining enemy forces for him to appraise casualties. In planning, it was assumed they would be high. All he could do was hope they were not too high.

Two hundred feet ahead and to his left a dark brown eagle suddenly flashed into flame. The prince heard the mingled screams of bird and rider as they tumbled toward the earth. They burned like paper in the embrace of the salamander.

Rann cursed. Special vents were tapped in the rear of

each fire sprite's jar so that its eager chittering would tell the bird rider when it was fixed on target. The fire elementals sensed the presence of inflammable substances and sped directly for the most volatile when released. Some fool of a eagle rider had pulled the trigger without being certain what his elemental was tracking. It had struck a comrade instead of a foe.

There was nothing Rann could do about that. Nocking an arrow, he put Terror into a circling dive toward a fat orange sphere rising from Kara-Est.

The black iron frame bucked like a wild beast as the bow of the ballista slammed to. Engineer First Class Juun held her breath as she watched the missile's flight with eyes scarcely less keen than a bird rider's. The eight-foot spear reached the top of its arc, tipped down and punched between the ribs of a war eagle as the creature's wings rose to gather wind. The bird convulsed in midair. Cheers rang from the tiles of the roof as the creature plummeted, its rider falling at its side in a helpless flailing of limbs.

Two burly assistant engineers, bare backs gleaming with sweat in the hot sun, spun the double windlass to recock the ballista. Making herself relax, Juun scanned the skies for another target. She had two kills that morning. The bounty would mean luxury for years.

She gestured with a gloved left hand. The platform on which the engine was mounted began to revolve, turned by more assistants. As it turned she caught the eye of her friend Falla manning a ballista mounted on a turret at the other end of the building. Two more engines were mounted on the other corners but these lay out of sight behind the pitched roof. Falla grinned and touched the tip of her nose; she had seen Juun's kill. Juun laughed and waved back, then turned to peer through her sights.

She shut her ears to the shrieks as a ludintip fell like

a meteor in the next block. The damned Sky Citizens had hellish magic on their side, but even that wouldn't bring them victory over the freedom fighters of Kara-Est. The elite rooftop artillery would exact a far heavier toll of the invaders than their limited population could afford.

She heard a thump, glanced reflexively to her left. A round lump the size of a bushel basket had dropped on the catwalk connecting the two emplacements. Near Falla's end thick greenish black smoke roiled from the ball. Juun turned her attention back to the skies as the rattle of bootheels on stone told her the fire-control crews were rushing to douse the smouldering projectile.

A buff-colored bird entered her field of vision, swooping in on a rising ludintip, its rider launching a stream of arrows at the gasbag's nucleus with breath-taking speed. Shouting broke out to her left, the sounds of struggle. She ignored it, gesturing to her crew to position the weapon. Juun had only a heartbeat before the bird was lost behind its quarry. She drew breath, pulled . . . the missile arced and fell past the bird's fanned tail. She groaned as the eagle went out of sight, its wings almost brushing the taut bladder of the ludintip.

She didn't hear the creaking of the windlass working against the mighty pull of the bow.

"Snap to it!" she shouted.

A gurgling scream answered her.

Juun spun in the saddle, snatching at her dagger. The man on her left was sitting down staring at the shaft of a ballista dart that jutted from his belly. Figures writhed together on the catwalk, some obviously fighting to the death, others naked or partly so, striving belly to belly. In the eyeblink she had to absorb the strange scene, Juun saw others dancing drunkenly around Falla's engine, laughing, singing. A ballista server tottered an instant on the stone railing before plunging to the street eight stories below in a flawless swan dive.

A swirl of smoke curled around her face. It was aromatic; without meaning to, she inhaled deeply.

Her surroundings began glowing with a light of their own. She perceived a world behind the world she had known before, and this was a world she could almost enter. But not quite. Frustration brought hot tears coursing down her cheeks.

When Falla came to her with knife in hand and laughing, she welcomed her friend as she would a lover.

Above the battle for a moment, Rann gulped in great lungfuls of air. Though the sun was well past the zenith, the air up at a thousand feet was stinging cold and cut down his throat like a knife. His whole body tingled with manic energy. His every sense thrummed to the surging strength and pungent smell of the bird beneath him, the stinks and sounds and sights of the battle raging around him and below, the wind in his face. Even the burning line across his back, where an Estil archer had almost punched through his light mail, filled him with fierce exhilaration. Torture and intrigue, battle and flight, these were his loves, his fulfillments, the only ones available to the eunuch prince.

He experienced the latter pair to the utmost now.

Pressure from one knee made Terror drop his left wingtip and go into a steep bank. He surveyed the grim situation below. But it differed little from what he had expected.

Things had gone well for the City in the Sky. The staged "rout" of their ground forces had feinted a good portion of the defenders out of Kara-Est. The burning bundles of Golden Barbarian vision-weed had been shot from the City's walls with commendable accuracy. Hits and near misses had incapacitated a quarter of Kara-Est's rooftop artillery. Rann had learned about the drug when he had been a field marshal of a combined City-

Quincunx army that had defeated an incursion of the Golden Barbarians into the Sjedd almost six years before. Whoever breathed its vapors forsook the real work to travel in a realm of visions and delusions—or perhaps in an alternate realm, depending on which school of philosophy one heeded on the subject. What mattered to Rann was that the victims' minds went elsewhere while their bodies provided conveniently helpless targets. High as he was, high enough to drift over the skywall into the City itself, he caught the resinous tang of the vision vapors.

"I hope everyone remembered to take the antidote," he muttered to himself, the words inaudible even to Terror due to the rush of wind past his lips. The antidote to the drug was more costly by weight than gold. Synalon had grumbled over the expense, but Rann had persevered and knew himself now to be correct.

The assault had gone according to plan. Even so, three quarters of the rooftop engines still spat death. The water battery of warships anchored in the harbor were virtually untouched and the Estil forces, as diminished as they were, still outnumbered his own three to one.

He raised his eyes from the conflict below and peered at his City. A black and silver clad figure stood alone on the prow of the vast stone raft, gesturing with slender arms.

Synalon.

He wheeled, keeping her in view. He again wondered if she had as much of the Dark Ones' favor as she believed. He knew his royal cousin, knew that she was the most powerful magician in the Realm and most likely in the entire world, knew also that she was capable of overestimating her power.

He watched the mystic gyration of the sorceress's arms. Briefly he felt the age-old pang, an impotence predating his emasculation. For magical power, like political power, passed along the female line of the Etuul clan. He had no innate magical ability, nor the aptitude to learn spellcraft, though he excelled in every other thing he attempted.

"I should be able to feel the power flow, to know if Synalon's magic works or not," Rann mumbled. But that was as inaccessible to him as knowledge of his own destiny. He was utterly at the mercy of his demented cousin, the monarch he loved and hated and, always, served.

He reached for another arrow and set Terror into a long, steep dive. Battle still raged.

Sun-heated stone stung the soles of her feet. Cold wind caressed her bare limbs. Synalon Etuul, Queen of the City in the Sky, shut her eyes against the sun's intrusion and strove to put her soul in touch with darkness. Her guards stood about her fingering their weapons and nervously watching their ruler poise herself on the tip of the skydock with nothing but sky an inch in front of her toes. She ignored them as she ignored the arhythmic thunk of catapults arrayed about the walls, and the tumult of noise that beat like surf against the floating City.

Black hair snapped in the wind like a million tiny whips. Synalon wore a harness of black leather, a web woven about her otherwise nude body, leaving bare her breasts and the dark, furry tuft of her loins. What seemed to distant Rann some silver garb was only her own skin, as pale as moonbeams.

A black dot appeared in the center of her being. It grew quickly, and with it grew pleasure. Soon it was a sun, a black sun, consuming her in ecstasy and darkness. Her Guards cried out in alarm seeing black flames begin to stream from their mistress's body. She threw back her head and shrieked like a soul in torment. With an oath, a Palace Guard leaped onto the dock and raced to her.

Naked bones clattered on stone as the black flame scoured flesh from his skeleton.

The queen did not notice. Unholy pleasure possessed her. Yet through the midnight fires of orgasm burned the cold hard light of Will.

Come to me, the Will commanded. *You are mine. Take form before me that my enemies shall be destroyed. By my Power, by the City in the Sky who have chosen me for Their own, I bid thee—come!*

Out over the bay a swirling stirred the air.

CHAPTER EIGHT

"Behold," said Erimenes. "The City in the Sky, precisely as Jennas predicted. *Now* do you believe her visions, Fost? I've told you all along to heed them."

Fost glanced at Erimenes. The genie leaned jauntily on the weatherworn railing of the ship, as though the splintery, faded wood actually propped up his insubstantial form.

"You did no such thing," growled Fost.

"Don't quibble. I hadn't thought you so smallminded. I've held all along that Jennas truly was receiving inspiration from Ust the Red Bear. If I didn't say so, it was only because I deemed it so painfully apparent to any thinking being as to require no comment."

Fost paid no attention. The courier stared into the sky and tried not to be sick.

In any kind of sea, the caravel Miscreate rolled like a pig in mud. Fost and Jennas had turned green the minute she warped out of Port Zorn and stayed that way until the walls of the easternmost lock of Dyla Canal shut behind the Miscreate's round stern. On the sheltered waters of Kara-Est harbor even a beast like Ortil Onsulomulo's slatternly ship rode as smooth as a dream. It was the commotion of the sky beyond the pastel buildings on the waterfront that made Fost's gorge yearn once more for wide-open spaces.

The Sky City was exactly where Jennas had predicted. And it floated in the middle of a battle of awesome proportions.

"Now you know why no one else was willing to haul

your carcasses down the coast," came a voice from behind Fost.

Fost turned to the Miscreate's captain. He was something to behold.

The foremost mariners of the day were the black-skinned Joreans of the continent lying northeast of the Sundered Realm. The fact that Ortil Onsulomulo was half Jorean tended in Fost's mind to balance the disreputable appearance of both him and his vessel.

Joreans believed that each sex possessed its own peculiar essence and that these essences were best not intermingled. Thus, except for purposes of procreation, Joreans tended to eschew intercourse with members of the opposite sex, taking those of their own gender as lovers instead. However, like most folk, the Joreans were not insensible to the lure of a little perverse fun. Sailors being what they are, the Jorean mariners were inclined to go all-out when indulging their taste for the unconventional.

Thus Jama Onsulomulo, master of the cog Swift, begot a son with a sallow, blonde-moustached Dwarven woman of North Keep.

With a Jorean's strong moral sense, Onsulomulo had taken it upon himself to see to as much of the lad's upbringing and education as he could. As a result, young Ortil spent half his time on the decks of Swift and half sweltering in the warrens and foundries of North Keep. The boy became a mass of unresolved conflicts between the openness and intellectualism of the Jorean and the dour materialism of the Dwarves. Ortil Onsulomulo became a sailor of notable skill while at the same time flaunting the fact that his vessel was a ghastly ramshackle tub that only a landlubber could possibly mistake as seaworthy.

As Fost, Jennas and Erimenes looked on with expressions ranging from bewilderment to glee, winged shapes and bloated balloons battled across a smoky sky. Anchored off the bow of Miscreate, broad-beamed carracks of the Estil navy flung a hail of darts into the air. One bird rider tumbled from his saddle and another pinned a rider to his eagle for a long fall into the greasy water of the harbor. Farther away, a ludintip shot sideways, its tentacles spasming to drop gondola and crew into the central plaza.

"A nucleus hit," Erimenes said sagely. "Some bird rider got either lucky or smart."

In a single prodigious bound, Onsulomulo leaped to the railing of his ship. He swayed this way and that on the precarious perch. The half-Dwarf kept his balance with almost contemptuous ease, as if hoping to be flung overboard to his doom.

He waved a stubby arm at the sky.

"Swine! Rogues! Devil worshippers!" he screamed. "You'll go too far, mark my words. The land has rejected you, the sea won't have you, and soon the sky itself will cast you from its bosom!"

He looked strange and wonderful standing there with his bare feet splayed on the railing. He was the height of a short man, massive of torso and head, childlike of limb. His hair was a curly orange brush, his skin reddish gold, his eyes liquid amber. Finely chiseled Jorean features mingled grotesquely with the Dwarven lumpishness of his body. Watching him, Fost wondered if he was in one of the manic spells that had gripped him periodically during the journey—or if he, like Jennas, were touched by some higher power.

A sharp bronze beak lanced through the water toward them. Fost barely made out the low black hull of a galley, its gunwales almost swamped by its own bow wave as twenty pairs of oars rose and fell with the same easy unison as an eagle's wings.

The courier cried a warning. Onsulomulo capered on the rail and shouted crazy laughter. But the black ship was not trying to ram them. It swept by, as clean and quick as a shark, rocking the much heavier caravel with the power of its passing. Streaming out from the

mainmast in the stiff breeze cracked a familiar ensign:
a red field emblazoned with a tentacled black triangle,
from which glared a single red eye.

"Cowards!" Erimenes shouted at the fleeing ship.
"Go about! How can you flee from a handful of over-
grown sparrows?"

Onsulomulo cackled laughter, a surprisingly ancient
sound from one who looked to be Fost's age.

"Never in my hearing has anyone ever called the
sailors of the Tolviroth Maritime Guaranty cowards,
smoke-man," he said. "They've completed their com-
mission of guiding some fat merchant fleet to safety. No
one's paying them to stick around and fight the flyers."

A rock cast from the City landed on the waterfront
and bounced like a bowling ball along the pier. It struck
an anchored merchant ship, scattering spars and sailors
like eightpins. Fost gulped, acutely aware that he was
heading into a witch's cauldron of battle from which
the redoubtable warriors of the TMG were fleeing.

He felt Jennas's eyes on him.

"What now, Longstrider?" she asked calmly.

"We get the captain to put us ashore," he said with
no great enthusiasm. "Then we try to find a way into
the City."

"Then we try to stay *alive* long enough to find a way
into the City," corrected Erimenes. "You must beware
of imprecision in speech, friend Fost. I've told you before . . ."

An unearthly moan froze Fost's blood in his veins. It
came again and he realized it issued from his war bear
Grutz's capacious chest, who sat man-fashion on his
rump on the deck not far away. The bear stared into
the air beyond the Miscreate's aft rail and hunched his
head down between his shoulders.

"Look!" Jennas's brawny arm shot out.

Fost squinted. He made out a disturbance in midair.
Ghosts of color danced within as though the sun's light
were being broken into component colors. As he

watched in uncomprehending fear, the disturbance grew and a tail dipped toward the surface of the bay.

"Ust preserve us," breathed Jennas. "A sylph!"

The spinning tail of the air elemental touched water and a waterspout loomed above the vessel, a thousand feet tall.

Though he expected it, Rann's lips drew back in a grimace as the waterspout blossomed in Kara-Est's harbor.

"She *does* have the power!" he exclaimed in wonder.

No one had summoned an air elemental of that size in centuries, perhaps not since the War of Powers. The Sky City's magicians traditionally dealt with fire sprites. Though Air and Fire were by no means inimical principles, it was testimony to the growth of Synalon's power that she could summon an unfamiliar breed of elemental outside the confines of a laboratory. And one so huge!

As if gravity had been reversed, an Estil war galleon leaped abruptly into the air. The water tornado sucked up another vessel, and another. From several miles away, Rann heard the screams of the doomed seamen, even above the roaring of the elemental.

The menace of the water battery was broken. That still left most of the rooftop-mounted ballista intact. Synalon claimed she could deal with those, too. What she had in mind was even more ambitious than summoning a sylph tall enough to peer over the parapets of the Sky City itself. Though Rann still doubted, he had little choice but to turn Terror's head around and start the bird climbing toward the City to execute the next stage in the conquest of Kara-Est.

Drinking air that intoxicated like wine, Synalon knew the exaltation of pure power. She had summoned a giant sprite and bound it to her will, as docile as a pup. Her creature sported in the harbor, scattering Estil ships like so many broken toys. But there were still the defenders on the pitched roofs of Kara-Est to eliminate. The sylph might be able to deal with them but not without endangering Synalon's bird riders—and perhaps the City itself. The sorceress-queen had another conjuration in mind that would better eliminate the Estil artillery—and at the same time demonstrate her own power in a unmistakable way.

She staggered slightly and clutched arms around her body. Pain grew in her like a metastasizing cancer. She clamped her teeth to hold back a howl of agony. The black sun had turned to red, and there was no pleasure in the fire that ate at her belly and limbs. Battle raged, her body the battleground and her mind and soul the prize. But still her Will shone brighter than the fire. Gripped by distress that transcended mere physical pain, Synalon shouted a word of Command.

A ball of fire enveloped her. Her guards fell back, throwing up their hands to shield their faces against the dreadful searing heat. Something had gone wrong. Their queen was being reduced to ashes before their eyes.

Then the flame vanished, rushing away across the doomed seaport as the giant salamander Synalon had conjured within her own body was set to do her bidding. It etched a line of death through the air, leaving ludintip and eagles alike flaming in its wake.

It cast itself into the waterspout.

Windows exploded in the two cities as the salamander's scream of agony burst like a bomb above the harbor. Water was the foe of Fire; Synalon had brought forth the sprite only to hurl it to horrid death. But not immediate death. Tottering, going to her knees on the lip of the pier, Synalon forced the salamander to remain in being, denying it the surcease of death that was its only desire.

Steam hid waterspout and harbor. Naked now, her glorious black mane charred to a smouldering, crackling stubble, Synalon clung to the stone of the pier. Though her body was drained of strength, though her skin stung as to the touch of a hot iron, she continued to work her Will upon spirits of Air and Fire, while her servitors watched in horror from the skywall.

Misty tendrils began to billow from the swirling cloud. Though the wind had been blowing out toward the harbor, they crept into the streets of Kara-Est, swallowing the city like a vast white amoeba. The surviving artillerists shouted in dismay and disbelief as the cloud engulfed them, hiding the sky from their view.

With an eagle's cry of challenge and delight, Rann launched Terror once more from the rim of the City. Behind him flew a hundred of the elite Sky Guard. Huge protuberances grew from the docks, became the sausages of giant balloons, silks gleaming in the sun. Though salamander-heated air filled the gasbags almost to the bursting point, they could not successfully lift the freight of men and arms that swung below. Five balloons towed by a score of straining eagles carried five hundred men toward the Hills of Cholon and the Ducal Palace in the wake of Rann's attack.

The Palace garrison saw them coming and sent a frantic signal for reinforcements to watchers in a spire atop the Hall of Deputies, who were only just visible above the unnatural fog. Then the bird riders struck. An arrow storm swept engineers from their emplacements. Detachments veered to land at preassigned parts of the Palace, while Rann and a dozen men attacked the tower.

Duke Morn awaited them. Somehow he seemed to fill his suit of plate and chain as robustly as he had before the death of his beloved wife and his heir. He held his head high. When the Sky Guard came for him, he killed six with a greatsword that flickered featherlight from side to side. The seventh he faced was Rann, and the duke did not prevail.

* * *

Still convinced the day was his, General Hausan despatched most of his defenders to aid the duke. Neither Tonsho nor Marshal Seuma shared his optimism.

"Yes, yes," the general cackled like a hen sitting on an egg. "This will be the finest hour for the city. The very finest. We triumph on all fronts! The bird lovers are being repelled on all fronts. Oh, yes, a fine day. Fine."

Sky Marshal Suema drew Tonsho aside.

"The plan, Excellency," Suema whispered in the Chief Deputy's ear. "Shall we execute it?"

Tonsho nodded jerkily. Her teeth chattered too violently for her to speak.

Claws scrabbled on stone as Grutz heaved his bulk out of the water. Fost let go of the animal's stubby tail to hoist himself onto the dock. He scrambled into the saddle and turned back. Chubchuk appeared, with Jennas still aboard his broad back.

A cloud covered the harbor like a fleecy white roof. Sounds echoed eerily beneath: screams, shouts, the crack of splitting timbers, the roaring of the sylph. From above came the hideous keening that had sounded since the fireball from the City had plunged into the depths of the waterspout.

"A fire elemental, I do believe," said Erimenes from his jug. "Quite amazing. Synalon's position as foremost enchanter of the age is assured now beyond all doubt."

"How nice for her," said Fost. "Let's get the hell out of here."

"I think getting the *Hell* out of this scene is quite beyond your powers, friend Fost." The spirit chortled eerily as the two bears broke into a soggy, squishy run.

The waterspout had cut through the anchored naval vessels like a scythe. Then it began to rampage at random across the harbor, picking up ships and flinging them to the points of the compass.

Even the slovenly Miscreate did not escape its attention.

Fost saw Ortil Onsulomclo. The golden Dwarf had climbed up the Miscreate's rigging and clung with one hand while he shook his chubby fist at the elemental. Then the wind funnel caught the vessel. Fost had a final glimpse of Onsulomulo hurling defiant curses at his enemy before man and ship vanished.

Fost turned away. He was all too aware of moisture on his cheeks that had a taste different from the rank water of the harbor.

Leading the way, Fost rode for the southern fringes of the seaport. He had no particular reason for heading that way. All he knew was that the center of town wasn't going to be a healthy place. Battle raged furiously in the thickness of the fog.

They rounded a corner and steel hissed reflexively into his hand before his brain had time to evaluate the situation. A brown eagle, its chest a blaze of white, swooped straight at them. Grutz snarled a challenge, and Jennas unslung her greatsword.

The bird paid them no heed. It set down lightly in the middle of the block and stood gazing over its shoulder at the rider clinging to its back. The dark-haired woman rider slumped over the bird wore the armlet of the Guard.

As he and Jennas watched, the woman swayed and toppled to the ground. Fost dismounted and approached, sword in hand. The bird beat its wings and screamed at him. He jumped back, then looked closer at the prostrate form of the Sky Guardswoman and sheathed his sword.

The bird let him near the rider. The osprey-feathered shaft of an Estil arrow jutted out just below her collarbone. A trail of blood ran from a corner of the full-lipped mouth.

"I tried," she told Fost, gazing up at him from beneath sagging eyelids. "I . . . tried."

"You did well." There seemed little else he could say.

She coughed pink foam, sighed raggedly, seemed to shrink. Fost thumbed her eyelids closed. The eagle raised its head and uttered a single, lonely cry.

Fost straightened, casting his eyes warily up and down the street. He heard the clamor of voices and arms off to his right, toward the center of town. But under the fog which formed a few feet above his head the streets of Kara-Est were deserted.

He drew a deep breath, a decision made.

"Jennas. We've found our way into the City."

The hetwoman looked from him to the eagle, standing with its fierce head wreathed in mist. Fost took a step toward the bird. It opened its beak in challenge.

Jennas brandished her sword.

"Ho, bird, here!" she shouted. Grutz and Chubchuk growled and lumbered about menacingly. The bird turned its head to glower at them, allowing Fost to vault into the saddle.

The bird cried in fury.

"Settle down, bird, there's nothing to fear. I mean you no harm. Damn!" The last word popped out as the feathered head swiveled to slash at his leg with a black beak. Fost drew his sword and pressed the tip to the side of the bird's neck.

"I mean you no harm," he said again, enunciating each word carefully. The eagles were intelligent and understood manspeech even though they couldn't speak it. "I must travel to the Sky City. If you try to hurt me, I'll defend myself."

The head bobbed. Fost hoped that meant assent.

"Come on aboard," he called out to Jennas.

The woman hesitated, took a step forward. The eagle hissed. She stopped.

"I can't."

"Certainly you can!" Fost twisted in the uncomfortably small saddle, keeping a sharp watch for interlopers. It was unlikely that soldiers of either side would be friendly to armed strangers in the streets. Anyone in the street would be fair game. "Get aboard."

Her approach was again met by shrill whistling from the eagle. It batted at her with its wings as it stepped backward, clumsy under the courier's weight.

"It fears her smell," said Erimenes. "I don't think it likes bears."

"It accepted me. Jennas, for Ust's sake, hurry!"

"With all due respect to the lovely and capable Jennas, you're hardly as steeped in ursine essences as she."

At the mention of the Bear God, Jennas's face had gone thoughtful. She stepped back and let her greatsword slump until its tip rested on the granite cobblestones. She had reached a decision of her own, no less painful than the one Fost made.

"I am not meant to go," she said. "This journey is yours alone, Fost."

Wings thundered overhead and the voices of men floated down through the fog. Fost's bird screamed. It twisted about under him, its wings beginning to flutter nervously. The bird longed for the air. Fost cursed and jabbed its neck, expecting the Sky Guards to start dropping through the misty ceiling. None came.

"That's ridiculous. *Get aboard.*"

"I couldn't," she said, her brown eyes gleaming wetly, "even were it intended that I do so. Yon beast can't bear both our weights."

"She's right, Fost. That dead girl's a foot shorter than you, and no doubt weighs half what you do."

"Shut *up,* Erimenes." A catch in his voice almost choked him. He tried to lie to himself that it was due to eagerness to see Moriana again. He knew better.

"Nor can I abandon our faithful bears in the streets of this strange city," she went on remorselessly. "You can manage on your own. Nor are you truly on your own, O Chosen of Ust."

"Jennas. . . ."

She turned and mounted Chubchuk, her soft, "Good-bye," coming back to haunt Fost.

"My sainted self, Fost, quit dithering!" Erimenes shouted.

Face a mask of anguish, Fost nudged the eagle's flanks with both knees hoping this was the proper signal. The bird understood. It stretched its wings, hopped, thumped the air vigorously in an effort to raise the unaccustomed weight. The courier's heart almost stopped as the bird dropped from beneath him, but the next instant the wings caught air and smoothly bore him upward into the mist.

"Good luck, Jennas I . . . I hope we'll meet again!"

"We shall," she called after him. "But not in happy reunion. Fare thee well, Longstrider. I . . ." The words became garbled by distance. Fost thought she added "I love you" but couldn't be sure.

A moment of flight both timeless and weightless through the veiling clouds and then Fost was blinking in hot sunlight. The roofs of the buildings were completely covered by the fog. Off to his right the salamander still died in agony within a thrashing spiral of steam. Hoping the bird had sense enough not to veer in that direction, he pressed himself against its neck and clung.

Off to his left where the blunt cliffs of the hills shouldered out of the cloud, he saw the distinctive shapes of the Sky City cargo balloons dropping down with bird riders circling protectively above. Just ahead, a greater number of the sausage balloons dropped toward the Central Plaza. The gondolas beneath bulged with armed men in the livery of Bilsinx. Though he didn't know what was happening, he knew enough of both tactics and of Rann to make a fair guess. With the fog to cover the maneuver, the prince had launched a feint attack on the Ducal Palace; when the Estil commanders sent troops to relieve the Palace, the main attack fell against the reduced forces in the Hall of Deputies, the nerve center of the defense.

The sky was nearly clear of eagles, though more balloons hung near the City bearing loads of arrows and javelins for the riders to replenish their ammunition. Most of the birds Fost saw were spiralling down among the assault balloons. That confirmed his guess that he was witnessing the killing stroke.

But what of the score of balloons rising upward toward the City in the Sky?

"Easy, easy," he told the eagle, mainly to quiet his own nerves. To his surprise, he was not reduced to jelly by the knowledge he was alone on the back of a potentially hostile bird half a thousand feet in the air. Since first encountering Erimenes and Moriana, he had been through any number of appalling adventures, including several of the aerial variety to rival this hellride to the City through the combat all around him. That and the emotional numbness remaining after his escape from the wrath of a captive elemental a hundred stories tall accounted for his seeming calm.

He couldn't bring himself to even think of Jennas left behind in the now defeated city so far under his feet.

"Erimenes," he whispered, knowing it was lunatic since none could hear him. "Erimenes, why are so many Sky City balloons climbing back to the City? The battle's at its climax."

"Guardian was right. Your eyesight is weak, indeed."

"What?" Why was that confounded genie prattling about the sentient glacier guarding Athalau?

"Don't you see those 'balloons' are orange and round? They aren't balloons, they're ludintip."

"Oh," said Fost, "and we're flying right up into the midst of them."

"There's always the opposite direction."

Fost swallowed hard.

Singlemindedly, the bird beat its way upward. None of the ludintip's passengers seemed to be looking their way, Fost noted with relief. Their attention was fixed upward. A few eagles flying combat patrol around the City's perimeter swooped down, only to be clawed from the air by whirring flights of arrows. Then the living gasbags were above the rimwall, pouring lethal arrows on the startled faces of the attackers turned defenders.

Fost's eagle climbed up into the midst of the beings in time to see a flight of small black birds billow upward like smoke.

The five hundred men and women riding beneath the ludintip had not the slightest expectation of living to feel solid earth beneath their bootsoles again. Their only aim was to sow as much death and devastation as possible in the City itself before they fell. Synalon and Rann might triumph, but nevermore could it be said that the City in the Sky was immune to reprisal from the ground.

Dropping with her squadron of bird riders and Sky Guards, Colonel Dashta Enn was astonished to see the ludintip sprouting from the mist like red-crowned mushrooms and go rushing upward so fast that she and her flyers only had time to loose a futile scattering of arrows.

The audacity of the attack took away her breath.

Trained by Rann, she did not hesitate. The colonel was committed to the attack on the Hall of Deputies. That assault might succeed. Then all that remained would be the mopping-up of scattered, disorganized and leaderless forces. If it failed, all Rann's genius and the sorceries of Synalon could not alter the fact that the Estil armies still outnumbered their foes hugely and would crush them like a giant swatting a fly if they regrouped.

The City had to fend for itself. She swooped down to battle. Her eagle's talons raked cotton, then fell on unsuspecting prey.

* * *

Synalon sat on the stone pier, head hanging listlessly with her chin on her breastbone. It took all her powers of concentration to keep the sylph and the dying, screeching fire sprite under control. She didn't know if they were still needed. She dominated them now simply to prove her power.

Something brushed her cheek. It whined like an insect. She slapped at her face when she felt the sting.

"Your Majesty, beware!" screamed one of her bodyguards from the skydock behind her. Additional words were lost in a bubbling, gurgling moan.

Her fingers touched wetness. She pulled her fingers away in dismay. It took a few seconds for her inwardly directed eyes to register smeared blood. Her own. Someone dared to attack her, Queen of the Sky City! And within her own territory!

She flashed to her feet. Her concentration broke. The waterspout leaped upward, dissipating in air with a great shout of joy at the destruction it had accomplished, leaving nothing behind but a rain of muddy water and debris. The salamander hissed relief as oblivion swallowed its agony.

The sky was filled with gaseous ludintip.

"Maggots!" Synalon screamed. "You dare attack my City!" The rage burned her brain as the salamander had seared her flesh.

All that saved her life was the amazement gripping the Estil archers after their first volley when they realized that the wild, scorched, nude figure was Synalon herself. Now came clouds of arrows.

Screeching in fury, she waved her hands before her, covering herself with a shield of fire in which the arrows flared and disappeared without reaching her body. The survivors of her bodyguard shot back, but they were vastly outnumbered. Even as the raging queen blasted a second volley of arrows, a ludintip gondola bumped down on the gray stone. Howling like fiends, armed men and women poured forth. For the first time

since the human capture of the City in the Sky, its
ramparts felt the tread of an invader's feet.

Even with the allies she had and the death spells
she commanded, Synalon could never hope to with-
stand such a fanatical attack singlehandedly. So savagely drained of energy that she could barely stand,
Synalon teetered on the brink of the skywall. Hidden
reserves of power were fed by her anger.

"Up, my children, up!" she screamed, her voice wild
and fierce and mad. She threw her scorched arms up
over her head, then pointed to her intended victims.
"Rend and slay the invaders, the groundling maggots!
Slay them!"

Obedient to their mistress's command, the ravens of
the Sky City burst forth from their rookeries. A boiling
black cloud of death, they swept over the invaders like
a firestorm from the guts of Omizantrim. Beaks pecked
at the vulnerable membranes of the ludintip, plucked
eyes from warriors battling impotently with bows and
spears. Their talons slashed at the Estil commandos
and each contact of claw with skin meant inevitable
death. As Synalon stood and laughed while balancing
precariously on her spit of stone, daring gravity to
claim her in the moment of her triumph, her ravens
slew the intruders to the last man and woman. Though
the Estil soldiers killed the black attackers by the hundred, each raven that fell was replaced by a dozen more.

At last the screaming died. Only the sound of the
wind could be heard over the ripping of flesh by a
thousand black beaks.

Somewhere in the City a war eagle left alone by the
ravens who mistook it for part of the City's forces
touched down bearing a rider whose senses reeled with
horror at the sight he had just witnessed.

The battle was quickly finished. Convinced of his
triumph to the end, General Hausan was shot by Colonel Enn while posing for ten artists dashing off sketches

to mark the epochal event of Estil history. Pudgy Sky Marshal Suema led a gallant delaying action against the bird riders while Tonsho, her nerve broken by the nearness of physical danger, fled downstairs to her private apartments in the south wing of the Hall. Suema and his men fell quickly. Scimitar in hand, Enn led the pursuit of the real ruler of Kara-Est.

They found her cowering among cushions and fine tapestries pulled from the walls. Her pretty-boys fought bravely but futilely; after a brief exchange of swordcuts Enn called for archers. The Chief Deputy's lover-bodyguards were feathered to fall among the silks. The scent of blood mingled with a dozen rare perfumes.

Tonsho cowered in the midst of luxury.

"No, no, don't hurt me," she moaned, her eyes screwed tightly shut. "For the love of all gods, *don't let Rann have me!*"

"Do you yield the city of Kara-Est?" Enn demanded sternly.

"Y-yes," sobbed Tonsho.

And the thing was done.

CHAPTER NINE

With the unfamiliar, harsh syllables of the *Zr'gsz*
tongue hissing in her ears, Moriana lay on her belly
and watched. The jagged black stone beneath her stung
with heat even through her sturdy tunic. Whether the
heat came from the sun hanging low in the western sky
or the fires burning far below she couldn't tell.

She stiffened as she sensed a presence nearby.

"Anything?" asked Darl Rhadaman r'Harmis, lowering himself beside her on the crest of the undulating
line of cooled lava.

Moriana pointed with her chin. The main camp of
the Watchers lay below. It was a somber place, reflect-
ing its purpose. Walls of dressed lava rock holed like
cheese supported flat basalt roofs. The windows had
been hewn from the same green-black stone as the roof-
ing. Moriana knew why. Wood, sod or thatch, anything
combustible, couldn't safely be used as building ma-
terial here on the northeastern slope of Omizantrim
where hot sparks or ash might descend from the Throat
at any time. A fresh dusting of gray ash overlay the
compound, a remnant of Omizantrim's eruption weeks
before.

The princess set her mouth. The Watchers' architecture might be practical but it did nothing to alleviate
the grimness of the task they performed throughout
long generations.

She saw them going about their everyday tasks. Men
and women ground wheat together turning the man-
high millstone in a granite bowl with the strength of
their own backs. Some knelt to whet the edges of spears

and shortswords. A sweating, straining, curiously silent crew manhandled casks of fresh water gathered at springs below from the bed of a wagon built to survive the brutal broken terrain of the badlands. Over by the long oblong mouth of one of the underground bunkers in which the Watchers weathered Omizantrim's outbursts, a sturdy woman with sunbleached hair drawn back in a bun slit the throat of a squealing deer and began to give a group of children a lesson in butchering and dressing meat.

"It's like a combination military camp and monastery," remarked Darl in a low-pitched voice that carried only a few feet. Moriana glanced at him, nodded slowly.

Since their arrival in Thendrun, Darl had emerged from the cocoon of self-doubt and despair that had wrapped him since Chanobit. On their second night in the emerald keep they had once again become lovers. Whether Darl knew or not what had occurred between her and Khirshagk, he said nothing of it. Moriana felt tempted to ask Ziore if he suspected. She didn't. That would be an invasion of Darl's innermost privacy.

Still, there was something about him that disturbed Moriana. Was it fatalism, discouragement or simply feeling the onset of middle years, the slowing that comes inevitably to even those as robust as the legendary Count-Duke of Harmis? He had held up well on the rapid march from the keep of the Fallen Ones, though. When they had to leave their war dogs behind to advance silently through the badlands, he walked with a firmness and sureness of step that put Moriana, a decade and a half his junior, to shame.

"Where's the creature?" he asked.

"It generally stays in the vicinity of the camp. Sometimes it moves in the dead of night. No one ever sees it. In the morning, it's simply gone, only to turn up elsewhere."

"Foraging?"

"Apparently not. The Ullapag doesn't eat. It seems to derive its sustenance from the mountain itself."

"The same animal has survived for ten thousand years?" Darl shook his head in wonder. "We deal with potent magic."

Mariana said nothing.

Something scraped stone behind her. She turned her head slowly to see Khirshagk approaching gingerly over the sharp lava. The height of a tall man, the *Zr'gsz* leader moved with surprising grace. However, he and all his kin were less skillful at silent movement than the humans in the party.

After a council of war with the followers who had remained faithful into the depths of Thendrun, Moriana had decided to send one knight back across the Marchant into Samazant to muster men for a new attempt on the City. Darl had been afraid they'd used up their stock of sympathy among the men of the City States. But last night Moriana's crying spells had revealed the Sky City occupation of Kara-Est. News of the seaport's fall would have reached the Empire by the time Sir Thursz reached his home country. Those tidings would make men reconsider the princess's pleas for aid.

A Nevrym forester had gone north down the trail from Thendrun to his home woods to consult Grim-peace, the head of the woods runners. The foresters lacked the instinctive fear of the Hisser that most of the Realm harbored, but they were known also as redoubtable foes of the Dark. This reassured Moriana that her appraisal of the *Zr'gsz* was accurate. It also let her hope the Nevrymin might aid her, especially since she had promised a substantial gift of gold in return. Like their neighbors the Dwarves of North Keep, the foresters had a healthy regard for specie.

"Have you located the hellbeast yet?" asked Khirshagk, lowering himself beside the humans. His limbs sprawled in a way the princess found disconcerting. His dark hide blended with the black rock and evergreens around them as if he had been bred in such surroundings.

"Not yet," said Darl.

A file of men and women appeared abruptly below and to the left. They wore drab clothes like the folk in camp, with the addition of mottled green and black cloaks. The *Zr'gsz* were not the only ones practicing camouflage. Not even the four keen-eyed foresters accompanying them had known of that patrol's nearness.

"This country works both for and against us. You can hide an army in these folds. Not even the Watchers have a way of overcoming that." Darl rubbed the dark stubble on his jaw. "We may be able to bring this off, after all."

"I hope you are right," said Khirshagk.

Moriana reappraised her companion. After his bullheadedness and refusal to take her advice had helped lose the battle at the creek, she had fallen into the error of dismissing his military judgment. Now she was reminded that he knew more of infantry-lore than she; her greatest experience lay in aerial warfare. When the Watcher patrol appeared she had experienced near panic. Her imagination had peopled the tortured black landscape with hordes of Watchers closing unseen on them. Darl had restored perspective. If the intruders moved warily, the Watchers would only discover them through a stroke of luck.

"Maybe their vigilance has flagged," she said, thinking out loud.

"No," said Khirshagk simply.

"But . . ."

"Khirshagk, get back! It's looking this way!" At the urgent whisper from Ziore's jug, the lizard man slithered back down the slope. Moriana flattened herself on the rock and looked around wildly.

"What is? I don't see anything."

"The Ullapag," said Ziore. "It sensed Khirshagk."

"Can it read thoughts?"

"Poorly. Enough to feel the alertness come into its mind. I deflected its attention, set it at ease. I think."

"I wonder if it can communicate with the Watchers?" asked Moriana.

"Probably," answered Darl. "But I don't think it has." The routine below dragged along calmly.

The two slipped away to join Khirshagk in a fold of the lava. A caprice of wind carried acrid smoke from a fumarole uphill to them. Moriana and Darl coughed and blinked back tears.

Khirshagk rocked on his haunches. His eyes had a faraway gaze.

"The Heart. I taste its nearness." Unconsciously, his tongue flicked from his thin-lipped mouth. It was forked. Moriana felt a disquieting tingle in her loins.

Moriana opened the lid of Ziore's jar. Pink mist spilled from the satchel, became a whirlwind of dancing bright motes and finally shaped itself into a woman, tall, serious and quite lovely despite advanced age.

"Which direction?" she asked. The *Zr'gsz* pointed a black claw south, past the camp. Ziore looked grave. "The Ullapag lies that way as well."

"It's guarding the Heart?" asked Moriana.

"So it seems."

They made their way down the gulley to where the others waited. The four Nevrymin waited with the Fallen Ones. Moriana sat on an outcropping of lava and let Darl explain the situation.

"We can't wait for night?" asked Quickspear, a narrow man whose habitual grin was rendered lopsided by a long knife slash down the left side of his face. He cradled the weapon that gave him his name, fingers nervously dancing along its shaft.

"My people do not function well in the cold." The *Zr'gsz* weren't true reptiles. They fell somewhere between mammals and lizards—furred yet scaly, nursing their young though oviparous, warm-blooded but inclined to become sluggish when the sun went down.

"We've only two hours of sunlight left us," said Darl. "Here's my plan. . . ."

Vapors streamed upward from the molten rock that bubbled in a pit cut like a slash across the mountain's flank. On a broad expanse of rock above the fumarole sat a vast creature, as unmoving as the lava beneath it.

A tall man could lie comfortably in the space between the bulging half-lidded eyes. Its hide was warty, green dapples on black mimicking the pattern of the Watchers' cloaks. Its immense body lay among four legs that seemed unable to support its bulk. It had the sloped back of a toad instead of the crooked back of a frog. Obsidian eyes stared out, missing nothing.

Moriana scarcely believed the thing lived. No motion of breathing stirred its bloated sides. But she felt its presence in her mind, alien and imposing.

She studied the natural amphitheatre scooped in the side of Omizantrim. Fifteen yards across and forty deep, its open side faced the Watchers' camp several hundred yards downslope. The fumarole lay at the inside end of the amphitheatre, with the Ullapag's rock raised like a dais above it. At either side of the opening stood a single Watcher. Two more Watchers stood in the rocks above the monster, armed with bows and spears. Though the pit's stinging fumes blew in their faces, they showed no sign of discomfort.

The four Nevrym Forest men were sneaking up on the four sentries. Moriana, Darl and Khirshagk, with several of his men, waited hidden on the northern wall. Though the foresters assured her they could capture the sentries without difficulty, she worried. She balked at killing any of the Watchers, and she didn't trust the *Zr'gsz* to be scrupulous in avoiding the slaying of their ancient antagonists. The bulk of the party of Hissers waited in concealment around the Watchers' encampment to bottle up any attempts at aiding the Ullapag. But that had to be done, moral niceties or not.

If the sentries were alerted before the foresters reached them, Khirshagk and his men would have to deal with them willy-nilly. Moriana and Darl had to confront the Ullapag, by means mystic or mundane as required.

She still had no clear idea what the Ullapag did. It looked too ungainly to run down the fleet *Zr'gsz* in rough terrain like this. One thing it did attempt was to detect the nearness of the Hissers by a special sense. Ziore hovered beside Moriana, dulling the Ullapag's mental sensitivity to the presence of a hundred of the very beings it was meant to ward against.

A flicker of movement not far away caught Moriana's eye. It was Brightlaugher, a young blond boy painfully proud of the skimpy golden fuzz on his chin. He moved up on the nearest of the Watchers. He was almost in position for the quick final rush.

"Moriana." The low voice was so distorted by effort she almost didn't recognize Ziore. "Moriana, you must help. Can't hold by myself any more."

"What?" she whispered back. Darl and Khirshagk stared at them.

"The Ullapag. Help me blanket it."

"But . . . I can't!"

"You can!" Ziore snapped. "Since I've known you your power has increased steadily. Help me, or all is lost!"

The princess wondered if the nun was right. Then she shut her eyes and concentrated.

She didn't have to grope to find the Ullapag's mind. It loomed bright, short of sentience, but old, old and very watchful. A bright thread of suspicion shimmered in the creature's mind. Moriana felt Ziore's presence and realized that the genie couldn't soothe the sense of wrongness troubling the Ullapag. She stretched out her own mind, soothing without words.

The doubt-thread vanished.

I did it! Moriana thought. The realization exhilarated her. Had her power grown because she'd slept with Khirshagk? He said her ancestor namesake hadn't perceived true magic *herself*. Had she gained something her forebear hadn't?

Hidden within her tunic, the Destiny Stone turned black. A rock loosened, twisting away beneath her foot. She stifled a yelp of alarm but couldn't save herself from falling.

The guard below turned and saw Brightlaugher rising from behind a bush twelve feet away. The Nevrym boy lunged. The spear came down, and the boy gasped as he ran onto its broad point.

The other guards shouted alarm. One standing above the Ullapag nocked an arrow and drew. Sprawled among the biting edges of the lava, Moriana recovered her grip on her own bow, drew, fired.

The Watcher stiffened and pitched forward, falling past the Ullapag's perch to disappear into the boiling lava.

Foresters wrestled with the other two. One of Khirshagk's warriors, overcome by battle-lust, leaped past Moriana and struck down the Watcher as he struggled to free his spear from Brightlaugher's belly.

The Ullapag screamed.

Moriana heard it as a bass thrumming, almost below the level of hearing. The *Zr'gsz* standing over the sentry jerked as if struck by an arrow. He began to twitch and his head twisted to score his own shoulders with his fangs.

"Unnghh." Khirshagk's body was bent backward like a bow. His jaw was locked and his eyes rolled wildly. In spite of the agony gripping him, he ground out words between his teeth. "You must . . . slay it. Or . . . we . . . die!"

She stared at the Ullapag. It had grown until the

princess realized it had lifted itself upward enough to allow a huge throat sac to expand beneath it.

"It's producing a vibration," Ziore shouted. Moriana barely heard her, though the hum of the Ullapag wasn't loud. "It'll kill the lizard men."

As if to prove her right, the *Zr'gsz* who had dashed into the open fell to the ground beside his victim. His eyes stared upward. His mouth shone darkly with his own blood.

Moriana drew another arrow from her quiver and shot, aiming for an eye. The broadhead flew true.

It was four feet from target when a pale tongue leaped from the Ullapag's mouth and snagged it in the air like a fly.

Darl was up and running, broadsword in hand, shouting, "Victory! Moriana and victory!"

The moist eyes swiveled and fixed him with their baleful gaze. The throat sac expanded further, the humming came louder. Moriana's body tickled all over and her throat hurt. The monster's vibrations obviously affected humans, but not as they did the *Zr'gsz*. The uncontrollable contractions of Khirshagk's muscles were breaking him like a thief on a wheel. His men rolled on the ground at his side, hissing in terminal anguish.

The Ullapag was puzzled. Here was a man running at it with hostile intent. Yet its deathsong to *Zr'gsz* had no effect. Was it possible a human might attack it?

The Ullapag pounced.

Darl escaped being crushed under the monster's bulk by inches. The Count-Duke rolled and came up running. He charged. Swinging his sword doublehanded he hacked at the bloated, warty flank.

His sword rebounded with the sound of a stick striking a poorly stretched drum. The monster's lipless mouth opened and the tongue shot out. Instantly sword and swordarm were tangled in loops of wet, pallid flesh.

Darl tried to pull away. The tongue held him fast. It

began reeling him inexorably inward. He twisted, slashed at the tongue with his dagger. Green blood sprayed his chest.

A mental squeal of agony made Moriana and Ziore wince. The Ullapag raised a foreleg and clumsily clutched Darl, trying to hurry him forward into the pink cavern of its mouth. Darl dug in his heels and locked his knees but lacked the strength to resist for more than seconds.

It earned him life. Moriana needed no more than a heartbeat to fit a new arrow, draw and aim, to let fly.

With the monster's tongue coiled like a serpent around Darl, nothing hindered the arrow's flight. It struck the eye and sank to the fletchings. The Ullapag reared, hauling Darl off his feet. A second arrow followed the first.

The tongue uncoiled, spilling Darl onto the hard lava. Even as he fell he struck at the monster's throat sac. The blade cut through the membrane.

A third arrow sang its shrill song of death. The other eye exploded. Darl rocked to his knees and drove his sword into the moss-green belly.

The Destiny Stone turned white. The dying Ullapag fell to the right, rolled onto its back away from the kneeling warrior. Its legs kicked spastically at the air.

As though dropped by an invisible hand, Khirshagk fell limp among the rocks. His men lay about him, frozen in attitudes of ghastly death. Moriana knelt by his side.

His eyes opened, looked into hers, then he said, "Thank you."

She was up and running to Darl's side.

"How could you do it?" raged Ludo, the Chief Warder of Omizantrim. "For a hundred centuries we've kept our faith with Felarod for all humanity. How could you betray us?"

"Don't talk to the princess in that tone, pig," snarled Darl. He came forward, face dark with menace. Moriana waved him back.

"No, Darl. He has a right to speak that way." The words threatened to congeal in her throat. "Listen carefully, Warder Ludo. I'm not betraying anybody. I must explain."

Ludo spat at her.

"Calm down, old man," Quickspear said softly, bouncing his spear suggestively in one hand. "Brightlaugher was my sister's husband's cousin, and well-loved."

"He got what he deserved." The old man's blue eyes were merciless and as fearless as a hawk's. "He was a traitor to men, embarked on a traitor's errand."

Quickspear raised his weapon.

"Hold!" shouted Moriana. "Quickspear, leave us." The dark-haired forester scowled at her, weighing rebellion. He was no fool. He left.

Moriana slumped on her stool. She massaged her face with long, slender fingers. She suddenly snatched them away, screaming. They were drenched in blood.

But it was only a trick of the candlelight.

"I am Moriana Etuul," she said, "rightful Queen of the City in the Sky."

"Pah! You live with the stink of Vridzish magic. What else can we expect of you, witch?"

At a warning growl, Moriana spoke without turning her head.

"Please, Darl, let me finish." He subsided. "Thank you, Darl." Leaning forward, she told the entire story to the Chief Warder, of her sister's usurpation of the Throne of Winds, of Synalon's dabbling with the blackest of magics and her desire to make a compact with the Lords of Infinite Night.

"So it is to fight the Dark Ones that I march against the City," she told him earnestly. "The *Zr'gsz* are no more foes to men. They know their time is past. They aid me to recover ancient treasures they were forced to leave when exiled from the Sky City." She inhaled deeply. "When they have those things, they'll return to Thendrun in peace. Khirshagk, Instrumentality of the People, gives me his word on this."

Ludo fixed her with an eye as frosty as the Southern Waste.

"You're either a liar or the most accomplished fool I've ever encountered." He jerked his head at Darl. "You can have your bully-boy kill me now."

"No one's going to harm you." She started. Ludo stared past her shoulder, his eyes wide.

She turned. A *Zr'gsz* male stood there, a torch gripped in his talons.

"Khirshagk want you," he said. "Come. Now. Pleezzz."

Moriana and Darl looked at one another. Then they followed the messenger into the cool, starry night.

CHAPTER TEN

Their guide led Moriana and Darl from the camp up the slope to the fumarole over which the Ullapag had stood guard. A forest of torches around a sprawling building that had served the inhabitants as school, temple and assembly hall showed where the *Zr'gsz* guarded the captive Watchers.

Arrows and slung stones had greeted the Watchers when they tried to come to the aid of their fellows and the Ullapag. The Ullapag had given throat then and the Hissers surrounding the camp had collapsed in agony. Before the Watchers could slay more than a handful of the helpless lizard men, the Ullapag's song had been stilled. Shocked by the Hissers' return to activity, the Watchers had emotionally crumbled when Moriana and Darl called on them to surrender. The fact that their immortal co-guardian was dead, and that humans had aided *Zr'gsz* in slaying it, shattered their morale. They threw down their weapons and obeyed.

Khirshagk's control over his folk was good. Less than a score of the Watchers were killed or injured. The other encampments would send patrols to investigate when no word came from the main village; Moriana was worried but Darl assured her their small detachment could hold until reinforcements summoned by Khirshagk's sorcery arrived from Thendrun. Moriana was puzzled by this—she had been under the impression that so few *Zr'gsz* had accompanied them because there *were* so few alive. The great crystal keep had fairly rattled from emptiness, and she had scarcely seen a soul other than the Instrumentality and a few silent

150

servants until they were ready to march. But Khirshagk told her more men were on the way, and she deemed it impolitic to question her ally too closely.

A dozen *Zr'gsz* stood around the fuming lava pit holding torches. The sun was down but this didn't keep the People from their chores, whatever they were.

"I greet you," said Khirshagk from the platform that had been the resting place of the monster. "You have done a great service for my People this day. It is fitting that you witness this, the culmination of years of waiting, of longing."

Moriana and Darl looked at one another. Stepping forward as near as they dared to the fumarole, they stopped and waited. Their hands found one another.

Still in loincloth and mace-belt, Khirshagk no longer looked the rude savage he had appeared by day. In the smoky torchlight and lit below by the hellglow of melted stone, he was weird and magnificent, the king-priest of an ancient people, an ancient faith. Moriana wondered what ritual he enacted here. She tensed in anticipation, feeling forces mounting all around her.

Khirshagk raised his arms and threw back his head. A wind rush of syllables blew from his lungs. Moriana couldn't understand the words, not fully. But the clicks and hisses and unvoiced vowels struck strangely half-familiar chords within her mind, tantalizing her with hints of understanding. She stole a look at Darl. He watched with curiosity but with no trace of comprehension.

Moriana forced the name to form in her mind: *Ziore?*

I can make nothing of this speech, child, nor can I read the emotions behind it.

That negative reply caused Moriana's unease to grow. Powers definitely beyond the pale surged in this stony amphitheatre.

Moriana sensed excitement growing in the *Zr'gsz* though their expressions remained unreadable behind

masks of torchlight and alien musculature. Khirshagk
finished his oration in a cry that was almost a sigh, a
breath expelled toward the stars, expressing transcen-
dent passion. The *Zr'gsz* thrust their torches into the
face of the night with a wild sibilance.

Moriana's nose wrinkled from the brimstone fumes
drifting out of the fumarole. A crust of partially cooled
lava rode the turbulent surface of the pool and cracked
in a not quite regular pattern like mud dried on a flat.
Yellow-orange glare burned along the fracture lines.
Bubbles of gas rose from the depths of the mountain
popping loudly to vent noxious vapors and spit glowing
hot gobbets in all directions. One struck stone near her
boot. The heat stung her even through the thick leather.

Khirshagk stood silent, looking from one *Zr'gsz* to
the next. In spite of the undercurrents of emotion about
her, Moriana suppressed a yawn. It had been a long
day, and her body demanded rest.

Darl squeezed her hand.

"I hope they finish soon with whatever they're
doing." She caught his eye and grinned. Perhaps she
wouldn't rest so soon.

"My friends." Almost guiltily they looked at the Instrumentality who had called to them in manspeech
across the seething pit. "You are about to witness an
epic moment in the history of the People: the recovery
of their Heart, lost to us these ten thousand years."

A tall, slimly built *Zr'gsz* cast away his cloak. He
walked to the edge of the pit, looked down a few seconds, turned to face his leader. She couldn't be sure,
but the princess believed the look on his face to be the
pure rapture of a religious experience.

Khirshagk pointed with an arm circled in rings of obsidian and jasper. The youth nodded and waded into
the lava.

Darl gasped. Moriana stared. Step by step the young
lizard man descended into the fumarole. The tendons
on his neck stuck out like columns.

"Gods, is he immune to heat?" Moriana whispered.

Darl didn't reply. He only licked dried lips and continued staring at the sight.

The lizard man raised one leg high to wade over an irregularity in the bottom of the lava pool. The meat hung loose on his bones. The bubbling lava reached his groin, his waist, his sternum. His face never lost its look of transfiguration, not even when the liquid stone reached his chin, his lips. Steam poured from his nostrils as he cooked inside from the awful heat.

He went deeper.

Moriana looked away as the lava reached his eyes. The stench of burned meat clutched at her stomach like a groping hand.

She forced herself to look back. There was no sign of the youth. Moriana assumed he had finally received the benison of death. No creature could desire to survive after having been cooked alive like that. The other *Zr'gsz* gazed eagerly at the roiling surface, Khirshagk among them. The princess knew she would never let him touch her again, not in exchange for any or all powers, magical or temporal.

A platelet of solidified lava slid to one side. A hand thrust from the lava—or the remnant of a hand. Naked bone gleamed in the torchlight but that skeletal hand clutched a jewel, an immense black diamond that smoked from immersion in the molten stone.

Great Ultimate! Ziore cried in Moriana's mind.

Moriana couldn't respond, either with mind talk or vocalized words. She was too stunned by what happened.

Hand and diamond sank from view. The watchers hissed consternation. At a nod from Khirshagk a second lizard man plunged into the fumarole, eyes fixed on the spot where the gem had disappeared.

He brought the diamond five feet nearer shore before he succumbed. Six more *Zr'gsz* made the horrendous journey into the boiling hell of the fumarole before the last handed the great diamond to the Instrumentality and fell back to sink in a cloud of steam.

Khirshagk cradled the gem in both hands. His mighty arms trembled as if it were too massive to hold. He spoke to it fervently in his own hissing tongue, and then turned to Darl and Moriana to address them in their language.

"Ah, this day shall live as long as night comes to cover the land! The Heart is returned to us!"

The diamond glittered darkly from a hundred facets. Smoke streamed from it. The surviving *Zr'gsz* threw themselves down and writhed in rapture.

Unspeaking, Moriana and Darl backed off and then almost ran down the stony path. The princess felt anguish emanating from Ziore's jug, a mental keening. She pitied the genie. It would be horrible to have been cloistered all one's life and then be subjected to such a spectacle.

She saved some pity for Darl and herself. The sight of the young lizard men wading deeper into the killing heat of the lava would live in their dreams as long as they lived. Tomorrow Moriana would attempt to evaluate this shocking demonstration of the gulf that existed between the human owners of the Realm and their inhuman predecessors. Tonight they would cling to one another to maintain their sanity and would seek forgetfulness in the sharing of flesh.

"In High Medurim," Fost told the faces upturned in the dusty gloom of the warehouse, "this type of technique is called the push-pull. Originally it involved a mature thief and a juvenile apprentice. The urchin, whose appearance was carefully made as scruffy and dirty as possible, would jostle a noble walking the streets. The noble, and guards if any, would either seize the urchin to chastise him for his effrontery or give chase if he was agile enough to evade them." He allowed himself a self-satisfied smirk. "I was only caught once. The best record for any 'pusher' in The Teeming. However it went, both the mark and his or her retinue were sufficiently distracted for the well-dressed adult thief to make the 'pull,' that is, lift the victim's purse. Though manual dexterity was useful, as a general rule the mark was so set on avenging himself on the presumptuous brat that a blind man could rob him without being noticed."

He leaned back against the cool wall.

"Now, since I didn't drag you through that discourse simply to show you what a fine apprentice thief I was as a lad, who among you can tell me how a variation of the classic push-pull can be employed against a Monitor armory guarded by a dozen armed men?"

Blank looks met him. He crossed his arms, arranged a knowing and superior smile on his lips and waited. On his last sojourn to the City in the Sky he had fallen in with the Underground who resisted Synalon's rule. He hadn't been notably impressed by their competence. In fact, their ineptitude had almost cost him and Moriana their lives when he rescued her from the Vicar of Istu's lustful clutches during the Rite of Dark Assumption. Now he did his best to help them grow more professional and effective. As Luranni, golden-eyed daughter of High Councillor Uriath, had told him, he had little real choice.

He caught Luranni's eye. She sat on a stockfish barrel at the back of the audience of would-be revolutionaries. She smiled at him. He held back the urge to wink in reply.

His eyes slid to the youths of both sexes seated in the makeshift classroom. Their garb was of far humbler quality than that of the people surrounding Luranni. Patches were much in evidence and here and there a ragged hem of tunic or skirt caught his eye. In spite of their less than splendid appearance, it was from among these young people that Fost expected an answer.

He got it. A girl with black hair cut square across her

forehead and a piquant prettiness offset by thick eye-brows raised her hand.

"You· set children to taunt the guards. Make'em good'n loud so a crowd gathers. Pretty soon all the Monitors'll be able to think about's the way the brats're making them look foolish. While their cods are shriveling inside their trousers, your team can slip inside." Her brow wrinkled. "To think on it, might be still better to have the kids fling rocks'n garbage at the Monnies. That way they're likely to leave station to give'em chase."

Fost smiled in appreciation at a correct answer.

"Very good, ah—I'm afraid I don't know your name."

"Syriana," she replied. She smiled at his quizzical expression. "I was named for the Royal Twins, Sir Longstrider."

"Fost will do, Syriana—and for the rest of you, as well." He glanced at the high, narrow windows of the warehouse and gauged the slant of the sunlight falling through dusty, musty air. "It's getting near dark. We'll wrap things up for the day."

The class gave him a ripple of polite applause and rose to file out. He thought it nice to be appreciated.

Fost Longstrider, revolutionary, had such a nice ring to it. Even if he hadn't volunteered.

As the students split up in ones and twos to slip from the building by different exits to avoid attracting attention, Syriana approached Fost with a shy expression.

"Sir . . . uh, Fost," she said. "Is it true you, um, you killed a war eagle? All by yourself?"

A rustle of silk, a waft of cinnamon and Luranni's arm slipped cool into his.

"It is indeed true," she said. "He's quite a man, my Fost." Luranni smiled more widely than necessary.

"I, uh, I see." Syriana licked her lips, then turned and joined the file of departing students.

Luranni looked up at the courier, a glint in her eyes. "You weren't thinking of letting that lowborn fluff turn your head?" she asked in a fierce whisper Fost was sure must be audible all the way to the Palace of Winds. "I'll have to braid another knot in my hair to bind you more closely."

He smiled reassuringly at her. The smile ran no deeper than his lips. He wondered what would happen if—when—Luranni discovered that he was still devoted to Moriana. Given the perilous nature of his very existence in the Sky City, where discovery meant a lingering death at Rann's hands, there was danger of more than an unpleasant emotional scene if Luranni became jealous of the princess.

He donned a cloak, pulled the hood up to obscure his features and let Luranni lead him out into the narrow streets of the Sky City. Sunset was beginning to tinge the western horizon in outlandish colors. Despite the promise of cooling evening breezes, Fost sweltered inside his cowl. Still, this was better than roasting over a grill lit by Rann.

He had killed one of the gigantic eagles of the City's armed forces in single combat. But he hadn't intended to. He had meant to ride up to the City on his captive bird and slip away into the maze of streets hoping to meet some member of the Underground who could tell him where to find Moriana. Only later did it occur to him that he had let fatigue and horror cloud his judgment. The bird could communicate to its keepers in its own speech that it had been forced to bring a groundling into the Sky City. There was no reason for Rann or his secret police to guess the identity of the intruder, but they'd turn the City inside out looking for him. This of all times, the City's rulers couldn't afford to allow possible spies to roam at large.

After flying over the grisly battle between the poison-taloned ravens and the Estil suicide squad, the eagle had touched down in a sidestreet near the starboard beam of the City. Fost had leaped to the pavement.

"Look out!" Erimenes shouted from his jug.

Fost flung himself face down, not even pausing to ask himself why the genie had warned him again of impending danger. Perhaps the long-dead philosopher thought a fight would be small entertainment if terminated at the first stroke by the great decapitating sweep of the eagle's sharp beak that swooshed inches above his back.

Fost rolled desperately. The bird struck again, scoring his hide and striking the flagstones with a jarring screech. Yellow talons groped. Fost got his legs under him and sprang away.

The bird advanced, its eyes bright with the determination to shed his blood. It was bright enough to know Fost must try to kill it; it had struck the first blow. Fost fell back step by step, weighing his chances. He didn't care for them at all. The bird was almost twice as tall and fast, very fast. If he stood, the beast would shred him with beak and claws. If he ran, it would be on him in an instant like an owl falls on a fleeing mouse. The street was little more than an alley between hostelries and shops shuttered for the battle. He had little room to dodge and no place to seek refuge.

"Go *past* him, you fool!" hissed Erimenes. Unquestioning, the courier obeyed.

Shrieking rage, the bird whirled as Fost dived past its legs. The great white head struck a jutting cornice of gray-green stone. As the bird reeled, stunned, Fost regained his feet and closed to make a quick kill with his broadsword.

Bleeding from wounds he didn't remember receiving, wounds dating back to those given him by the demonbird in the Black River, Fost ran. Most of the City's police and military were occupied on the walls, but it still took every bit of streetcraft he'd learned growing up in the poverty of High Medurim's slums to reach the familiar short building with its wood facade. The door inside the triple arched entryway was barred by magical means.

"Allow me," Erimenes said with sardonic satisfaction, and the door swung open to admit the courier.

Luranni's eyes showed no astonishment when she had later entered her third floor flat to find him lounging among fat cushions she used for furnishings.

"I knew you'd come," she said, a smile spreading across her face. "I made magic to bring you to me. See?" She reached and undid a braid of brown hair which had been wound around her head. The intricate plaiting made it hard for Fost's eyes to follow.

"Well?" Luranni asked. "What are we waiting for?" She let her gown drop to the floor.

With an unusual degree of discretion, Erimenes viewed their lovemaking from within his bottle without tendering his normal lewd commentary. When Fost and Luranni paused to rest, he introduced himself. Once again Luranni showed no surprise. Naked, she pulled the philosopher's jug from Fost's satchel and examined it.

"I've not met you before, have I?" she asked. "But you spoke to me when I met Fost and the Princess Moriana and guided them to where their eagle waited."

"Just so," replied Erimenes.

"So," she said, turning coin-colored eyes to Fost, "this is the property Moriana stole from you."

"Yes." Like her well-born comrades in the Underground, she may have lacked a sense of the realities of intrigue and insurrection, but she was a highly intelligent woman who had earned high responsibility in her father's import-export business because of her abilities. It was well for Fost to be reminded in a minor matter.

It might mean his life if he didn't consider her in more ways than one.

He had to be circumspect in what he told her. Praying that Erimenes wouldn't see fit to contradict him, he explained that he and Moriana had gone off in search of some unspecified treasure, pursued all the way by Rann's bird riders. In Athalau, deep inside the glacier that called itself Guardian, they had become separated. Fost had been trying to catch up with the princess ever since.

"I just missed her at Chanobit Creek," he said, lapsing back into truth. "We found a survivor of her retinue. He didn't live long, but before he died he told us that Moriana was coming here. And so I came to find her."

"But she didn't come here," said Luranni.

Fost groaned. His stomach turned over.

"Wh-where is she? Are you sure?" he demanded when he recovered from the shock.

"Synalon claims she has gone to make a compact with the Fallen Ones in Thendrun," she said. "It might be a lie. You know what our beloved queen is like." Fost knew. "But my father says she appeared to be speaking the truth when she told the Council of it. She was in a rare fury. Sparks were flaming off her the way they do when she's angry, like hot wax from a taper. Poor Tromym got his sidewhiskers set on fire. A servant had to pour a beaker of wine over his head."

"How did Synalon come by this information?" Erimenes asked. "I only enquire to expedite this discussion," he added with a courtly bow, having insisted on being let out of his jug, "so that Fost can get back to sampling sundry carnal delights with you as soon as possible."

Fost winced. Luranni only smiled. The courier noted the broad patches of her areolas and the way her nipples stood erect again.

"She divined it, she said. It was hard to tell what

made her more furious, her sister betraying humankind
or the Dark Ones betraying her. She seemed to think
they allowed the Fallen Ones to ally with Moriana in
spite of promising to aid her."

"Mightn't the Vridzish have decided to take matters
into their own hands?"

Luranni shrugged, then said, "Synalon seemed not to
think so." She went to a pewter bowl on a shelf, took
up a long slender fruit and began to peel it. "She spends
most of her time brooding and trying to make contact
with the Dark Ones, and occasionally torturing some
poor soul to death to take her mind off her problems."

"Synalon has grown rather exalted in her own es-
teem," Erimenes remarked, "if she thinks she can summon the Lords of Infinite Night like some lower caste
djinn." He stroked his nose with a skinny forefinger.
"But enough talk."

Luranni took a bite from the fruit she held.

"I agree," she said, reaching for Fost.

Not only did the Sky City woman not seem to mind
Erimenes's appreciative presence, she went out of her
way to indulge in erotic variations that left Fost gasping
for breath. The philosopher was elated.

To each her own, thought Fost, then settled back to
enjoy.

Since then he had found himself a full member of the
Underground. He had been less than enthusiastic until
Luranni pointed out that Fost wanted to join forces
with Moriana again, and that Moriana, one way or another, was bound for the Sky City. He might as well
lend a hand in the interim both to further the princess's
cause and pay for his keep among the City's resistance.

Behind his normal congeniality Luranni's father had
not been overjoyed to see the courier again. Fost took it
for granted that if he did nothing to justify his continued existence, the High Councillor was fully capable of

having him dropped over the skywall some night when the moons were down. In fact, he suspected Uriath might not be beyond hinting to the Monitors where a prize Rann would value highly could be located, but he kept that suspicion to himself.

Fost soon found himself enjoying his role as revolutionary. The subterranean life was far from unfamiliar to him. He had spent his early years dodging the Emperor's police and the goons of the various guilds until opposition to authority had become a part of him. Wandering through the Grand Library of Medurim under the guidance of Ceratith the pedant, Fost had come upon many works on the theory and practice of revolution. He had read them with the all-consuming eagerness with which he approached all learning in that halcyon stage of his life.

His first suggestion had been resisted vigorously by Uriath and the senior members of the Underground. Fost wanted the resistance to be broadened to include middle and lower classes as well as the noble-born.

"I'm a sorceror," Fost told Uriath, "and I can teach your people the secret of invisibility." By that, he explained, he meant that the Underground was ignoring the best source of intelligence in the entire City.

"Who pays attention to servants? More than that, who heeds the glaziers who repair broken windows, the workmen who clean and polish the building stones, the maids who dust Queen Synalon's bedchamber?"

Uriah looked skeptical. Grinning, Fost gestured past the High Councillor. Plying a feather duster over the elaborate wooden screens hung on the walls stood a servant in the yellow and blue livery of Uriath's own household. Uriath turned a deeper red and agreed to try Fost's scheme.

It had borne fruit. Through workers in the barracks of the bird riders, the Underground had made contact with malcontents in the City's military, the first such breakthrough in the movement's history. Actual armed insurrection against Synalon became for the first time more than a dream as unreal as any evoked by the Golden Barbarians' drugs.

His spectacular rescue of Princess Moriana from the Vicar of Istu gave Fost a reputation with the Underground. It was enhanced by rumors of his victory over a war eagle, which he saw no need to balance by pointing out that the bird had smacked its own fool head against a building. When in spite of initial sullen resistance to the idea of recruiting members of the service class into the movements Fost's outrageous scheme produced results, he could do no wrong.

He'd made further innovations. The Underground's internal security was little more than wishful thinking. As far as Fost could judge, the only reason it survived was that Rann was too occupied with planning and executing Synalon's grand scheme of conquest to give much mind to the business of spying on Sky Citizens. Additionally, the leaders of the movement were too highly placed and valuable to the running of the City bureaucracy for Synalon to arrest without concrete evidence. So far, all the Underground members had died before revealing the names of anyone important.

But it was only a matter of time.

In the existing organization, the damage was done; each member knew the identities of too many comrades. For new recruits, including servants and disgruntled soldiers, Fost introduced a cell system. An individual never knew anyone outside his own three-person cell and those whom he or she recruited. Contact with superiors was done through those who had recruited the cell members themselves, and the recruiters kept their own identities secret. In this way the damage would be minimized if a captured rebel lived long enough to spill his figurative guts along with his literal ones.

While Fost played rebel leader, Erimenes consulted with various mages in the Underground about means of short-circuiting Rann's magical surveillance net. By using captive fire elementals, Palace sorcerors spied on any events near the direct glow of fire. It netted a fair number of disaffected citizens overly fond of sitting down before their evening fire and spouting off about the oppressions of the crazy queen.

Since that was unlikely to remain the only trick in the secret police's repertory, the fifteen-hundred-year-old sage was also trying to foresee and forestall new approaches of the opposition and to come up with ideas of his own. Though Erimenes's powers were limited, only coming into full potency when he was near his natal city of Athalau, he possessed what Fost grudgingly had to admit to be an excellent knowledge of the theory and practice of Athalar magic, magic involving the intrinsic powers of one's own brain. The Athalar, and Erimenes, were less knowledgeable about extrinsic magic involving the manipulation of powers external to oneself, such as elementals or demons. But even here Erimenes was a fount of useful lore.

To all appearances Erimenes was enjoying his role as hugely as Fost was his. He didn't even seem to mind that his own labors and researches prevented him from watching the carnal antics of Fost and the willing Luranni, which grew increasingly more frantic as time passed and the inevitable but as yet unscheduled confrontation neared. Through the grapevine Fost heard intriguingly lubricous rumors about orgies among the younger mages and apprentices fomented by Erimenes. He didn't ask the spirit if there was truth in them. If there was, Erimenes would tell him in vastly more detail than he cared to hear.

But Fost worried. In the past, the genie's sole allegiance had been to gratifying his own lust for vicarious experience, particularly sex and violence. Back in the days of a more innocent eon, when Fost had been a mere courier delivering a parcel of unknown contents to a sorceror, Erimenes had repeatedly gotten Fost into trouble by calling pursuers down on him when he sought to hide. To hear the philosopher, he saved Fost from a life of cowardice. Fost knew Erimenes merely wanted to enjoy the ensuing bloodshed. When Moriana had stolen the jug from Fost and returned to the City to make her fateful reconnaissance, Erimenes promptly transferred his loyalty to the princess. And when Moriana was captured by Synalon, again Erimenes had switched his perfidious loyalties, seeing in Synalon and Rann the chance to sample their offerings of perversion and sadism.

After the escape from the City he helped Fost and the princess. But he had aided them because they provided him legs and the chance to gain for himself the life-restoring Amulet of Living Flame. Since then, he had befriended Fost consistently, though he was always ready to provoke a good fight whenever he found things dull. Erimenes seemed to be genuinely on Fost's side. But the courier could not forget Synalon's determination to exhaust the possibilities for perversion nor Rann's dark genius with knife and heated iron—or the attraction their activities had for a shade of Erimenes's tastes.

As long as Erimenes acted helpful, there was nothing Fost could do about him but worry. Which he did.

Like metal in a forge, the days warmed and stretched as summer came on. Fost taught urban guerrillas in the day and engaged in sweaty sexual encounters every night. He started losing weight and growing dark circles under his eyes. Sometimes he worried about Jennas, who had helped and loved him, even knowing that she could never truly have him. And he thought of Grutz, his war bear; he had grown fond of the beast. But he told himself worrying was both futile and unnecessary. Jennas could care for herself, as could Grutz.

As time passed, he thought less and less about the hetwoman. But all the time he thought of Moriana.

He was not the only one preoccupied with thoughts of the princess.

"But Uriath!" Tromym's whiskered jowls bobbled mournfully above his goblet. "The princess is laying plans to march against the City with the thrice-cursed Hissers. She might actually win. And then what becomes of us?"

Uriath sat at apparent ease, fingers steepled, allowing his eyes to rove over the screens adorning the walls of his study. They were quite ancient, depicting the Three and Twenty Wise Ones of Agift: Gormanka with his Wind Wheel, Ust rolling the ball of the sun, lithe Jirre and her lyre whose music was irresistibly aphrodisiac, Ennisat blessing the first human settlers of the Realm with the knowledge of double entry bookkeeping, along with the other nineteen. Uriath used the pictures for both relaxation and as an excuse not to meet Tromym's eyes.

Uriath sighed, thinking what a congenital fool Tromym was. And fools quickly outlived their usefulness.

"She might, Tromym. She might also lose. Our most exalted queen has fought three major battles in as many months. And won each, but every time at a cost. What will remain of her strength after the final confrontation with her sister?" He blew out a long breath. "And if Moriana wins, how strong will she be? In the disorganization following the invasion of the Sky City, it will be easy enough to eliminate her." He picked up his own goblet and sipped. "We might become heroes for doing away with her. She's turned traitor to her kind, after all, by enlisting the help of the Hissers."

He belched lightly, rose, went to the window. It lay open to admit a breeze heightened with the sweet growing smells of the plains a thousand feet below. The two moons hung above the lower reaches of the Thails, pink and blue, casting the High Councillor's shadow behind him and across the table where Tromym sat.

"Don't forget the gift that subcurator of the Palace library made us. We have magical forces at our disposal now, too, ones our own mages don't even know of. That could give us the needed edge."

"Do we understand these forces enough to tamper with them?" Tromym gulped his wine so hurriedly he choked.

"I am of the Royal Blood, Tromym, even if removed from the present rulers. Sorcery is in my genes. This book reveals some of the secrets of the earliest Etuul. It was written by the original Moriana's daughter, Kyrun." He turned from the window with a grand sweep of his arm. "Someday, I shall become a sorceror to equal any, Tromym. When my daughter sits on the Beryl Throne, then shall I make my true mark in the history of the City."

Tromym looked away nervously. He reached for the decanter of wine, then saw the trembling of his hand and rang for a servant to refill his goblet for him.

"Who'd have th-thought it," he said, "that enlisting the help of the rabble would profit us so."

Uriath gave him a tight smile.

"That damned barbarian my daughter's taken for a pet has proved useful."

"Y-you think he might be a fit consort for her? Robust barbarian blood might spice up the line a bit, eh?" He tried to wink at Uriath but wound up opening and shutting both eyelids alternately so that he appeared to be trying to blink a message in code. Uriath's cold blue eyes staring back at him chilled to the bone.

"Do you seriously suggest for an instant that my daughter could conceive of forming an . . . an arrangement with a *groundling?*" Uriath's biting tone indicated he'd judge Synalon's famous hornbull a more likely choice.

"No-no, Uriath, not at all. Making a joke, that's all. Ha, ha." He squinted into his wine. "Damn, this thing's empty again."

A steward entered at Uriath's summons.

"Bring the Councillor a larger vessel at once. And see that the sluggard who provided him such an inadequate thimble is soundly whipped." Wordlessly, the servant bowed and withdrew.

"Where were we? Ah, the Northblood messenger boy. He'll have to go, I suppose. He's too likely to have some sentimental notions of loyalty to Moriana—to say nothing of the possibility that he might fancy himself to have some claim on Luranni's affections." The steward returned bringing a soup tureen for Tromym and refilled his master's cup.

Uriath watched and waited for the steward to leave, his fingers working on his fringe beard.

"If only that young fool Chiresko had done as he was told, we wouldn't have the problem of this Longspider or whatever he's called confronting us now. Or of Moriana, either."

"Do I hear my name spoken, O good and loyal Uriath? In a favorable context, I trust."

Wine dyeing his sidewhiskers pink, Tromym raised his face from his bowl to compliment his friend on his uncannily accurate imitation of Moriana's voice. The words congealed in his throat when he saw Uriath's face turn as white as his beard.

Experiencing the same endless falling sensation that had come over him when Synalon's silvered sphere approached him at the victory feast, Uriath gaped at the features of Moriana Etuul, laughing back at him from the surface of his wine.

"Dark Ones," he muttered, fighting down panic. Had she heard?

"Y-your Highness," he stammered. I didn't expect—"

"Naturally not. Synalon doesn't expect it either. She

believes her magics screen my perception from the City. But I have learned much since I saw her last." Moriana smiled, her teeth rippling as Uriath's hand trembled and conveyed the motion to the surface of the wine. "It will be pleasant indeed to show her how much I've learned."

"We all await that time most fervently."

"We will take your protestations of devotion for granted, Uriath. Now listen. There is much to be done. . . ."

CHAPTER ELEVEN

The Sky City crossed first Brev, then Thailot, while the inhabitants of those cities stared up in apprehension. It was wasted emotion. The City passed in gray, stony silence and was gone. It turned northeast at Thailot toward Wirix.

An army of five thousand *Zr'gsz* camped on the shore of Lake Wir. Their numbers were swelled by a thousand foresters from the Great Nevrym Forest, and roughly the same number of adventurers recruited by Darl on a whirlwind tour of the City States. After the fiasco at Chanobit, it was miraculous that any harkened to Moriana's claw and flower banner. After her alliance with the Fallen Ones became known she would have said it was impossible. But the fear of the Hissers was an ancient one. Fear of Synalon burned hot and immediate. And Darl did work miracles. None who heard him failed to be stirred, and those who had heard him before said he spoke as he never had, as no man had. He spoke like an angel come to deliver a new revelation, and his words drew men's hearts like a magnet.

Moriana did not hear his stirring speeches on her behalf. She busied herself preparing for the prodigious battle with the City in the Sky. A thousand details claimed her attention. Food had to be arranged for her growing army. The skystone mines on the slopes of Omizantrim required constant administration. The imprisoned Watchers proved a nagging dilemma. Groundlings had to be drilled in the use of the Hissers' skyraft.

Then there was diplomacy. The Wirixers weren't happy at the presence of the Vridzish. However, they understood which Quincunx city would next feel the might of Synalon's men and magic. With Bilsinx and Kara-Est occupied, and Brev and Thailot having thrown themselves at the City's mercy, the Sky City could take all the time it needed to build its forces for the conquest of Wirix. The mages of the lake city were mighty, but they doubted their ability to master magics such as Synalon commanded. And if Kara-Est's aerial defenses couldn't preserve her from military defeat, Wirix's strictly landborne defenses meant little more than walls of sand. The Hissers might seem unworthy allies but they and Moriana offered the only hope of survival for Wirix.

Nonetheless, the Wirixers were glad when Khirshagk and his retinue turned down their offer to visit their city on its island in the midst of the great Lake Wir.

The City girded itself for war.

It would be a war unique in the City's long history. For the first time since the Human Conquest, the City itself would be the principal object of attack. In the many small squares and parks dotted about the Sky City, the citizens gathered in little knots and gazed at the northeast horizon until masked Monitors drove them on with curses and cudgels. Though they had grown cautious about speaking their thoughts aloud, most wondered whether the victory of either side in the impending conflict might be a loss for them.

Rann drilled his forces hard. From Terror's back he led the bird riders back and forth across the sky in exercises designed to bring them to perfect fighting pitch. Even his own elite Sky Guards grumbled at the severity with which he drove.

He drove himself harder still. He had had to work out the details of the occupation of Kara-Est mostly on his own. Fortunately, Chief Deputy Tonsho had been taken alive. She dreaded physical pain above all things, which meant Rann himself was the perfect threat to keep her in line. Just thinking what exquisite agony the deputy must be going through, knowing herself at his mercy, brought a smile of pleasure to Prince Rann's thin lips. But such smiles were rare and shortlived. Tonsho was a woman of character as well as ability. Sooner or later she would overcome her cowardice and wreak harm on her city's oppressors. But not soon, he judged, and that was all that counted. For the time, a military governor and a strong garrison sufficed to insure her cooperation.

Such cooperation was vital now. Kara-Est had to start functioning again as a seaport and trade center as soon as possible. Moreover, there were matters that would take all of Tonsho's diplomatic skills to straighten out. Since the City was not yet in a position to go to war with such powers as Tolviroth Acerte, the Empire and Jorea, there were reparations to be made for damage to neutral shipping, and the rights of noncombatant citizens had to be guarded. There were problems such as that posed by the ship's captain, half Jorean and half North Keep Dwarf whose vessel had been deposited intact in the Central Plaza of Kara-Est as a prankish parting gesture of the air elemental Synalon had summoned. The outlandish halfbreed demanded recompense far beyond the value of his vessel. In the meantime something had to be done about the ship sitting in the middle of the city. Rann was pleased to have someone, anyone, tend to such matters for him.

Synalon sulked because she felt the Dark Ones should have prevented the Vridzish from allying with Moriana. Several of the queen's advisors pointed out that the Fallen Ones might have fallen into apostasy toward the Elder Gods since the Dark Ones' patronage hadn't benefited them before. Those advisors were not perspicacious enough to realize the fallibility of the Dark Ones wasn't something Synalon wished to be reminded of just now. She had ordered them all exiled through the Skywell to the earth a thousand feet below.

In the meantime Synalon contributed almost nothing to preparing for the conflict with her sister. In a way, Rann found that a blessing, since she was prone to fantastic whims. But it did leave more of a burden on his slender shoulders. Particularly when it became apparent that organized subversion had increased in the Sky City.

Sometimes, however, the queen herself took an interest in the affairs of her City. . . .

Flesh parted to the caress of a blade. The naked young man bucked and screamed.

"There, my love," said Synalon, patting sweat from his forehead with a moist rag. "Tell me what I wish to hear. Who are the traitors?" She smiled tenderly and caressed his cheek. "The pain can stop any time. Then you can love me. Tell me, have you ever seen anyone more beautiful than I?"

The Sky Guard lieutenant looked up at her with the eyes of a snared rabbit. They were lovely eyes, really, she thought, the deep dark blue of a winter sky at sunset. Her captive was a handsome youth, taller than normal among the short, wiry Sky Citizens, leanly muscular under tanned skin, his hair glossy brown with blond highlights from spending time in the wind and sun on an eagle's back. His cheeks and eyes were sunken from the terror of confinement following his arrest, but to Synalon's taste that merely accented the aristocratic quality of the facial bone structure.

Her breath came shallow and fast, as if after lusty exertion. The aroma of her own excitement was hot musk in her nostrils. She wore a pearl gray silk smock that came halfway down her sleek, silvery thighs. It was opened midway down the front. Heavy, well-shaped breasts with skin like fresh cream hung mostly in view, crested by burgundy nipples taut as a drum with arousal. The young man showed little inclination to look at them.

From below came mutterings, scraping noises, an occasional high, sharp cry. The vast aeries of the City, honeycombed below the level of the street and the very Palace itself, buzzed around the clock with avian activity. The almost subliminal sound transmitted itself through the stone flooring of the dungeon and Synalon's bare feet to tickle its way up the inside of her thighs. She enjoyed the melange of sensations, the sounds of martial preparation and breathing with the jagged catch of panic in its rhythm, the erratic orange light of torches set at the bases of arches which formed the groined ceiling of the torture chamber, and the smell of sweat and blood and her own hunger.

The captive sucked in his breath as Synalon trailed fingers along the tight skin of his belly to toy with his limp penis.

"There, there, I wouldn't hurt *that*," she said. He quivered as she bent to kiss it. "Not until the last—*if* you don't tell me what I want to know. . . ."

He looked resolutely toward the far wall. Synalon frowned and slashed. Another scarlet line appeared across his chest. He howled in pain.

She worked on his body with passion and artistry. True to her promise, she left his genitals alone. She would break this young buck, and then she would enjoy him. And she would make him enjoy her, despite his agony.

It was rumored in the open air markets and the bird riders' barracks that Queen Synalon could bring a corpse to orgasm. The rumors were not far wrong.

"Damn Rann," she hissed. The pink tip of her tongue peeked out of the corner of her mouth as she studiously flayed a strip of skin from the bulge of the lieutenant's left bicep. The young man ground his teeth on the leather strap she'd fastened in his mouth to keep him from biting his tongue. His buttocks slapped convulsively against the stone slab to which he was fastened. The bonds were leather, lined with velvet padding; no chains or manacles for Synalon. They might damage the subject by accident. Synalon regarded randomness the bane of artistry.

Reconsidering, she wondered whether she ought to curse her cousin. All bird riders were tough and well-trained, but the Guard was a fanatical elite, handpicked and then honed and polished like the finest North Keep blades. Synalon knew that only philosophical principle would cause a Guard officer to betray the throne. The young fool had decided Moriana would make a better ruler for the City than she. And what a Guard decided on principle, he would adhere to with all the fortitude Rann was so expert at inculating.

No, she shouldn't curse Rann. She loved a challenge.

The secret police who had arrested this young man had evidence which led them to believe he knew the identities of the leaders in the conspiracy against her. That was why she chose to interrogate him herself; also, she needed surcease from the screaming frustration of beseeching the Dark Ones to tell her: *why?*

By layers she stripped away resistance. The apparent carelessness of cuts she had first made was belied by the way she played on them to create a pattern of pain, of blood and tanned skin. And finally, sobbing uncontrollably, the captive was ready to tell everything the silvery, seductive voice coaxed him to reveal.

Then the change began.

At first Synalon blinked, thinking it a trick of the light or of sweat dripping in her eyes. It was no illusion. The skin blackened before her eyes.

She drew back with a startled exclamation. Did the young man have some loathsome disease that had just entered a climactic stage? Her fingers traced glowing patterns in the air in front of her. She chanted a spell of protection even as the writhing of the bound body became a writhing of the very contours of that body, a change of mass and outline more profound than any wrought by Synalon's knife. The chest expanded, grew so muscular that it was grotesque. The legs shortened and thickened, swelling with muscle until the straps around thighs and shins parted with explosive cracks. The arms grew thicker, too, lengthening so that the huge muscles of the upper forearm burst asunder the straps that had restrained the captive's wrists. The forehead bulged, the jaw became a slab, the nose twisted into a sardonic beak. Eyes like portals to an infinite pit regarded her with infinite amusement.

It was a black Dwarf which lay on the torture table. But a Dwarf taller than any man she knew. The sturdy stone table groaned beneath its weight.

"Don't you remember me, little sister?" The Dwarf shook his gigantic head. "And after all the caterwauling you've been pouring into the Void I shouldn't think you'd greet me with those paltry protective canthrips you're muttering beneath your breath." He smiled showing huge perfect teeth. "Or has it occurred to you that your behavior toward my Masters, alternately whining at Them and demanding that They offer explanation for what you take to be Their deeds, has been scarcely calculated to win Their approbation? And have you thought, lovely one, that the mildest of such punishments I might mete out for your impertinence would have you offering your kingdom and your soul for the chance to trade places with that unfortunate who occupied this berth before me?"

She fell to her knees. Fear and ecstasy numbed her brain, and her heart raced out of control.

"O Messenger of the Dark Ones, forgive me! I didn't realize it was you." Her hands caressed the gnarled thighs, working upward to their juncture.

The Dwarf chuckled and swung to a sitting position.

"Much would I enjoy giving way to your inviting blandishments. You definitely have your uses, though you've given little evidence of that lately."

"What do you mean?" She flinched back. "Haven't I served the Dark Ones well? The mightiest seaport of the Realm lies an offering at Their feet. And how do They repay me? By allowing Their chosen folk to make compact with my sister to drag me from my throne, the throne I consecrated to the greatness of the Lords of the Dark!"

The Dwarf threw back his head and laughed like the rolling of a great brass bell.

"How quickly your ire makes you forget the humility appropriate to a lowly servant." Beams of scarlet stabbed from his eyes. Synalon's smock flashed into flame. She shrieked and leaped to her feet, clawing at the fiercely burning garment. Her fingers blistered as the fabric resisted a moment, then gave way. She flung the smock into a heap by the wall. It flared to intolerable actinic brightness and vanished, leaving only scorch marks on the wall. All the time the Dwarf's laughter washed over her like oily surf.

Her belly and breasts showed a fiery pink, as though from long exposure to the sun. Her rump felt as if it had been branded. The rancid smell of burning hair choked her. She beat at her head and the juncture of her thighs until the smouldering stopped.

And then the realization struck her like a mace.

The Messenger read understanding on her face and smiled.

"Yes. You thought you had mastered the fire long ago, and yet in its most primitive form it almost consumed you. Think on that lesson, beautiful child."

He folded maul-like hands across his bulging belly and leaned back onto his elbows.

"Now. What was it you wished to ask of the Masters?"

She took a moment to conquer the fear and rage seething within. She almost blurted out another accusation. She turned it into an exhalation of breath and started again, to the accompaniment of the Messenger's knowing grin.

"I have done my utmost to serve the Dark Ones," she said as evenly as possible. "None could have served Them as faithfully. Now They—rather, now it *appears* that They have chosen to air my mortal enemy against me. I dem—That is, I most humbly beg to know why They have done this thing. And what . . . what redress I must make to regain Their complete trust."

The black head swung ponderously from side to side.

"O, ye of little faith," the Dwarf said. "Is this truly how you venerate the Eldest? By leaping to the conclusion that They have betrayed you?" He clucked. "It is a sore disappointment to our mutual Masters. They harbored great hope for you."

"But . . . but the Vridzish are worshippers of the Dark Ones! Aren't the Masters permitting them to come against me?"

"The Fallen Ones worshipped the beautiful principle of Oneness which is the Endless Night—ten millennia ago. Because of their own carelessness they lost their power among nations. They chose to blame the Dark Ones, who so loved them that They gave Their only begotten child to aid the *Zr'gsz* against the interlopers. So they turned away from Grace."

Synalon stared.

"The Fallen Ones no longer worship the Masters of the Void?"

"Think how easily your faith was swayed. The Hissers lost a world. One can understand their deviance. Almost."

She ran her fingers through the stubble remaining of her hair. It was brittle and broke with tiny sounds like the snappings of a thousand minute twigs.

"You're saying the Dark Ones have no influence over the Vridzish?"

"Not necessarily. But like their opposite numbers, the Dark Ones work almost exclusively through those who chose to do Their bidding. Much depends on the vagaries of mortal servants on both sides, and even of those who take no side."

Her nerve returned and with it a measure of defiance.

"Then let the Dark Ones aid me against my sister. It should be sweet indeed for Them to taste complete vengeance against those who have forsworn Them."

The demon tipped his head back and studied her down his nose before saying, "It isn't that simple. You are on probation. Your behavior has caused our Masters doubts . . . grave doubts." He shook his head. "Only the worthy may receive the blessings of Darkness. You must prove yourself, my dear."

"But . . . but Moriana has the magic of the Hissers to draw upon!"

"And haven't the Dark Ones given you many gifts of power and wisdom already?" He sat up and rested his heavy chin in the palm of one hand. Unlike a human, his palm was as ebon-dark as the rest of his body. "Our Masters chose you because They deemed you the most powerful enchanter alive. Do you believe your sister is stronger?"

"Moriana?" She spat out the name. "That pale-haired bitch-slut? Never!"

"Then you will have no trouble besting her. And in the process, reaffirming the Dark Ones' faith in you."

He turned and lay down full length on the table.

"Perhaps the next time the Masters will allow me to accept the tribute you tender so well," he said, a touch of sadness in his voice. "But until that hour. . . ."

"Wait!"

"Farewell."

The heaving, undulating transformation didn't reverse itself. Instead, white light exploded from the Dwarf, dazzling Synalon and throwing her back against the wall.

When her eyes opened she was on her knees again.

The shape of the captive reclined on the table in a pose of mortal agony.

But not in the flesh. What lay on the dull stone was an obsidian likeness of the traitorous officer, perfect to every feature depicting each incision Synalon's knife had left, even showing bloodspills trailing from the wounds.

As such portentous events are prone to do, it happened quite by accident.

Fost dropped by one of the field headquarters Uriath had set up in a safe house after the courier pointed out that the High Councillor might not want the attention of Monitors drawn to too many comings and goings from his own mansion. Fost enjoyed appearing unannounced. It irritated Uriath, but the High Councillor could scarcely refuse to see someone as important and highly regarded in the movement as Fost.

"Time to clench your teeth and loosen your purse strings again, Uriath," the courier said as he entered the basement of the chandler's shop which was the current secret command post. "We've a contact who has blackmail goods on old Anacil's chief assistant chamberlain. Seems he's been diverting funds from Synalon's warchest."

"Who's that?" a voice asked sharply, apparently from nowhere. Uriath looked up from what appeared to be a large pan of water resting on the table in front of him. The look of annoyance on his face quickly changed to surprise.

Fost's heart bounced into his throat. Frowning, unwilling to believe his ears, he moved forward to stare into the pan.

He found himself face to face with Moriana.

"Uriath, what . . . Great Ultimate!" The image wavered as the princess fought to control herself. "Whoever you are," she said in a quavering voice, "you bear too close a resemblance to someone I once knew."

Fost grinned.

"I don't know whether you'd call it resemblance so much as identity," he said.

"Ah, Princess Moriana, we meet again," said a voice from Fost's hip. "I've never seen you lovelier. Treachery and murder agree with you, it appears."

"Erimenes?" She gasped. "Then it's—oh, Gods, Fost!"

"Guilty." The word cracked across and the flippancy left his face. He opened his mouth only to shut it again. "Are you well?" he finally asked, and instantly castigated himself. He'd had months to form a proper greeting and had done no better than a lovesick adolescent.

The princess visibly strained to hold back her tears.

"I didn't think I'd ever be grateful that I didn't strike true," she stammered, "but now, oh, Fost, I'm so glad you're alive!"

"Don't chide yourself about your aim, Moriana. There's something I need to tell you. You don't have . . ."

His voice stopped. His lips moved but no sound emerged.

"Fost? There's something wrong with the enchantment. I can't hear you."

"You don't have anything to worry about, my dear," he heard his own voice say. "I'm working with the Underground to pave the way for your glorious return."

She frowned at his peculiar choice of words.

"I'm pleased to hear it. I'm laying plans with Uriath now so that we may strike coordinated blows to bring Synalon down." She seemed about to say more, then glanced out of Fost's field of vision. "I . . . I have to go now."

The breaking of the connection hid a choked sob.

"Erimenes," hissed Fost, picking his way from shadow to shadow through the streets. "Why in Ust's name did you take over my voice? And how did you do it? This far from Athalau?"

"Necessity," the philosopher said haughtily, "is an excellent aid to my already significant ability. And it was urgently necessary that I prevent you from blurting that Moriana had the Destiny Stone instead of the Amulet of Living Flame."

"But why? By the Emperor's rouged ass, she has to know!"

"Do you really want Uriath to know?" The courier fell abruptly silent. "That's better. Someone might hear you—hsst!"

A footfall came to Fost's sensitive ears. He melted back into a doorway and concentrated on imitating shadow. A moment later a pair of Monitors swung around the corner and came right at him.

"And then I said to her, 'If you'll just be reasonable, it might not be necessary to take you in, my sweet.'"

His companion laughed loudly, an ugly, distorted sound through his mask.

"So wha'd she say? Huh?"

They passed by. The first Monitor elbowed his taller companion in the ribs. Fost's fingers tightened on his swordhilt.

"What do you think, Nalgo? 'Oh, you Monitors have always been my ideal, so strong and brave! I'll do simply anything for the service of my Cit—'"

They rounded the next corner, going in the opposite direction from the candle shop Fost had just left by a back door. He let himself breathe again and set off down the street.

"I don't trust Uriath farther than I can throw him," Erimenes said as if nothing had happened.

"A vaporous entity would be hard pressed to throw a man that portly."

"My point exactly. I think he suspects Moriana ventured to Athalau in search of a talisman of some sort. Whether or not he knows she was after the Amulet is irrelevant. If he thinks she got something powerful, he might just decide to lay hands on it himself."

Fost chewed his lips, rolling the problem around in his mind.

"I wouldn't put it past him," he conceded.

"And if he finds she's got the Destiny Stone—and if he has any idea of its properties—he may just decide to have nothing to do with her. At all."

"You mean the thing's that potent?"

"Potent beyond imagining." *Was* it imagining or did Fost sense trepidation in the genie's voice? "It's vastly stronger than the Amulet ever was. But it was always valued less because its powers were uncontrollable. In my time some theorized it possessed a sentience of its own."

For once Fost wasn't yawning at one of Erimenes's lectures.

"But we've got to tell her."

"Agreed," said the spirit. "But can you suggest how we might go about it without sharing the information with the great and noble Uriath?"

"I'll think of a way."

"You hope."

"Ziore?"

Yes, child.

"I . . . I feel strange."

She felt rather than heard gentle laughter.

You kill the only man you've ever loved, only to behold him healthy a half year later. Did you not feel strange, that would be the strangest thing of all.

"Did I do right, Ziore?"

"Do you think what you did was right?" came the genie's soft voice, both to ears and mind.

"I did then. But now, I don't know." She sat up in bed. A moon balanced on the edge of the Thails, laying a golden trail across Lake Wir. In the distance a night-bird sang to it. "But somehow the decision to ally myself with the Fallen Ones came easier because . . . because I killed him."

"Because you felt you'd already soiled yourself."

"Yes." Moriana hooked a thumb around the silver chain she wore always around her neck and fished the Amulet into the moonlight. As usual its surface balanced white against black, revealing nothing. "Now I hate myself more. Fost's being alive almost makes things harder."

"I know." The words came soft, caressing, soothing.

Moriana kneaded her face with one hand. "I do love him," she said softly. "How can I find myself resenting that he's alive?"

"You're human."

"It's easy for you to be so glib, you who've never known human passion!" She stopped, horrified at what she'd said. "Gods, Ziore, I'm sorry. I didn't mean . . ."

"You did," Ziore said with a trace of sternness. "If nothing else, I've learned too much to heed words spoken in anger." A moment's silence, then, "But speaking of anger, I confess I was angry when I heard you address Fost's unseen companion as Erimenes. If you hadn't had things of more import to say, I would have told that vile charlatan a thing or two!"

Moriana grinned wryly at Ziore's vehemence, so unusual to the placid spirit. In an oblique way the nun was chastising her. It was the fault of Erimenes's philosophy that Ziore *hadn't* known human passion.

"I'm glad Darl's away," said Moriana. "I . . . I couldn't face telling him yet."

"I understand."

"Thank you." The princess let the Amulet fall and lay back down. The pillow was cool and sweet-smelling beneath her head. "To think I'll see him again!" she whispered. "Oh, Ziore, I'm not a murderer!"

But a voice in the back of her skull asked: *am I a traitor?*

CHAPTER TWELVE

In increasing desperation, Fost attempted to tell Moriana that the talisman she carried was not the Amulet of Living Flame but the mercurial Destiny Stone. The opportunity eluded him. As the City moved toward Wirix and the waiting army, the press of preparation drove each of them ever faster. Not infrequently Fost was on hand when Uriath and Moriana were in communication. They exchanged a few hurried words, looks which Fost *hoped* meant certain things but couldn't be sure.

But Uriath was always there, somedays bland, sometimes avuncular, always giving the impression of something hooded coiled inside him. Even with Erimenes there to hold his tongue for him, Fost found himself unwilling to speak of the Amulet and the Stone with Uriath near.

As the City crossed the Thail Mountains and began to descend from the height to which it had climbed to clear the peaks, Moriana's army broke camp and moved southwest from Lake Wir to meet it. The Wirixers didn't want the battle fought over their heads and were unwilling to take active part in the action. They had given Moriana's forces the right to stay for a time and had provided her with supplies. More than that they wouldn't do. It mattered little. The battle for the City would be fought in the City's own element: sky.

It was the last day before the two sisters met, doomsday for unspecified numbers on both sides. Fost had gone without sleep for three days trying to accomplish a million things at once, laying out tactics for the joint invasion and insurrection, trying to keep the morale of his untried revolutionaries from disintegrating totally at the prospect of battle, dodging the last-minute push by the Monitors that wiped out a quarter of the Underground's cells overnight. He stumbled like a zombie when he entered Uriath's current catacomb to confer with the resistance chief.

A silent youth guided him down a slippery flight of stairs. Rank and humid smells clogged his nostrils. Why did Uriath pick a mushroom farm for his new command post?

A door streaked with a rainbow array of fungus was pushed open. Fost caught a glimpse of Uriath slamming a book closed and slipping it into a compartment on his desk. The courier was too exhausted to care what the volume was or why the High Councillor acted so furtively.

He nodded to Uriath, spotted a blond wood stool, navigated to it as the door shut behind him with a groan like an arthritic giant. He gave the stool a quick once-over before sitting. The wood was warped and water spotted but showed no signs of mold. He sat and leaned back against the wall with a sigh.

"I think I've got the damage patched up," he said without preamble. "Rann, or whoever is handling internal security for Synalon, actually struck too soon. We didn't give out the final assignments until this afternoon, which means no one they netted knows our exact plans or dispositions. As a bonus, it's easier to change assignments and then distribute them instead of changing them abruptly after they've been issued and confusing hell out of everybody."

"Your idea," said Uriath, more curtly than usual. Crediting the courier irked him.

"All our reports indicate Synalon's going to be locked up tight in the Palace, working her magics from there. So I've cut the number of people on other squads, the ones attacking the aeries and Monitor stations, to get the full complement for our push at the Palace. What we really need . . ." ·

A chime shimmered in the air of the room. Hairs rose on the back of Fost's neck though the sound was now familiar to him. He still wasn't used to sudden tones issuing from tubs of water.

Energized again, he stood and went to peer into the tin vessel. Uriath swiveled in his chair, gave Fost an annoyed look, and bowed his head to the water.

The surface turned murky. The cloudiness began to swirl without stirring the liquid. The murk coalesced into Moriana's tired but radiantly beautiful visage.

"Fost," she said smiling, "you're upside down. Good evening, Uriath. I trust everything proceeds according to plan."

"We have experienced some difficulties, Princess," said Uriath with a sigh, "but we are persevering, even in the face of such great adversity."

Fost saw that Moriana tried hard not to laugh at his sententious manner.

"It pleases me to hear that, good Uriath. Now, as for our plans tomorrow, we must coordinate . . ."

A door opposite the one through which Fost had entered swung inward on oiled hinges. Councillor Tromym entered unsteadily. His nose glowed the color of Uriath's florid face.

"Uriath, I have to talk with you," he said with the meticulousness of the truly inebriated, seeming to pick each word out precisely and exactingly with a pair of tweezers. "It is about this . . . oh. Ah, well, yes. Hello."

Fost grimaced. Tromym showed every sign of collapsing completely under the strain. In the courier's opinion the best thing the whiskered little man could do was climb into a rumpot and stay put until the shouting was over.

Uriath was visibly unhappy.

"Tromym," he said sharply. He heaved his substantial bulk from the chair. "If you'll excuse me—I'm sorry, Your Highness. I'll be but a moment."

Moriana nodded graciously as the pair left her line of sight. Fost looked at her wondering if she was eager to have him gone so they could speak privately. He held his own passions in check. He had more important things to tell her.

"Listen, I've got to tell you something," he began.

"No, I have something I must tell you," she said. "Oh, Fost, I can't express how it makes me feel to see you. When I stabbed you, I knew I was doing the right thing, though part of me died with you. Or when I thought you died."

In his befuddled state it took him until now to realize that what he'd taken for a necklace about her neck was the all too familiar pendant, a big-faceted stone in an elaborate silver setting. Half of the stone's surface shone white, half radiated blackness. He had only seen the gem once, briefly, but was unlikely to forget it.

"But . . ."

She raised a hand, cutting off his words.

"No, you need say nothing. Even though you didn't die, I can never atone for what I did, not in my own heart." A tear welled from one eye and rolled down her cheek. "I . . . I'll try to make it up to you, Fost. I promise!"

But the courier wasn't listening. He stared in horror as a wave of black slowly washed over the Destiny Stone entirely blotting out the white.

"So," a voice said from the outer doorway.

Slowly, Fost turned though he knew what he'd see. He would have felt better at meeting Istu himself awakened from a ten-millennium-long nap. Luranni stood there, her gaily colored smock in sharp contrast to the dull gray of her expression. She looked as if she'd just been struck in the belly.

"Fost? Fost, what's wrong?"

He didn't answer Moriana. Luranni's oval face was stricken. She knew. As Fost opened his mouth hoping some inspiration would make the proper words come forth, she turned and ran.

He caught her in the antechamber of Uriath's office, at the foot of the slimy stairs. Rows of mushrooms stood at attention in boxes, rank on rank until they were lost in the gloom. An eerie pallid glow rose from some of them to mingle with the green shine of the tube filled with miniscule luminous beings that lit the room. Other than sunlight and moonlight, the light vessels provided the only form of illumination by which it was safe to conspire in the City.

He seized her wrist as she tried to race up the stairs. Her arm seemed ridiculously skinny against his scarred fist and burly forearm. He thought with a pang how such restraint wouldn't be possible with a woman like Moriana.

"Wait," he said. "I can explain."

Her eyes called him a liar. He felt shame at uttering the faithless lover's age-old plaint.

"You still want her," she accused. Her voice, normally so musical, rang out in the cellar as husky, broken.

"I do." He released her slender wrist and moved closer to her rigid body. "I'm sorry, Luranni. We . . ."

"Don't say anything. I thought you believed in our cause—in me."

He took a deep breath and let out a sigh.

"I *care* for you, Luranni. But I came to the City to help Moriana. I chose to help the princess because of . . . the way I feel about her, and because I fear what Synalon intends."

"But I thought you believed in our revolution! Don't you want to bring popular government to the City?"

He hesitated, unsure how to answer.

"I guess my upbringing warped me. When I look at any government, no matter how popular or benevolent, all I see is the field of spearpoints holding it up."

"*So you did it all for the love of her!*" she cried. She was gone before he could deny it.

But then he could never have denied so plain a truth.

The tattoo of her steps faded up the stairs, ended with the bang of a door. He turned back and raced for the office.

"Moriana, you've got to listen to me! The pendant . . ."

"Yes? What about a pendant?" Uriath's eyes glittered.

Fost looked into the tub. Water. He turned and walked out without another word.

Evening settled on the camp of Moriana's army. The clink of the armorer's hammer drifted to the ridge of the humans' camp, along with the murmur of talk around the cooking fires, occasional snatches of song. From the dark pavilions of the *Zr'gsz* nearby came only silence, as ominous and complete as that in which their oblong skyrafts flew. Rarely, she heard a stacatto burst of syllables, and once came a chanting in a voice she recognized as Khirshagk's.

"Come," she said, taking Darl's hand. She led him down the far side of the rise, toward the stream above where it curved around the bluff to run beside the twin encampments. The cool, moist air danced with the smell of growing things, and the songs of crickets and frogs and tree lizards hummed and reverberated. Once below the lip of the hill, it was impossible to tell or even believe that within half a hundred paces beings of two races prepared for war.

She led him to a fallen log by the river, shaded and covered with moss. They sat together, watching the sun light the nearby Thails with evening colors. Darl looked robust and heroic in tight whipcord breeches and a silken tunic of the palest blue. This evening Moriana dressed feminine and soft in a long beige gown that made her eyes glow like emeralds.

She hadn't worn her swordbelt; at her waist rode a sheathed poignard. No satchel bounced at her hip. Many things had to be resolved, and she would speak of them herself without having Ziore to soothe her.

"There's something I must tell you." Her thoughts echoed Fost's earlier in the evening: *I care so much for this man. Why can't I think of anything that's not inane?*

"I know," he said, a tiny smile wrinkling his lips.

She looked at him in surprise.

"You do?"

"Yes. I've know for some time." He laughed at her stricken look, took her chin in his hand and kissed her. "A blackness lay upon your soul, Moriana. When I came back from the City States, it had vanished. I don't know how it happened but one thing alone could have lifted that burden from you."

"He lives." Her whisper tried to lose itself amid the sighing of the stream.

"I told you before," he said, his arm encircling her, "he must be a man indeed to leave so deep a mark upon you." He smiled lopsidedly. "I wish that I could meet him."

"Oh, but you can! Tomorrow, if . . ." She couldn't bring herself to say *if either of you live.*

He shook his head.

"I have but one tomorrow remaining to me."

"What do you mean?"

He pointed to the evening star twinkling on the saw-toothed edge of the wall of the mountains to the west.

"I shall not see the Crown of Jirre again, Bright Princess. I know this."

"How can you know?" She wanted to jar him from this prophecy, but a thought jarred her instead. "You have the Sight."

"It may be so. I've felt at times I have a Gift. How else could I stir men as I do with simple words any can utter?" He hugged her tight, kissed her forehead. "But don't grieve for me, Bright Princess. The end comes for us all. And this I know—tomorrow I shall have that which I desire most. No man can ask for more than that. And many receive much less in their lives—and deaths."

"You're rationalizing," she said weakly. "You're trying to spare my feelings." She tried to convince herself that Darl's belief he wouldn't live out the next day was only morbid imagination. Something within her knew better.

"Will you love me one last time?" she asked, her voice barely audible above the rippling of the stream.

"Princess, I'll love you forever," he said.

Tenderly he touched her breasts, dipped his head, nuzzled her cheek, touched his lips to hers. Her mouth opened to his. In the last light of day they stripped and made love beside the river, with the bittersweet languor of those who know there will be no other nights for them.

A trumpet skirled from the highest tower of the Palace of Winds as the dawn spilled over the rim of the Central Massif and fell upon the swarm of shapes rising from the hills ahead. A thunderclap broke the City's stillness as four thousand eagles seized the air with eager wings. For a moment, they hovered like a feathered cloud above the buttressed towers of the City in the Sky. One eagle broke to rise above the rest, a huge bird as black as the bedchamber of Istu but for the scarlet crest blazing on its head. The tiny figure on its back waved a lance. Eight thousand throats, men's and birds' together, answered him with a fearsome cry. Then the aerial legions of the City in the Sky formed and flew to meet the attack of Moriana and the Fallen Ones.

Moriana's heart quailed as she saw the arrowhead flights streaking toward her. She had known all along that her quest must end with this. She faced the eagles of the City in the element they had ruled for eighty centuries. More than anyone else she knew how near that course skirted outright suicide.

But the skyrafts had plied the air for uncounted generations before the first of the giant war eagles were bred by Kyrun Etuul for the armies of Riomar shai-Gallri, first human queen of the City. More than a thousand of the rafts formed Moriana's aerial armada, from small swift two-man flyers to great stone barges mounting powerful war engines and carrying scores of men. Her own raft fell midway. It was thirty feet long and fifteen wide, ringed with a stone bulwark that came waist-high on the princess.

A wooden box atop the bulwark gave added protection. With her rode forty men in the green and brown of the Nevrym foresters. The only Hisser aboard was the pilot, a stunted male in a loincloth who hunkered at the stern, moving his clawed hands over the surface of an obsidian ball. The globe somehow steered the craft. Moriana had felt magic tingling beneath her palms when she had handled one experimentally, but she couldn't attune herself to it.

It was Vridzish magic, like the skyrafts themselves.

Most of the craft were less well protected than hers. Most made do with movable screens of wicker or wood, and some augmented the stone ramparts with sandbags. It wasn't solely to protect the princess that her craft carried so much cover. Along with four other craft similarly equipped and crewed, hers would be running the gauntlet of the defenders in advance of the main force and land in the City to link up with the Underground's rebels. The other rafts would engage the bird riders while Moriana fought her way into the Palace of Winds and the meeting with her twin.

The princess looked to her right. Darl stood resplendent in plate armor, the golden slanting sun turning him into a demigod. He had one booted foot on the bulwark of his raft and his head was thrown back, grinning into the wind with his long brown hair streaming out behind. He saw Moriana, brought hilt to lips and kissed it. She mocked a smile and waved.

To her left rode Khirshagk. Like Darl's, his raft was mostly open and like the Count-Duke's his vessel had a mixed crew. There seemed two classes of *Zr'gsz*: tall, well-built males who were possibly nobles and resembled their Instrumentality. The other type of lizard men was more numerous and seemed of the same caste as the pilots. They were smaller and armored rarely, if at all. They carried shortbows, slings, javelins; another was assigned to every noble, Darl included, and bore only a large shield.

Here and there on the other rafts Moriana glimpsed the paleness of human skin. There were many more of the green Hissers. She wondered where they had come from, as she had many times since the first columns marched to Omizantrim from the keep at Thendrun in strength greater than she would have believed the *Zr'gsz* could muster. This was no time to question their presence; the eagles were on wing and she could only be thankful for the numbers of her allies.

A wedge of birds flew straight for the three long rafts in the lead. Moriana appreciated having the three paramount commanders each on a different skyraft—she had insisted on it—but at the moment she wished fervently she had Darl at her side.

Or Fost.

Spears, stones and arrows arced to meet the attacking formation. From the way the bird riders flew, Moriana knew these weren't Sky Guards. She nocked an arrow but kept her attention high. Far overhead an echelon lined out with mathematical precision. The Guard, no doubt led by Rann himself, waited for the

common bird riders to draw the attention of the enemy
so they could swoop and kill.

"Above!" she called. "The Sky Guard. Rann!"

Darl turned, then shouted back, "I see them! Thank
you, Bright Princess!"

She had to shout again to attract Khirshagk's attention. The king-priest of the Hissers solemnly bowed but
didn't look above. Moriana considered shouting again
to be sure he understood, then decided to save her
breath.

He would discover soon enough what he faced.

The nearest attackers were three hundred yards away
and closing fast. Without thinking, Moriana drew and
loosed. The lead bird rider somersaulted over his
mount's tail feathers and fell, flailing his arms in a futile
attempt at flight. Moriana heard a buzz of admiration
from the Nevrymin. A half-dozen of them had shot and
none of their shafts had found a mark. They considered
themselves fine shots, and so they were—by groundling
standards. The princess was a full-fledged Sky Guards-
women and could put fifteen shafts into a palm-sized
mark at two hundred yards in a minute's time.

The foresters loosed another volley. This time one
eagle fluttered groundward and another shrieked mourn-
ing for its fallen rider. Only a few of the Nevrym men
could shoot through the firing slits at a time. The others
hunkered on the deck and grumbled. But they weren't
meant to shoot it out with the bird-borne marksmen.
They must be preserved as shock troops for the landing.

"Well shot," she called to her men. They turned rue-
ful smiles in her direction. She obviously outshot them.
They applied themselves to the attack, concentrating in
an attempt to better her towering skill with a bow.

Shooting methodically, Moriana emptied four more
saddles with five shots. Then the eagles were rushing
past in a whirlwind of sound. A bluff blackbearded
forester to her right gurgled and sank with an arrow

through his neck. Arrows fell like sleet against the plank protection of her raft.

She darted a glance at Darl's raft. He still stood exposed, his foot on the low wall.

"You fool!" she cried out.

"But a magnificent fool," said Ziore from her secure spot at Moriana's hip.

The powerful eagle Terror uttered a brief cry to its master.

"I see her, old friend," Rann said, leaning forward to pat the sleek black neck. It took eagle-keen eyes to make out the princess's slim form through the slits of the covered raft. Rann's tawny eyes were second only to those of the great bird he rode. He smiled, raised a gloved left hand. Then he put Terror into a steep dive.

Moriana glanced up, saw the Guards peeling from their echelon formation and streaking down. She widened her stance, nocked a new arrow, waited.

"Damn the bitch!" cursed Rann. "She sees me." But to his surprise, the prince found himself laughing in sheer delight. He had personally trained his cousin. He would hate to have her disappoint him. He nocked his own shaft, grinning a taut grin devoid of all humor. This would decide so very much. Him against her, arrow against arrow, teacher against prize pupil.

"Goodbye, Moriana," he said softly. "If only I could consummate my love for you at greater length."

He drew.

Darl's raft bucked upward. Before either cousin could loose an arrow, his craft had swung protectively over the princess's. Rann shrieked a curse and shot at Darl. He'd at least take care of Moriana's damned lover.

He didn't.

Darl watched the arrow, calmly awaiting death. With contemptuous ease, the *Zr'gsz* at the Count-Duke's side thrust up his shield. The arrow thunked into it. Darl stared at the malformed head gleaming an inch from his breastplate.

"My thanks," he said dryly.

The lizard man grinned.

Moriana tracked Rann the instant Terror plummeted past Darl's raft.

"Die, you devil!" she screamed, and shot.

The Destiny Stone went black. The glue binding one of the three feathered vanes to her shaft gave way. The arrow slewed wide. Moriana wept with frustration as Rann and Terror were lost to sight beneath her sky-stone raft.

More bird riders rocketed in. Archers Zr'gsz and human got the feel of aerial shooting and took a grim toll of the attackers. But the Sky City riders took a toll of their own. Men and lizard men fell writhing on the decks. Red blood mingled with green.

A clump of riders bore down on Khirshagk's raft. He stood as defiant as Darl. The Heart of the People smoked in his right claw. Only one rider reached the raft and that one died as he flew overhead. But he cast down the heavy clay vessel he carried.

It shattered on the prow of the Instrumentality's raft. The Zr'gsz leader turned at the acrid odor of turpentine. Four hundred yards away, three bird riders dropped fire lances, heard the chittering of salamanders, released them.

Moriana gasped as three lines of blinding fire reached for Khirshagk. He revolted her, ally or not, but it was hard to see him die in this diabolical manner.

Khirshagk uttered a laugh that resounded above the clamor of battle. He held the Heart high. Smoke boiled into the sky. The salamanders streaked straight into the core of the huge black diamond and were absorbed without sound.

Deadly quiet filled the sky. Watching from her throne room in the Palace, Synalon choked out an obscenity and raised her arms in invocation. The sleeves of her robe flapped like wings in the wind streaming through the open windows.

"It's time!" Moriana cried to her steersman. He shook his head in *Zr'gsz* affirmation and the raft plunged ahead. She heard a wolf cry from the Nevrymin foresters in the skystone rafts behind as they sped up to keep pace.

"Moriana and victory!" she heard Darl cry.

She raised her bow in salute. There were no words adequate.

Rann's death plunge had carried him far below Moriana's raft. Levelling out at the bottom of his attack, he found himself in the midst of an angry swarm of two-man rafts. Rann's bowstring snapped in a furious exchange of arrows. Terror finished that duel by clutching the stern of an eight-foot raft with his mighty talons and bodily flipping the craft, sending its occupants tumbling to their deaths.

Angrily Rann flung the useless bow away. Not even he could restring a bird rider's bow in flight. He satisfied himself that the rafts were being dealt with successfully—even at the high cost of half his elite flight—and put Terror into a climb, searching the sky above for Moriana's raft.

He found her. A mile in advance of the others he saw the five wooden-clad skyrafts, almost to the ramparts of the City itself. There was little point in pursuing now. Rann allowed himself a sardonic smile. Synalon would soon be learning the extent of the powers she'd accepted from the Dark Ones.

He drew his sword and led the flight steeply toward the armada floating overhead.

Eyes as wild as an animal's, Fost glared up and down the street. He had hacked down three Monitors in a storm of blood without being aware that he did so. Erimenes still cheered hysterically.

He tested the heft of the round shield he carried. This was his first real, full-dress battle. He wasn't fool enough to go into it with no more protection than his broadsword and chainmail shirt.

"Back!" cried Erimenes. Fost jumped into a doorway. An arrow splintered the doorpost near his head. A girl with close-cropped red hair popped out of the next doorway and let fly her arrow. The sniper did a high dive from a minaret across the cobblestone street. His scream ended in an ugly thump.

"Excellent shot!" applauded Erimenes from his jug. Fost's lips curled back from his teeth in a wordless snarl. The genie's bloodlust sickened him, but Erimenes still seemed inclined to help—and help he had. He'd just saved Fost's life.

"Where's Luranni?" came the inquiry from the street.

Fost cautiously peered from his niche. Two young men trotted toward him surveying the heights all around. He recognized Prudyn and Chasko, two of the ablest of the lower caste recruits. Short and stocky Chasko carried a javelin and bird rider's target shield. Prudyn loomed over him, holding a bow with professional ease, brown eyes keen beneath the rim of a stolen helmet.

"I don't know," Fost replied as the two ducked into the niche with him.

"We thought she'd be with you," said Chasko. Fost shrugged and turned away. He'd futilely sought her at her apartment the night before and wound up sleeping with his assault squad in a warehouse. By the time the unit had to move, the High Councillor's daughter hadn't shown up.

A sea-gray eagle flecked with brown swept over the rooftops. Prudyn whipped up his shortbow and shot. The rider tumbled off and disappeared behind the buildings. Prudyn whooped delight. Chasko and Fost pounded him on the back.

They calmed enough to take stock. The tumult of street fighting raged all around. Smoke sprouted from a dozen fires. To his right, the soaring architecture of the Palace lorded it over lesser buildings. Two hundred yards away, Fost judged. He had an appointment on the steps of that edifice. He prayed fervently to gods he still didn't fully believe in that the other party would arrive unharmed.

The door opened behind them.

They jumped into the street snapping weapons around. A pudgy feminine-looking hand reached out holding a green glass bottle. Prudyn hesitated, accepted it and lifted it to his lips and drank.

"Thank you kindly," he said. The arm withdrew and the door closed once more.

The three passed around the wine bottle until it was drained. Fost called for the rest of his squad and they moved toward the Palace.

A melee raged among the rafts of the People. Sky City men had birds shot from under them and if luck favored, they managed to drop to the decks of the enemy rafts and continued the fight at close quarters. Others, out of arrows or simply eager to come to grips with the ancient enemies of their kind, landed deliberately to fight side by side with their birds. Riderless eagles plucked *Zr'gsz* and Nevrymin from the skystone slabs and cast them down.

Both sides fought with fanatical intensity. More than a few of the bird riders passed under rafts after firing their arrows, only to have the hissing Vridzish fling themselves onto them so both fell, struggling viciously until the hard earth mingled their substance and rendered all issues moot.

Darl's great blade reaped lives like grain. A war eagle knocked his shield-bearer to the deck and disembowelled him with his talons. Darl decapitated the bird with a single cut and spun to split its rider's skull to the teeth as the man closed with a spear.

The deck teemed with battling men and near-men. A green-clad giant loomed over a knot of wiry little bird riders, flailing at them with his bow. So great was his strength that he batted three of the black and purple clad troopers over the edge before the others brought him down.

Darl leaped upon the giant's slayers. They turned as quick as serpents, but their speed and skill meant nothing against the Count-Duke. They died.

Behind him Darl heard a boom of wings, a scrape of talon on stone.

"Very well done, my good Sieur r'Harmis," came a cultured voice. "We seem to find ourselves alone. Shall we?"

Darl turned and slowly smiled at Prince Rann Etuul.

In eerie suspended silence, Moriana's raft soared over the rimwall of the City in the Sky. She fancied she floated on the wings of dream until a ballista thrummed and a barbed iron head punched through the wooden shielding to kill a Nevrymin. She came out of her reverie and shot an artillerist as he bent to the windlass of his engine.

Eagles screamed and circled. Arrows hammered the walls and roof. Moriana cast aside an emptied quiver and stooped to pick up another as a sweating forester drew his dagger across the throat of the howling man with the ballista-bolt in his guts. She said nothing. She understood battlefield mercy all too well.

Quiet and outwardly untroubled by the carnage around him, the *Zr'gsz* steersman guided the raft between the airy spaces of the City, making for the Circle of the Skywell in the center of town. Moriana peeked through the slit to check on the craft following hers.

She saw only three. Something had happened to the other; its pilot slain perhaps or it might have been knocked down by the catapults. As she watched, the next raft behind hers careened abruptly to the right. She caught a glimpse of its steersman slumping from behind his globe, arrows sprouting from his back.

The raft brushed a thin tower and brought it crashing into the street. The impact caused the raft to straighten.

"Please, survive," the princess said quietly. She had little hope they would.

It ran headlong into the forward wall of the Lyceum and disintegrated, flinging Nevrymin about like dolls. And then there were only two rafts remaining.

She felt the deck tip beneath her. Her heart missed a beat but a quick glance aft showed her steersman intact and in control. She looked out again.

The Circle wheeled lazily below. The Skywell opened onto a pastoral landscape a thousand feet below. The pilot banked to follow the Skullway to the very portals of the Palace. To the left she saw armed men and women racing for the Palace. Ahead a squad of Monitors fled toward the same destination, heedless that their feet were defiling the skulls of the City's past rulers.

Some sense made her turn and look back toward the battle she'd left behind. With terrible certainty she knew what she'd see.

A thousand yards ahead of the City's prow two figures fought back and forth across the deck of a raft crewed by corpses. Moriana knew the splendid black bird who stood to one side watching the humans; she knew the tall figure in shining armor who swung his broadsword with skill apparent even across the distance; and all too well she knew the smaller black and purple figure darting in and out while his scimitar parlayed with the huge straight blade.

As the princess watched, Rann tripped and fell back toward the bulwark of the raft. Darl rushed. Rann ducked under the blow and swung with his scimitar. Darl's plate was sturdy but Rann's strength belied his size. The curved blade sank into Darl's side.

The Count-Duke spun, snapping the sword from Rann's grip. Rann danced away. Darl's heels came against the bulwark. He raised his broadsword to salute his foe. Then he turned, looked at Moriana and saluted again.

And fell.

"He knew," came Ziore's anguished words. Moriana returned his salute with her own broadsword. Her eyes stung but she wouldn't cry. Tears would cloud her vision.

And then they were down.

CHAPTER THIRTEEN

Lungs burning, Fost pounded across the pavement toward the Palace. Fifty rebels raced at his side, while a score hung back among the buildings on the perimeter of the grounds to cover the attack with bow and arrow. As he ran Fost kept staring at the spectacle before him. One after another, three large slabs of gray stone flew over the Skywell and turned up the Skullway to approach the Palace.

The leading raft bumped to a halt. The walls fell away as foresters hacked at lashings with sword and axe. Green and brown clad men tumbled out—and one in achingly familiar russet and orange. Even in helmet and hauberk, Fost knew Moriana.

Shouting incoherently, he angled to meet her as she led the foresters up the Skullway. Her last trip along that avenue had been as a captive, jeered by multitudes as a traitoress, regicide, matricide. Now spectators had even better reason to name her traitor—but the only watchers on hand were the rebels swarming across the paved Palace grounds, and a platoon of Palace Guardsmen on the steps.

"Moriana!" shouted Fost. She cried his name in return and they flung themselves violently into each other's arms. Rebels and Nevrymin clasped forearms and pounded backs, instant comrades. The exuberance of the rebels was partly due to the humanness of their new allies. They'd expected green scaly skins.

Fost and Moriana wasted precious seconds in a kiss. They reluctantly broke apart, laughing, weeping, dabbing at the blood streaming from their nostrils. The Destiny Stone swung free outside Moriana's armor. It shone benevolent white.

Fost pointed at it.

"Moriana, that's not . . ."

"Eureka!" screeched Erimenes. "May this day be blessed forever! I've found a woman of my own kind!"

"Don't 'my kind' me, you perverted mountebank!" Ziore screamed back.

Dead silence. Moriana goggled at the satchel by her side. The foresters gaped, too, having come to recognized the princess's familiar as sweet and shy.

The sweet, shy presence proceeded to deride Erimenes with the profane bravura of an Estil fishwife.

When Ziore paused to think up even more insults, Moriana spun quickly to face the Palace Guards, who stood clumped at the portal to the Palace wondering what was going on.

"Surrender at once!" she ordered. "I, Moriana Etuul, your rightful queen, command it!"

For long seconds nothing happened. Then a Guard pivoted on his heel and split the chest of the man next to him with a stroke of his halbred. The Guardsmen quickly paired off and slew one another. Fost grinned. A little subversion was a wonderful thing.

Moriana raced for the portal. Fost followed, shouting for her to listen, that she didn't have the Amulet, that she carried another talisman instead, that her life depended on getting rid of the Destiny Stone. But Monitors poured into the far side of the Circle and men shouted and moaned and butchered each other on the steps of the Palace, and the mysterious shade Moriana carried still berated Erimenes the Ethical at the top of her nonexistent lungs.

A fleet-footed rebel darted past Moriana as she mounted the steps and heartily kicked open the centermost pair of doors. A flight of arrows buzzed out like angry hornets. Most of them struck the impetuous youth, lifted him from his feet and tossed him lifeless down the narrow steps.

The foresters' bows sang in reply. Screams echoed in the Palace's vestibule. Moriana plunged in, sword in hand. Fost followed. He prudently sidestepped as he passed through the door to prevent being silhouetted. When his eyes adjusted to the relative gloom, he saw a groined chamber radiating out in three directions. From the one ahead came the sound of running boots.

Moriana.

As he followed, from the hallway to the right poured a stream of Palace Guards. One lashed at him with a halberd. Fost took the blow on his shield, grunting as the blade split hide and metal and bit into his arm. He swung the arm violently, letting go of the shield's hand-grip. The halberd flew wide as the shield's mass carried it along. Fost lunged and slashed the Guard across the face.

Rebels and foresters were crowding through the doors. Two Guards attacked Fost from opposite directions. Prudyn shot one, then cast his bow aside as another Guard rushed him. Prudyn stayed alive by seizing the haft of the Guard's weapon and battling him up against a wall.

The other Guard intent on Fost lunged, the spiked head of the polearm spearing for Fost's midriff. Fost whipped Erimenes's satchel off his left shoulder and swung it. Erimenes screamed.

The heavy satchel knocked the halbred aside. Fost thrust. The Guardsman sank. Fost ripped his blade from the foeman's chest and ran for the corridor Moriana had taken.

Above the fighting, Synalon waged a battle of her own from the throne room. Even as Moriana's flotilla surged ahead of the other rafts, the air began to dance as the immense air elemental took form.

A tornado howled toward the armada sucking boulders and uprooted trees high into the air. Khirshagk brandished the Heart of the People. A beam of blackness exploded from the center of the jewel and struck to the core of the approaching whirlwind.

A frightened, gusty wail split the sky. The elemental diminished, drawn down the black tube into the diamond. In a heartbeat it vanished. A rain of rocks and trees spattered the countryside below.

Shocked, Synalon stared in wonder and dread. She spoke new words of Summoning. She pointed to the earth. It heaved, a hill appearing where none had been before. She pointed to the sky. The hill shot upward toward the raft carrying the Instrumentality.

Black rays from the Heart stabbed into the soaring hillock. It exploded in all directions sending out a cascade of dirt and stone lasting for long minutes. Synalon screamed. She waved her arms. Sinkholes appeared among the hills below as boulders buried underground winked out of existence . . .

. . . to rematerialize above the vast fleet of skystone rafts.

Now Synalon's magic took full effect. A dozen rafts were stricken and fell, dooming a hundred of the People and scores of humans. A huge boulder dropped straight down for Khirshagk's raft.

The Heart radiated black energy. The boulder slowed, then stopped in midair, defying gravity above Khirshagk's head. He gestured with the Heart. The boulder soared away toward the City to plow a furrow of ruin from the prow halfway to the Palace.

Synalon tore her robes to free her arms for uninhibited gesturing. The fleet drove inexorably onward. She shrieked and the heavens rained fire. Men died screaming in the embrace of flames, some of them her own bird riders; the queen was beyond caring who died as long as she blasted the monsters who dared assail her City. But the Heart emitted a funnel of total blackness into which the flamedrops were drawn. The smoking diamond absorbed the rain of fire and glowed with even greater energy.

As the queen hurled spell after frantic spell against the Instrumentality, the earthly battle raged with undiminished fury. Khirshagk's raft was the nexus of a cloud of eagles, diving and slashing as their riders swept the decks with arrows. Shield-bearers kept their leaders from harm, though they died with the regularity of the Heart's black pulsation.

Still holding the Heart, Khirshagk tossed down his shield and caught up his mace. A bird dropped at him, claws extended. He swung the heavy mace and crushed the eagle's breastbone with a single stroke.

His inhuman laughter rang across the battle-torn skies.

Synalon sent black clouds to confuse the invaders. Beams blacker still stabbed through them. With a hurricane wail the clouds were drawn inward. Fire and steel and plague she sent against the Fallen Ones, and a horde of winged demons from a lesser tenement of Hell. The Heart smote them all. The more power Synalon expended against it, the greater its own force waxed.

Unnoticed by Synalon, Moriana's rafts crossed the boundary of the City itself. Their route had been chosen with cunning. Once in the City, they had roofs to hide them. When they made their run-in along the Skullway the Palace itself hid them from sight. Singlemindedly, Synalon hurled destruction at the *Zr'gsz* only to see her every enchantment turned back upon itself. Many of the Hissers fell before her might. But the Heart kept Khirshagk inviolate and safe.

Rann stood on the lip of the raft, watching Darl's body turn end over end as it fell. Only when Darl struck ground did the prince swing back onto Terror's back.

Khirshagk saw the prince's mount take flight from

the deck of his sister ship. He dropped his mace and seized a javelin. Straightening, still holding the Heart in his right claw, the Instrumentality cocked his arm and flung the dart with all his might.

Impact jarred Rann's body. Terror coughed. The scars criss-crossing the prince's face tightened like a net as he stared at the spearshaft jutting from his war bird's chest a handspan away from his right knee.

The rhythm of its wingbeats lost, the mighty bird began to sink.

Synalon watched in horror as her cousin's mount spiralled earthward. Channeling her grief and rage and hatred, she called up a storm. Thunderheads gathered, rolled down on the *Zr'gsz* fleet with avalanche speed. Violet lightnings speared skyrafts from the air.

Energy raved from the Heart and the demon storm was torn apart, wisps of cloud spinning away to disperse in midair.

Synalon clenched her fists until the veins stood out on her forearms. She endured the agony of summoning a salamander of awesome proportions, a fire elemental so powerful that the hangings on the wall burst into flame, then the carpet and the wooden furnishings. The surface of the walls and the Beryl Throne itself began to turn soft and flow from the heat emanating from the sorceress-queen's body before the conjuring was done. Then her Will drove the elemental deep into the earth through crust and mantle in search of live magma. A new Throat of the Dark Ones would speak with an authority the Heart of the People could not refute.

The smouldering door to the throne room opened.

"Greetings, sister," said Moriana. She stepped inside, frowned.

Synalon felt the salamander she had summoned at such cost wink out of being.

"You've fought long and hard to come here," she snarled at her golden-haired sister. The charred fragments of her robe fell in a black rain at her feet. "I'll see you enjoy a death commensurate with your achievement."

Synalon spoke rapid words. Moriana felt a detonation in her brain and reeled against the wall. It seared her shoulder.

Rage gripped her. She knew the spell—Synalon had used it to subdue her when she had tried to kill Synalon with her bare hands on the eve of her sacrifice to Istu. It would not bring her down again.

She willed the pressure in her mind to go, and it was gone.

"You *have* learned things during your sabbatical," said Synalon in a voice like milk and honey. "I should have expected no less. Even you can learn, if given enough time." She raised a slender hand. "My demons shall . . ."

The words died in her throat. She tried to force them out. She failed. It was as if a hand closed on her neck and bottled the words inside her.

"You shall not call your demons, sister dear," said Moriana. "Your Guardsmen are surrendering below or being slaughtered like sheep. I will not suffer you to call for supernatural aid. There's no one to help you. You must fight me, Synalon, with what power you have within you. If you've any of your own, that is."

Synalon's eyes blazed.

"Don't . . . count yourself the victor yet," she gasped out.

The real battle for the City in the Sky began.

Fost was breathing hard when he reached the tenth floor of the Palace, and motes of blackness spun in his brain.

"This is the proper level," Erimenes told him.

"I know," panted Fost. "Been here before, remember? When Moriana and I . . . rescued you."

"Rescued?" Erimenes said, outraged. "I wouldn't use that term."

"Neither should I. As I recall, you were busy collaborating with the enemy."

"That's the true barbarian spirit," a familiar voice said. "Holding a colloquy with a ghost while the fate of worlds is decided around you."

Warily, Fost watched High Councillor Uriath enter the room. The tall, portly man had a massive volume tucked under his arm. He radiated a fey humor Fost hadn't detected in him before.

"I'm not a barbarian," said Fost.

Uriath laughed. It was the first genuine laugh the courier had ever heard him utter.

"Ah, but you are. A pathetic groundling barbarian. Also a fool." He giggled. "And in another moment—dead."

"Kill him, Fost!" Erimenes bawled. Fost brought up his sword and lunged.

Uriath had flipped open the book. His lips moved quickly. An unlit oil lamp set in a niche along one wall burst into incandescence. Fost yelped and fell back as the flaming oil drew a line between him and the demoniacally grinning High Councillor. A shape cavorted in the center of the inferno, sinuous and vaguely reptilian.

Uriath pointed at Fost.

"Kill him," he commanded.

The salamander sprang. Fost flung himself to one side. Stone exploded, spraying him with glowing hot fragments. The fire sprite backed away, hissing, slavering sparks.

Fost crouched, keeping his sword between his body and the fiery thing, even though this was puny defense against the elemental.

"Erimenes? What do I do?"

"You pray to Ust," the genie said. "And I'll try Gormanka."

The elemental darted forward. Fost danced aside. He screamed as the being grazed his side leaving his chainmail glowing in a yellow-white swath along his body. He could barely breathe from the pain. The monster's next rush would end him. The salamander hovered between him and the gloating Uriath. A wild rush at the High Councillor would buy him nothing except a death quicker by milliseconds.

"Father!" Was it his imagination? "Father, what are you doing?"

"Removing the next to last obstacle between you and the throne," Uriath said without turning away from his victim.

Past the intolerable glare of the hovering elemental, Fost saw that Luranni stood behind her father, her face a portrait in horror. Her eyes were ringed with dark smudges, and she still wore the same bright smock she had the day before when she'd interrupted Fost and Moriana in their conversation.

"So it's true, Father. You've intended to betray Moriana from the start." Her voice was firm, flat, low. It didn't sound like the romantic, vaguely mystical Luranni he had come to know.

Uriath laughed.

"Of course! The Etuul have grown decadent. Haven't they wasted the City's substance, threatened its existence—no, the very order of the world!—fighting among themselves?"

"And when Fost went to rescue Moriana from the Vicar of Istu, you ordered your people to hold back." The words spilled from her in a torrent of accusation. "And Chiresko and the others—you turned them in!"

Sweat streamed down Uriath's florid features.

"Chiresko had outlived his usefulness," he explained. "Just like that fool Tromym. Now stand back, child, and stop bothering me. This beast's fearfully tricky to control."

"I won't let you murder the man I love, Father."

"Love?" Uriath turned. "Him?" His laughter rang out mad.

"I mean it."

"Too much is at stake for me to indulge your youthful folly. Salamander . . ." he began.

"No!" As her father spoke his words of command, Luranni shrieked and drove past him through the dwindling wall of flame. She flung her arms around Fost, kissed him hard. The scent of cinnamon welled around him.

The world exploded in flame and pain and the smell of burned flesh.

The battle of powers was over. The vanquished sprawled senseless on the floor and the victor staggered, trying to keep her feet, trying to control the shaking of her hands and change double vision back to clear focus.

A tall figure appeared in the doorway.

"My heart rejoices to see you, Your Majesty," said Uriath. Though tears had left shiny trails down his cheeks, he smiled hugely. "This day's horrors have cost me my daughter, who meant more to me than life itself. But all of it is worthwhile if I can only receive the boon of being the first to hail the rightful Queen of the City in the Sky in her moment of triumph."

He came forward with a drunkard's step and fell to his knees before the City's monarch by right of mystic combat. Moriana gazed down at him, not quite understanding what he said. Why, she wondered in a daze, did he have a huge, ancient book tucked under his arm?

And why was the stone on her breast glowing black?

Uriath's hand shot out. Silver links snapped as he snatched the Destiny Stone from her neck.

"I have it!" he crowed, leaping up and away from her with an agility amazing in one of his bulk. "The Amulet of Living Flame! I've won! I'm immortal!"

Moriana sank to her knees beside Synalon's prostrate form. Defeat tasted of ashes on her tongue. So much and all for naught.

She had never even had to use the Amulet. She had

overpowered her sister, Synalon the invincible, whose powers of sorcery had always before outmatched her. She had won her birthright.

And lost it.

The book lay open in Uriath's palm. He did a little jig as he began to read. Moriana smelled the magic gathering about the tower.

The room grew warm. A strange crackling, wailing sound drew Moriana's attention to the window. Salamanders danced outside, whirling round and round the tower so rapidly she only saw them as lines of light, red and green and white, weaving a garland of fire about the spire.

She tried to dismiss them. A tiny electric blue spark danced from her fingertips. That was all the magic she could Summon. She lacked the strength.

"Foolish slut!" cried Uriath. "This is the book of the deepest secrets of Kyrun Etuul! For generations it's mouldered, neglected on the shelves of your Palace library. And now it has passed to my hands—where it belongs!" He stopped his capering and beamed down upon the sisters. Beside Moriana Synalon began to stir.

"Your time is through, Etuul witches. Perhaps the reign of women is done, too. Yes, I think so. It's an abomination that women should rule men."

"The people will never accept you."

"No?" He hugged the book to his chest and tittered. "They accepted Synalon, didn't they? And you believed they'd accept you, too, you who loosed the Fallen Ones upon the world again."

She sank back. Synalon rolled onto her side, moaning. Moriana took her hand. It felt cold and lifeless, more like marble than living flesh.

"Enough words," the High Councillor said. "Prepare to burn."

A scuffling sounded from the corridor. Uriath looked up sharply from his tome. An apparition stood in the doorway, manlike in form but as black as Istu save for the bared white teeth. A naked steel blade gleamed in a blackened hand.

"You can't be here. You're dead! Burned up! The salamander took you when it took my poor Luranni." He began to weep once more.

"You haven't finished me, friend Uriath," said Fost Longstrider, advancing on the High Councillor. "I'm still blood and bone under this char. And I'm about to spit you and serve you piece by piece to your own salamanders, you murdering fat bastard!"

"No!" It was the squeal of a child in terror. Uriath's chubby fingers flew as they flipped through the pages of the book. He kept glancing frantically from the pages to the courier advancing on him step by merciless step. "Ah, here, here!" he cried, and screeched an incantation.

A dome of flame surrounded him. Fost flinched from the killing heat. A moment more and a dancing veil of fire sprang up in the doorway.

"You've come a long way to die, Longstrider," said Synalon in a cracked voice. "Still, there are worse companions with whom to receive the Hell Call."

Fost gazed around the room. Outside raged the firestorm.

"Isn't there anything you can do?"

Wearily Synalon shook her head.

"Isn't it humorous? My sister and I spent all our energies contesting with each other. And for what? So this treacherous blubbergut can roast us to death and claim the Beryl Throne for himself."

It was getting hotter.

"Erimenes?" The answer was a formless wail. Fost thought he heard a new note to it, a note of real anguish.

Moriana pointed at Uriath, dimly visible through the orange and blue shimmer of his fire shield.

"He's building his control of the salamanders outside. When he has perfected his grip on them, they'll

—

come for us." She shook her head. The tears flowed freely now. "Oh Fost, my love, my only love. I'm sorry I brought you to this."

But the courier's attention fixed on Uriath. He coughed.

"Perhaps it's premature to apologize," he said in a parched voice. The heat rose around them like a clinging, choking blanket.

"What do you mean?" asked Moriana.

Her eyes followed his. The Destiny Stone was a black so complete it seemed to burn a hole through the fires surrounding the High Councillor. Synalon looked on, curious about all matters mystical even in the face of death.

The heating of the air inside and outside the chamber caused a miniature whirlwind. Burning shreds of cloth swirled up around them. Fost cursed and slapped at one that stung his cheek like an insect.

Uriath's voice rose above the rush of wind and fire, chanting in a long-forgotten tongue. A flake of ash was swept up over his bald domed head. It settled downward bursting into sudden fierce flame as it fell through his fire shield.

It landed in the middle of the page from which he read.

The page flared. Uriath's eyes bulged.

"No," he cried. "No, no! This can't be. This is the last page. It's almost there, it isn't fair. I . . ."

Fire roared. Lines of flame converged from the window on the magical dome, merged with it. Uriath dropped the book and stared at fingers burning like candles. Cackling, freed of human control, the salamanders turned on him with all the capriciousness of their kind. The screaming went on and on.

And from the midst of the conflagration while the fire sprites played and Uriath danced his insensate dance of death, the Destiny Stone cast a beacon of intense, pure white light that outshone even the werefire of the elementals.

Fost collapsed at Moriana's side. They clung to each other, watching mute as the fires burned down. Uriath melted like tallow. With his passing the salamanders dwindled. When they winked out, only a blackened spot on the floor remained of High Councillor, elementals or the pendant.

"But he had the Amulet of Living Flame!" exclaimed Moriana, shrill with the nearness of hysteria. "Why didn't it save him?"

Fost drew her closer.

"He never had the Amulet," he said. "No more than you."

CHAPTER FOURTEEN

"The Destiny Stone," said Erimenes, obviously enjoying Moriana's expression of horror. "A different item entirely." The bright flush the heat had brought to the princess's cheeks drained rapidly as the genie told her of the true nature of the stone she'd carried with her for so long. The shiny, treacherous bauble for which she'd murdered her lover.

"He really died?" she cried, clinging to Fost. "Then why . . ."

"Why is he alive? Simplicity itself. The other pendant, the plain lump of rock tied on a thong, so rude a thing you both scorned it at once as trash—that was the Amulet of Living Flame. With his dying reflex Fost clutched it as he fell."

"And does he have it?" Hope brought life flooding back into her features. "Perhaps some of those who fell today . . ."

Gently Fost shook his head.

"It used up the last of its energies reviving me."

She buried her face against his breast and wept.

"At the end, Erimenes, why did it glow white?"

The spirit chuckled.

"It was bringing the greatest luck of all its existence." Fost cocked a singed eyebrow at him. "It was removing itself from the world, dear boy. What more fortunate a thing could it do?"

"I see your point," said Fost, smiling.

Motion at the edge of vision caught his eye. Synalon! In the aftermath of the Destiny Stone's passing they had forgotten her.

She stood on the ledge of the outermost window gazing down, the wind stirring the stubble of black hair remaining on her head. Her naked skin appeared almost translucent in the brightness of the day.

"Synalon?" asked Moriana.

The dark-haired sister turned her head and smiled wanly.

"You've not yet started to wonder what to do with me."

Moriana licked her lips. For a moment Fost saw hatred burn in her green eyes. Then it faded.

"There's been destruction enough," she said. "You're free to go. But you must leave the City."

"Oh, I intend to," said Synalon, smiling crookedly. "But not as you imagine."

The two stared at her. She laughed at their blank looks.

"What a marvelous new generation you'll breed! You look precisely like sheep. Your offspring will go about on all fours and crop the grass." She raised a hand to cut off their angry retorts. "Save your breath. The City was my life; when I lost it, I lost all. And I prefer not to live as a groundling."

"Synalon," Moriana began.

Her sister stepped forward into space.

Moriana screamed. The tears began again, more than before. She clung to Fost and wept great wracking sobs, wept for all those who had died. Her mother, Kralfi the faithful retainer, Sir Ottovus and his brother the grand old hero Rinalvus, young Brightlaugher of Nevrym, poor dear Darl. And even Synalon.

When the grief had exhausted her, Fost helped her off the floor and led her downstairs to greet her subjects.

As the sun passed the zenith and started back down the sky, the crowds began assembling in the Circle of the Skywell. There were plain Sky Citizens, looking timidly about them as if at some alien vista. There were the prisoners, bird riders and Sky Guards and Monitors and Guards from the Palace, watched by vigilant men and women who wore strips of blue and scarlet around their arms to show allegiance to Moriana.

Resistance had long since ceased. When Rann fell from the sky, the heart went out of the bird riders. In a matter of minutes, some quick-thinking rebels had raised Moriana's claw and flower banner from the Palace flagstaff. While the sorcerous battle for the City had continued to rage, the physical battle for the Sky City had ended with this simple action.

Moriana stepped out into the sunlight. In a few seconds, the entire City had taken up the cry.

She gestured. Fost joined her. His hair was black and his gaze a heroic blue, and only those nearest could see the way his eyes shifted nervously. Having just lived through horrible ordeal, Fost Longstrider found himself suffering from stage fright.

Moriana took his hand and led him down the steps to the Skullway.

"Relax, Fost," she said in a low voice. "It's over. There's no need to be nervous now."

"I'm not used to this," he said, looking out over the crowd assembled to cheer and venerate Moriana—and him.

"They're friends, all of them," she assured him. And it seemed to be so. He saw Prudyn and Chasko, carrying weatherworn satchels containing Erimenes and Ziore. The muffled sounds of acrimonious dispute rose from within, each making vile and impossible claims about the other's actions. And beyond them Fost sighted Syriana and the red-haired young lady who was sudden death on rooftop snipers, and tanned foresters and bearded Northern men and even a few diffident men in the breastplates of Palace Guards.

As they neared the Circle of the Skywell, however, Fost's unease returned.

"Moriana, where are the Fallen Ones? I don't see a single one of your *Zr'gsz* anywhere."

"They're hardly *my Zr'gsz*," she answered. "They're in the catacombs inventorying their religious relics. I suppose they'll want to load them on their skyrafts and be gone as soon as possible. After all, it's been millennia since the *Zr'gsz* had much commerce with humans. All this must upset them greatly."

"It upsets me," said Fost, with feeling. But the nagging unease returned. What exactly was it that upset him? Perhaps it was nothing more than the presence of the Vicar of Istu in the Skywell. He peered suspiciously at the basalt statue. It remained immobile.

Then Fost's attentions were diverted to the ceremony. The crowd melted away to give Moriana room. A pimply adolescent knelt with her burden at Moriana's feet. Moriana bade her rise.

"As the youngest of the warriors who took part in the capture of the Palace of Winds," Moriana declared, "Ufri Tonamil has earned the privilege to crown the new ruler of the City in the Sky." The crowd roared agreement. Moriana knelt as the child fumbled with the wrappings on the package. She soon revealed the winged silver crown of the City's rulers.

Ufri Tonamil hoisted the crown high, held it a moment, then stepped forward to place it on Moriana's head.

"All hail Moriana!" she cried. "Queen of the City in the Sky, Scion of the Skyborn, Mistress of the Clouds!"

Moriana rose. The crowd went to its knees as one. Fost watched, then decided he should kneel, also. Immediately Moriana seized his arm and yanked him to his feet.

"No one need kneel before me," she proclaimed. "Rise, my people."

They did. They swept forward and raised their new queen to their shoulders. Fost laughed at her expression, then cried out as he felt hands raising him, too.

Moriana caught his eye. Her lips formed the words, "We won!"

And they had. They'd won not just the Sky City, they'd thwarted the Dark Ones themselves. The Second War of Powers Jennas had direly predicted would never happen. *That* was their true victory.

The boiling crowd turned Fost around. For a brief instant the Vicar of Istu flashed in his sight. His heart missed a beat. Then the crowd was bearing them toward the Palace of Winds, and its jubilation caught him up like the surge of a sea-wave.

And in the depths of the City, a Demon stirred.